MW00617156

Tia,

NOTHING
Matters
but Peace
& Love
ERICKA WILLIAMS

PUBLISHER'S NOTE:

This book is a work of fiction. Names, characters, businesses, organizations, places, events, and incidents are the product of the author's imagination or are used fictionally. Any resemblance of actual persons, living or dead, events, or locales are entirely coincidental.

Library of Congress Control Number:

ISBN: 978-1-7368347-2-5 (Paperback)

ISBN: 978-1-7368347-3-2 (E-Book)

Cover Design: Nicole Watts Studios

Editor: Latisha's One-on-One Editing

First Edition

Printed in the United States of America

Social Media:

Facebook: www.facebook.com/Ericka-Monique-Williams-389815499992

Instagram: @erickamoniquewilliams

"If your black life matters, you better put your fuckin' hands up right now!"

Brandon Phillips' heart nearly jumped out of his chest as he quickly put his hands up, wanting to turn around, but was scared to make any false moves and possibly lose his life. He fought the urge to wipe the sweat running down his forehead. Instead, he decided to speak up first.

"Can I help you with something? Is this a robbery?" Brandon asked the assailant who was yelling and pointing a gun at him like he was someone's target practice, or so he presumed. He was hoping it was a prank.

"Don't turn around yet. What are you doing here in this complex?" the voice of a white man responded. It sounded the way a cop would when exercising his authority.

"Listen, I'm moving in here as we speak. Can I turn around now?" Brandon never would have thought he would be held at gunpoint while moving into The Raven luxury condominiums in Montclair, New Jersey. This isn't the hood. He was stunned. This was supposed to be his dream come true. He had driven past this modern skyscraper regularly for two years, telling himself that he would live here one day, and he did all he could to make it come to pass.

"The moving truck is on the way." Brandon's voice quivered while trying to calm the owner of the aggressive voice down and de-escalate the situation that he was clueless about.

Questions swirled around in his head. Do I run? Where can I run? I'm in a fucking garage. Just turn around. The conversation he was having with himself was interrupted.

"Aaaaaaaahaaaaaaaa-haaaaaaa!" A loud, obnoxious, evil-sounding laugh echoed inside the parking garage. Brandon swung his head around and locked eyes with a white man who had his gun drawn and was laughing hysterically, lowering the piece of metal but still holding a tight grip. He wore a suit but looked dingy and dirty.

"Hey, dude, no hard feelings," he said calmly and arrogantly. "Nothing personal."

"What the fuck kind of joke is that? I don't even know you. You work here?" Brandon asked somewhat aggressively.

"Hold up, man. I still have this gun handy. One of the residents said she saw an unfamiliar face in the parking garage when she got out of her car. She was nervous, so I came to see what was going on."

"Going on? I told you, I'm moving in here. I'm waiting for my truck. Is this how this complex welcomes new owners? Because I shouldn't have my life threatened for moving in. Now, again, do you work here? And if so, would the management office condone you pulling a gun on an innocent person?"

"I'm going to have to tell you to calm down. Relax. Everything is okay now. You're moving in. Welcome. At least you know you'll be safe here," Mark Stephens, a fellow tenant, retorted sarcastically, again, laughing off his inappropriate actions.

Brandon was furious. He didn't make any moves except to turn around and face the asshole in front of him. "Listen, man. I don't know who you are, but I won't allow you to think you can pull a gun on me for nothing and then laugh about it. What is your name?"

"Let's just say that I may not work here, but I am a detective, and I am doing my job. Let's just forget this happened. I won't take this any further. You have a good day."

"I am not in the mood for any run-ins with any law officers because, clearly, you guys have a problem following the law yourself. I just want to move in peacefully. I hope that you won't harass me again because I may not feel so generous next time. What you just did was unlawful."

"I told you that an older resident felt nervous, and I came to investigate." Mark didn't like anyone challenging his authority, so he wasn't going to back down, and it seemed as though Brandon wasn't going to either.

"Mr. Detective, I know my rights. And I know that you just can't pull a gun on anybody because someone is nervous about seeing a black man in her building. I did nothing wrong. I need your identification."

"I guess you'll have to figure it out on your own." As Mark placed his gun back in his back holster, he walked past Brandon, watching him until he got around the bend. He grabbed his phone out of his pocket and rushed to call Jerry, one of the building's superintendents.

"Hey, dude. I need some info on a new tenant that moved in today. Black guy, he looks to be in his late thirties."

"Okay, but I need a cool hundred for that. You sure have asked for a lot of favors this month, and you don't like to pay," Jerry said, looking in his bathroom mirror, putting a card with cocaine on it to his nose and sniffing.

"Jerry, I've kept you out of a lot of trouble. That's your pay."

"Well, I need a couple of dollars. I'm not going to keep putting my job on the line." Jerry was fed up and tired of feeling like a gopher. Every time this guy wanted to bother somebody in the complex, he expected Jerry to be his intel.

"Just get me the information. We have a partnership. I wouldn't let you lose your livelihood. We've gotten some bad guys out of this building, and your compensation is that nobody knows you've aided in that. What's the matter? You forgot how much pull I have downtown? You can't get the accolades just yet because, remember, you're undercover like me, dude." Mark tried to butter Jerry up and keep him wrapped around his finger.

"Mark, you've gotta make it more worth my while. I can spy on people on my own; when I do it for someone else, it's called a job. If you want the name and apartment number, bring me the money." Jerry hung up the phone.

* * *

Brandon was so agitated that his whole mood changed. He dialed the moving company on his cell phone and let them have it.

"Yes, I've been waiting for my fucking movers to arrive at The Raven. My name is Brandon Phillips, and I will deduct money from my bill if my shit doesn't pull into this parking garage soon. They better show up in the next half hour!" He hung up and was ready to throw his phone but caught himself.

I can't believe this dirty-ass detective pulled a goddamn gun on me!

Brandon was startled when his phone rang as soon as he hung it up. He looked at the screen and shook his head when he saw it was his children's mother. Brandon didn't want to answer the phone. Ciara was his ex-fiancée whom he had broken up with six months earlier. Brandon had to get away from her. As much as he loved her, sometimes he despised her, so much so that he had been staying with his cousin Jarrod while saving to buy his condo.

Many thoughts were racing through Brandon's head, and he was fighting the feelings of discouragement that had him questioning whether he belonged at The Raven at this point. I don't need to live with people who hate me to prove to them that I am as good as them. He tried to shrug away his feelings of inadequacy.

By the time he answered the phone, Ciara had hung up, and he called her right back. "What's the problem, Ciara? What do you want? I'm not in the mood for your shit right now." Brandon paced back and forth, feeling more rage building. I am not in the mood for Ciara to act like she's my mother and like she knows everything.

"Brandon, I thought we talked about how you were going to address me better."

"Listen, not now, Ciara. I am not in a good mood, and I just had a situation. If it's not important, I'll talk to you later." Brandon wanted to hang the phone up and deal with her after this ordeal..

What a day he was having already. He was not expecting such a level of stress to come with a day he had been so looking forward to. He had to remind himself that moving, in general, was stressful. There were times like these that Brandon wished his dad was still alive. This void had shown itself at the most critical moments of his life.

"What else is new, Brandon? You're always in a bad mood. I was trying to see how your day was going with the big move, so that wasn't at all necessary. We now have two mortgages, which doesn't make sense. We could have—"

Brandon pressed the end button on the call. It was better than cursing her out. One thing he hated doing was getting out of character, but Cirara knew how to push his buttons. She was the only woman who could get that off, because he cared. Anything that affected her, affected his kids and he knew that. . He powered his phone down and then realized he needed to have it on for the moving people, so he turned it back on. Then he realized he needed a drink. A long sigh and deep breath were all he could get at that moment, to relieve some of his stress.

As soon as that thought entered his now cloudy and hurting head, the big moving truck was at the gate, honking, and his phone was ringing. He didn't answer but walked to the gate and hit the button to open it to allow the truck entrance. This lifted his spirit, to be in a building with a private garage. He approached the driver's side of the truck.

"So the garage is secure, but some Karen decides that someone who doesn't belong here is here. How?"

"What did you say? You're Mr. Phillips, correct?" the truck operator asked, confused and pulling farther in as Brandon directed him to the elevator lobby closest to his condo. The building complex had a separate moving entrance with large freight elevators. There were glass elevators on both sides of the building as well. The glass wrapped around to an outside view of Manhattan on the horizon. The privileged residents wouldn't have to walk too far to get to their homes. The Raven was luxury at its best.

Brandon walked behind the truck and approached as the two moving guys were opening the back doors. He kept replaying in his mind what had just happened with the son of a bitch detective. Brandon knew that situation had happened so often to other black men, but plenty of them ended up in the morgue, on a slab, over nothing. He was momentarily in a daze.

"Mr. Phillips, are you okay? I called your name a few times. Here's your invoice. Will you be waiting in your condo, or will you be stepping out?"

"Why? What difference does it make?" Brandon snapped, and the two white workers looked at each other. He figured they would be talking about the "angry black man" when they were back in their truck after moving him in, but so what. The very thing that triggered him was a white racist.

"My bad. I was just almost shot by a white cop who wanted to play a security guard, but it doesn't matter. You wouldn't understand." Instead of the two saying something stupid that would have ticked him off even more, he was glad they chose to ignore him and keep quiet. There was nothing they could say that would make him feel better.

"We were asking if you would be staying because we didn't know if you would leave us your key for the trips that we have to make back and forth or if you would be there to tell us where and how you want the boxes stacked. It was a simple question; no need for alarm."

"Alarm? Sir, let's just go upstairs, and I'll show you what I want before leaving. Is that okay? I mean, the boxes are labeled for each room, which was a requirement by your company."

Brandon rode in a separate elevator for their first trip up to the sixteenth floor. He knew he would need to leave because, if he decided to stay, he wouldn't be quiet about what transpired, and, in all honesty, it wasn't their fault. Maybe they weren't racist like the detective. Perhaps they were just lovely people who happened to be white and didn't understand his plight. Who would choose the black struggle if they weren't born into it, which was why many Hispanics didn't choose to identify with color but nationality. He decided not to leave so that he could direct everything. It felt good to give orders to two white guys and make them follow his orders.

This was going to be his peace, his sanctuary. He realized that he should be feeling joy, gratefulness, optimism, and pride. He was proud of himself. He was proud to be a black man in a world that hated him. He refused to beat himself up. He put a hip-hop and R&B mix on Pandora to change his mood.

"Now, where should I start?" he asked and then looked at the clock. It was already 6 p.m., but he had taken the week off to get settled in. Brandon Phillips was a thirty-eight-year-old advertising executive at Love and War, one of the top advertising firms in New York City. He had been with the company for more than ten years and after working a few different odd jobs after graduating college at twenty-two. He worked with mostly minority entertainers, athletes, and Internet sensations, taking their brands to higher levels, including international territories.

Brandon opened a bottle of gin, poured some in a glass with orange juice, and got to work. At six feet two, he was on the taller side and was dark and handsome, with the body of a twenty-eight-year-old due to keeping fit. Brandon had neatly kept dreadlocks that hung to his shoulders. He rocked a mustache and a short, light beard. His bronze skin made him resemble a modern-day Jesus, and women certainly treated him like a god. He had tattoos and a wardrobe that would easily attract any woman he wanted. His great character was more of an asset than his good looks because Brandon was humble and not arrogant or boisterous. He had a reserved demeanor but did not come across as a pushover. His presence demanded respect, and his achievements had him walking in the league of grown men.

Brandon wanted to sleep in his bed, so he began to unpack his room first, putting his suits in one of his two walk-in closets. He decided that he would have a work closet and a play closet. He put all his clothes that weren't for storage where they belonged. He would take the boxes to his basement storage unit later.

Brandon opened a box full of pictures, causing him to pause. He pulled out his son's baby picture. His name was Major, and he was nine years old. His daughter, Malika, was twelve, and for ten years, he'd raised his children with Ciara. It was one of his most significant accomplishments and most challenging responsibilities. He was twenty-six years old and in the prime of his life when Ciara announced her pregnancy. He took out a picture of the two of them when she was pregnant. He stared at the picture, and it took him right back to that day.

They were younger in mind than they realized and were unaware or unwilling to consider the challenging road that lie ahead. Both were in ignorant bliss. He looked at her breasts, which were only covered by her hand in the maternity photo, and spoke to her picture. "I ain't gon' lie, I wish I could still hit that now and then, but you're too damn emotional. One thing I never got tired of was that pussy. Your damn mentality, attitude, and mouth are what I don't miss. Well, when it was speaking, not when it was sucking or licking." Brandon laughed out loud. "I can hear you now. Oh, so after all of the years I proved myself to you, all you can think about is fucking me and me sucking your dick?"

Brandon shrugged his shoulders as if she was standing right there asking him the question, then said, "Why do women have to be so damn annoying and complicated? Damn, Ciara. We just couldn't get it right. I always tried to blame you for everything, and then you became the monster that I created."

His mind took him to one of their biggest arguments that made him realize, in his heart, they weren't going to make it. Ciara was a lost soul to him. She was always trying to please people because she had had such a hard upbringing. Her mother had too many kids and baby daddies, and Ciara was the oldest. She was treated like Cinderella, so she always catered to everyone. She catered to him, and he liked it and hated it at the same time. She was too good, and it was annoying. Brandon had to come to the realization he sometimes had toxic masculinity with a touch of narcissism. Sometimes he took the man role too far and was uncompromising.

Brandon found himself resenting Ciara for no apparent reason, except that her goodness made him feel like it required him to be more than he was, and he didn't want to. He wasn't a deadbeat dad, but a great father; he was paying most of the bills and feeling trapped. He was oblivious that he was taking his frustrations out on her emotionally and was mentally abusing her. She was his possession, and he felt like she should deal with anything he dished out to her because he loved her and because his mother had sacrificed herself for his dad that way.

"Brandon, what do you want to eat tonight?" Ciara began to massage his back.

"Whatever you want to make."

Her hands felt good on his back, but he didn't want her

touching him for some reason. He wondered why she treated him so well.

"Brandon, just say what you feel like having so I can make it or go to the store."

"I don't care. Damn, just make something. Why everything gotta be drawn out and extra? Just make some shit." Brandon got up and walked away. Ciara followed him out of the bedroom and into the bathroom and stood in the bathroom door as he stood in the mirror, admiring himself as if she wasn't there.

"Why everything gotta be drawn out and extra? Really? Why you gotta show yo' fuckin' attitude? Why can't you just appreciate someone that's good to you?"

"Shut the fuck up, Ciara. You're good to me, but you ain't the only bitch out here being good to a nigga!"

"What? Oh, what the fuck is that supposed to mean? You got another bitch?"

"Did I say that? I said you act like you doin' something you ain't supposed to do. You a woman; you better be a good woman. I ain't messin' wit' no slackin' ass bitch." Brandon brushed past Ciara and out the bathroom door.

"No, act like you should and appreciate it. I know what I'm supposed to do, and I do it. All you do is take it for granted. You think it's attractive that you treat me like that?"

"Who gonna treat you as good as me? I got you in this dope ass apartment, you hardly pay a quarter of the bills, and you always complaining. Be appreciative that you have a man that works."

"I'm not a bill or a job. I am a woman, and I need emotional support, not mental abuse. What part of that don't you understand? I don't complain; I tell you what I need and what I know I deserve, and I shouldn't have to tell you that.

You're a man, right? A real man knows that he should be gentle with his woman. He values his woman and makes his woman smile, not cry. You ain't a man; you a bitch yourself. You don't know how to love or care for a woman. You don't know how to give or get it."

Brandon looked at Ciara and felt like he wanted to spit on her. The disgust on his face was nowhere near the contempt he felt in his heart. "You gonna have the nerve to disrespect me when I'm in here paying bills and not out here fuckin' a whole bunch of women when I can? That's it. I'm done with you. You just don't know it yet." Brandon calmly walked out the door and didn't return until the next day, when Ciara was already at work.

Brandon snapped out of his reminiscing, determined to get back to his good feeling about the move. He still had feelings for Ciara but needed some time to get his thoughts together and figure out what he wanted to do. They had gone back and forth for years, and the relationship had run into a dead end. He was just glad to have some peace of mind, if there was really such a thing. Brandon struggled with anger and didn't always know how to control or defuse it.

Brandon finished his room and used the hand truck to take the boxes he wouldn't open from the bedroom down to his storage unit. He was feeling better and more relaxed after getting one room done. He decided to take down boxes after each room was complete, to view his progress. Plus, he wanted to ride the elevator and get outside of his condo for a few minutes. He loved that he could see the New York City skyline through the glass elevators.

He gazed in awe of the beautiful view as he rode the elevator down to his storage unit. He thought of how great it would be to ride it every day and find solitude, even on an elevator. He wished he could have a sexual encounter in it. Again, he amused himself with his thoughts.

As the elevator doors opened, Brandon was stunned to see his tormentor walking past, in the direction that he was headed. He stepped out and walked behind Mark, wondering if he was there to see where he lived.

Mark noticed Brandon out the corner of his eye when the elevator doors opened, but he kept walking. He slowed his gait down, and Brandon was startled by the loud and eerie-sounding whistle coming from Mark. He deliberately wanted to annoy Brandon to see if he could get a rise or reaction out of him to have part two of their first encounter.

Mark walked past Brandon's door—16M to 16R—before stopping as Brandon put his keycard up to the console. Brandon stopped as the door opened to see why Mark had stopped.

Brandon looked at Mark, who said sarcastically, "See you around, neighbor," then turned and proceeded to stroll while continuing his annoying whistle. Brandon stood there for a moment, envisioning himself running behind him and punching him out. He took a deep breath and stepped inside. He closed the door, leaning back into it, and thinking to himself, Lord, please don't let this be a nightmare. If this is going to be a test, prepare me to win.

* * *

Mark walked into his condo where his wife and two children were already eating dinner.

"What the hell? You guys couldn't wait for the man who puts the food on the table?" Mark walked to the bedroom.

"We are waiting; we were just sitting and talking! Come on, honey," Grace called from the dining room.

"Okay, I'll be there in a sec. You can start without me!" he yelled back, shrugging his shoulders. He went into the stash in his closet and took out two hundred-dollar bills.

Grace tried to hide her annoyance, but thought, Why on earth did you complain about us not waiting then? She didn't say a word. She started dishing out the plates while shaking her head.

"Are you telling me this son of a bitch lives on my floor? Yeah, this one is going to be fun. I know he's up to something, moving in here like he belongs. I can't wait to see what kind of pimped-out ride he's driving. He's too old to be a rapper or an athlete, so we know the next best thing is a drug kingpin." Mark was laughing out loud as his wife walked into the room.

"What are you laughing at, honey?" she asked, rubbing Mark's back. He brushed her off and moved away, walking toward the bedroom door.

"Oh, nothing. Just something that happened at work," Mark responded as he walked out of the room, Grace following behind.

"Where are you going now? We're about to eat dinner," she said, following him to the door.

"I'm going downstairs for a sec. I'll be right back. I think I left my wallet in the car."

On his way out the door, Mark heard Grace say that his wallet was right there on the couch's end table. He ignored her, quickening his pace to make it around the corner before she called him back in.

"Geesh, I sure may be on the right side of the law, but she lets me know what jail feels like," he said, shaking his head.

He walked to the elevator and took it down to the ground floor. He knocked on Jerry's door, putting the money up to the peephole. A few minutes later, Jerry opened, wearing only boxer shorts.

"Come on, Jerry. Don't be coming to the door like that. I don't want anybody thinking I'm fucking you in the ass or nothing." Mark hollered and laughed, pushing past Jerry, who had no intentions on letting him in.

"Hey, I have company. Here's the information on this piece of paper. I'm busy."

Mark walked into the living room to a half-clothed girl on the couch, who quickly covered up with a blanket.

"Oh, this is why you don't want me here. You got one of your hookers over tonight."

Jerry was the superintendent of The Raven and liked to drink and do drugs in between running the complex, like plenty of other superintendents did. The Raven had four superintendents, along with an outsourcing company that handled the big jobs. Each super covered a different wing of the monstrous, resort-like high-rise, and Jerry was the worst of them. He had no family, so his only recreation was recreationally destructive behaviors. Mark enjoyed using Jerry as his gopher and flunky.

Mark unzipped his pants and took his penis out. "Give me a kiss right on my pee-pee. Can you do that for me?" He moved closer to the filthy-looking girl.

"I don't do freebies. You got fifty dollars?"

"Jerry, give her fifty from the money I just gave you so I can get a quick fix. Y'all got all night. I have to go home to a nagging wife. Come on, loosen me up."

The girl sat up and leaned forward. She took Mark's limp penis in her mouth, and it was only a minute or so before he ejaculated. Her mouth jumped off him and let his semen hit the floor.

"Dammit, you're letting him cum all over my carpet," Jerry said, agitated, taking a swig from his beer. "Can someone clean that up?"

"Jerry, relax; your cum will be on top of it soon," Mark joked, zipping his pants up. "So what's this guy's story?" he asked as Jerry motioned for him to come down the hallway.

He whispered, "Stop talking around everybody. You know these hookers like to bribe you when they think they can hold something over you. So here; I wrote it down. His name is Brandon Phillips. I can't get his information until Lorraine is in the office. Brandy will tell if I try to look at the files. That's not in my job description. I'm here for maintenance, not intel."

"Just give me the paper and go get your dick sucked. I'll find out what I need to know, but if you get in that office and get more information, I'll grease your palms even more." Mark turned his attention to his ringing phone.

"What street? How many down? Okay, I'm there in fifteen," he said, hanging up. Turning to Jerry, he said, "I guess this is goodbye for now, neighbor. Duty calls."

Detective Stephens got in his unmarked Chevy Impala and began to drive to Newark, New Jersey, where the murder rate was high, and his adrenaline thrived on it. He called Camilla Strong, an officer on desk duty, another of his peons.

"Listen, Camilla. I need you to look up the name Brandon Phillips and see what comes back. I don't have any other information on him yet, so to make sure I have the right guy, send me all the pictures that pop up with that name."

He pulled onto Halsey Street, a dimly lit vacant block next to a public parking lot, and joined the homicide detectives and CSI team already on the bloody scene. He shook hands with his partner Paul Sirvillo and looked around to see if there were any bystanders but couldn't see any. It was ten o'clock on a Thursday night, in a commercial district, with stores that had been closed for hours. There were loft apartments in a converted warehouse, but not much traffic at that time of night. The parking lot wasn't even that well-lit, and he hadn't noticed a single surveillance camera as he walked to the scene.

"What we got?" he asked and was given the rundown on two young black men who were lying on the ground, dead and bloody, next to a hot yellow Maserati.

"I know that this is Slim and that's Slime. They were twin brothers. They were working for the Italian mob as security at one of their strip clubs in Passaic. They were either just getting out of the car or walking back to their parked car. We have to interview the parking lot attendant and see where the surveillance cameras are. So far, all he said is that a black van pulled in and fired on them. Maybe their bosses weren't satisfied with their work," Paul, an Italian, said sarcastically.

"I wonder how many baby mamas are gonna be crying and putting up bedsheets outside of their houses tonight for the neighborhood to come and write RIP on," Mark joked.

"Well, the liquor stores won't be upset to sell out of Hennessy tonight, that's for sure," his partner responded, both laughing.

Mark zoned out while the officer on scene was talking and answering their questions. He looked at the two brothers—two bodies—and started taking a mental inventory of jewelry and clothes. Mark began calculating the cost of the Breitling watch one of the boys was wearing and had no ounce of remorse or empathy over the fact that they had just lost their lives. He looked at the blood, spatter of brain matter, and tissue that had been expelled from the bodies and onto the concrete. It was a scene he had seen too many times before.

"Are there any other witnesses?" his partner asked the responding officers, who shook their heads no. They gave each other a look that seemed like they were sharing the same thought.

With his eyes closed and his hand placed around an imaginary beauty, Brandon slowly turned her around to dip her. He laughed to himself as one of his favorite Musiq Soulchild songs, "Love", ended. He lifted his dance partner back up and was suddenly looking into Ciara's eyes.

Shaking the thought away, he asked himself, What the hell am I thinking about Ciara for? He then answered, "It doesn't matter; it's over." Startled by the ringing of his phone and the screen showing it was Ciara calling made him chuckle. "Speak of the devil and she will appear."

"Are you still in a funky mood, or are you ready to be cordial? You know the kids want to come to see the new place, and you promised them they could stay with you tonight."

One, two, three, four, five... just don't react. Don't yell. Please don't curse, Brandon coached himself.

"Are you going to say anything? What do you want me to tell them?" Ciara continued, knowing that she was annoying him and not caring.

"Ciara, listen. I know I kind of flipped on you earlier, but I had a situation with a detective that lives in the building. He's an asshole and, unfortunately, he lives on my floor. You ain't gotta try to start with me; I know you want me to say something to give you an excuse to not bring my kids to me, but I refuse to feed into your shit. Tell them they can come tomorrow." He contemplated hanging up on her again.

"See, you're always telling them whatever. When are you going to—"

"Ciara, I know you miss me. I might just miss you a little bit too. I was just thinking about you—and don't get any ideas—but I was surprised to be thinking about the beginning of our relationship, when we used to dance and have fun. All you're doing now is reminding me of why I left in the first place. Tell my kids I love them." Brandon hung up.

He went to his playlist and changed to Hip Hop to get out of the romantic mood. Jay-Z was on the menu now.

"Shit, no more thinking about this chick... or any chick. In the Ferrari or Jaguar, switchin' four lanes, with the top down, screamin' out, money ain't a thang."

He picked up a new box he'd created for his storage unit and left the condo to take it downstairs. On his way back, he stepped out into the corridor and looked around to see if the dirty detective was lurking. Instead, a white woman with two children came around the bend with garbage in their hands for the garbage compactor. Brandon was unaware the woman and children were Mark's family.

Grace was startled by what appeared to be Brandon looking for her as she made her way in his direction. She hurried her children up as they passed by. He didn't want to look at them, as he understood how it might have seemed strange for him to be looking toward them as they approached, but he could feel their eyes on his back as he walked to his door and went in.

Damn, have these people never seen a black man in real life before? Shit. I better see a black person in this building soon, or I'll have to move out of this 'Twilight Zone.'

Brandon had a few more things to unpack for the kitchen. He picked up his box of cutlery and took it to the kitchen. For him, opening the box was like being a kid in a candy store. Brandon had spent the past six months very carefully picking out everything he wanted for his place, and now he was living the moment he had been planning for.

"Look at you, shiny little pots, you virgins. We are going to get dirty. Not tonight though. Tonight, I'll go out on the strip and see what's good out here on Bloomfield Avenue. This is supposed to be a bachelor's dream location. Lots of girls, bars, lounges, and restaurants right at my doorstep. I'm going to cook the panties off of one of these chicks around here. I didn't take cooking classes for nothing."

Brandon grew up in the small city of Englewood, and he was over the hood mentality. He didn't believe he owed anything to the streets. He owed it to his hardworking family to be the best he could be. Brandon was born in Harlem, New York, and his father worked hard as a janitor to move his family to the suburbs of New Jersey. He grew up in a black neighborhood, but his city and school district were mixed. He had friends from all races, and when he was nine, his best friend was a white boy named Max. Max's family had a lot of money, and they owned numerous homes. Brandon remembered what it was that made him want to move to Montclair in the first place.

One summer day, he was invited to a pool party at one of Max's homes. The house was enormous, immaculate, and one he'd dreamed about many nights. He always dreamed of the shiny pots Max's family's chef had used to make a smorgasbord of food Brandon hadn't seen outside of a restaurant. His pots at home were scratched, and the nonstick material inside them made him scared to eat because they were so damaged. He vowed from that day, at nine years old, to buy his mom new pots, and when he got his first job as a paperboy, he did just that. He also made the decision to one day move to Montclair, and he did that too.

That experience helped Brandon stay determined to live a different life. He grew up in a working-class family and escaped the establishment's systematic agenda by not ending up in prison or with a police record. When many of his male friends were dabbling in crime, he was beginning to dabble in girls. Brandon didn't give up on his love of women, but he didn't consider himself to be a womanizer.

He flashed back to a girl named Destiny, whom he'd been in love with before Ciara. He had been with her for two years and found out she had been cheating on him. He had been working two jobs to maintain his car note and help her with her bills and still be able to take her out on dates. Meanwhile, she was going out with a local drug kingpin of a neighboring city. He confronted her when he heard the news.

"So my hard work isn't enough for you? You had to humiliate me and make me look stupid?"

"Brandon, you're nice, and I care for you, but that life is just more exciting."

That was the beginning of his trust issues with women, and she went on to have two children with the guy, who ended up being murdered. Brandon shook his head and continued unpacking.

Four hours later—after finishing the kitchen, one bathroom, and the dining room—Brandon decided it was finally time to hit the streets. It was 10 p.m. on a Thursday night, the start of the weekend.

He put on a Gucci sweatsuit and matching sneakers. He admired himself in his foyer mirror. "Damn, nigga, are you trying to catch tonight?" He stepped out into the hallway and, again, looked to the right before going left to the elevator.

Brandon had asked his friend Jay to join him at Fume Cigar Bar and Lounge, but his wife was due with their first child any day, so he was remanded to solitary confinement at home. The walk from The Raven up Bloomfield Avenue was refreshing, and the night air was brisk but comfortable.

There was a small line outside of the establishment, with very grown and very sexy people waiting to get in. He noticed a group of ladies in front of him as he joined the line, and they all noticed him too. He checked out each one.

"You ladies look like you're ready to have some fun," he said as he stepped behind them. He knew out of the four, he would at least get some conversation from one. He was just looking for someone to talk to and ask questions about his new neighborhood. What he got was much more. They all turned around as he finished his comment, and one marked her territory.

"I know you!" a white blonde with the body of a sister yelled, as if she had seen her celebrity crush in person. Brandon knew this was going to be a good night.

"You do? Do I know you? What's my name then?" The girls all started laughing.

"What I mean is, I saw you. You just moved into my building. You live at The Raven. We're neighbors."

His mind started racing as he thought, Should I have a rendezvous with someone who lives in the same building, or should I try one of her friends? Damn, slow down, man. You ain't thirsty, he told himself.

"Do y'all all live there? My name is Brandon."

"No, just me. My name is Gabriella; this is Rebecca,

Selena, and Chavon." Each girl extended her hand, and Brandon shook each and told them it was nice to meet them.

They entered the lounge, and Brandon said he would catch up with them after going to the men's room. He really just wanted to see all the sand at the beach before planting his umbrella anywhere too fast.

He went to the bar and got a cognac shot and did a slow stroll, taking in the surroundings. He caught the eye of many females, but he convinced himself not to stop and make any first moves.

He went to the men's room just in case his first group of prospects were watching him closely. When he stepped out, feeling fresh and a bit tipsy, he decided on another shot.

"Hey, you can sit right here," a woman said, pointing to the empty stool next to her.

Brandon looked around and approached her, saying, "Are you buying me a drink too? I mean, since you invited me over, it would only be appropriate."

"Sure, I can do that. I'm not old-fashioned. I'll buy you a drink if you agree to take me out on a date."

"I'll agree to take you on a date after I talk to you first."

"What's that supposed to mean?" the woman, who appeared to be older, asked. She did look good and not lacking for money. She had expensive accessories and a bag he knew to be worth at least two thousand dollars.

"It means that I'm not thirsty. If you don't have a good conversation, there will be no reason to take you on a date when I'm already turned off by you." Her eyes popped out, and she looked as if his joke didn't do what he had expected.

"Don't take that the wrong way. You seem like a woman who has seen the world and who knows what to say and do.

I'm not turned off. I'm interested in learning more. I know I can't ask you about your age, so what can you tell me? And I will have a shot of Remy."

"I can tell you that I just got divorced, and I am looking to enjoy the rest of my life. I gave twenty-five years of my life to a man who did everything bad to me except physically murder me. No, wait. I can't start male-bashing; that's not attractive." Brandon and the older lady started laughing.

"That was funny, and this is true. I mean, you are attractive; you don't need to take away from that. And if you gave that many years to someone, what is it that you want from someone now?"

"I'll be candid. I have no idea. I'm just taking it one day at a time."

The bartender brought their drinks, and Brandon took a shot while asking himself if he should just get her number and move on. He looked at his watch. He had only been inside the lounge for a half hour. He didn't want to be rude. I'm going to get six numbers tonight: a cougar, a blonde, a brunette, two black chicks, and a Spanish one. Let's see if I can win my own bet.

He listened to Shantel talk about herself and was saved by the bell when Gabriella came looking for him. She looked at him from across the room, and he gave her a head nod to let her know she could interrupt. She came up and tapped him on the shoulder.

"Brandon, you're missing the party."

He turned around and looked toward Shantel. "I was coming to the bar, and this lady kidnapped me." He and Gabriella laughed while Shantel looked confused.

"Shantel, this is my neighbor Gabriella. She's having a get-together for her friend, and I was supposed to join them.

I don't want to be rude, so can we continue this conversation on the phone? Put your number in my phone, and I'll call you tomorrow."

"Did I pass the test yet?" Shantel asked, looking intently into Brandon's eyes and ignoring Gabriella's growing impatience. Gabriella started pulling Brandon away, and he pulled back and told her to hold on. He got Shantel's number, gave her a kiss on the cheek, and whispered in her ear that he would call her in a few days.

"Damn, that senior citizen was looking like she wanted to take you home tonight." Gabriella took Brandon's hand and led him to the outdoor patio where people were smoking their cigars. "Seems like I interrupted, but I thought I was rescuing you."

"I'm glad you came and found me because I planned on hanging out with your little crew." He wasn't about to feed into her leading statement or clarify whether she was interrupting or rescuing. He still got the number, and he didn't have to lie or justify. He was young, single, and free. Sometimes that was a good thing, and other times, he did miss Ciara and the kids, his family.

"Little crew? Don't underestimate what this little crew can do. We don't need your company; we want your company. Right, girls?" Gabriella asked, dragging him to their table and sitting down. She patted for him to sit next to her.

"Yup, we wanted you. We want to show you what Montclair is like. Where did you move from?" Chavon, the black girl of the group, asked.

"I'm originally from Englewood. I've lived in other places before moving into The Raven, of course. Gabriella, what's up with that detective who lives on the sixteenth floor?"

"Oh, he's a racist asshole. Don't even pay him any mind. He's always on an ego trip."

"How can I not pay him any mind when he pulled a gun on me?"

"He did what!" She sat down and picked up her drink off the table, sipping with her eyes wide open and her ears waiting. The other girls gave their attention as well, waiting to be told what had happened. Brandon quickly went through the story, deciding how much he should reveal to these chicks he didn't even know. I can't tell them everything. Who knows who they may tell, who they know, and who knows what my next move will be? I shouldn't have even said anything. But I need to know what's up.

He decided not to share everything. "So, I was coming back downstairs with the movers, and I saw this white guy in my truck, looking at my shit. I jumped up on the back of the truck and punched him in his face, and he pulled a gun on me." The girls cracked up laughing.

"What's funny? That's funny to y'all? Damn, y'all are fucked up. Dude shouldn't have been in my possessions, sneaking around." Brandon laughed on the inside. He had them going. He wasn't sure if they were friends of his new enemy, but he doubted it seeing as Gabriella just called him a racist asshole. Either way, that was his story at the moment.

"Brandon, oh my God. I was not laughing at the guy pulling a gun on you at all. I would never do something like that. Honestly, tell him, Gabriella. I am not a callous person. Right, Gabriella?" Rebecca, a brunette, apparently the airy one of the bunch, said. Brandon wanted to fall on the floor and laugh hysterically. This girl was apologizing for nothing. And she was serious. Gabriella gave her the eye as if to say, shut up and stop talking to him. I put my dibs in first.

"Brandon, I get it. I guess he pulled the gun because he

was scared. You made it seem like he just pulled a gun out on you for no reas—"

Brandon's eyes were now the ones widening in anticipation of how Selena would explain away that confusing statement. "What I mean is, it wasn't a reason to pull a gun on you, but like I said, maybe he was scared for his life. I don't know. He shouldn't have been in your truck. I don't know if you should have assaulted him first. Maybe you could have told him to get out?" Selena shrugged her shoulders as if to say 'fuck it if he don't get what I'm saying.' Brandon was amused.

"Shut up, girl. I know Mark, and he's an asshole. He deserved to get an ass kicking because nobody told him to be in someone's truck, but that's how he is. He thinks he runs the world and especially that building. But don't let it bother you. We'll talk. I'll tell you about him at another time. Let's just have fun. This is your welcome party! Right, girls?" They all stood up and started twerking and dancing all around Brandon. He eyed each one of them from head to toe, ass to tits, smiles, and hollers.

"Damn, I guess I'm in y'all circle now for real!" he yelled over the music and laughed.

"Yup. Instead of Bosley and Charlie's Angels, we're Brandon's Angels tonight," Chavon said, and they raised their glasses to toast him. He wondered if they were going to break out in prayer after their rants and chants. He gyrated on, twirled around, held hands with, and let them all 'back their things up' on him. He felt at ease; he laughed, danced, and celebrated. He felt good. Although his intention was to go out and see what was going on, on the famous Bloomfield Avenue, he didn't expect to be the honoree of the party.

Brandon was always the life of the party, but his day had been very stressful. He felt relieved, and the celebration rejuvenated that proud, excited feeling of accomplishing a lifelong dream. He was determined not to let this dream turn into a nightmare. No one was going to steal his dream. Fuck that nigga; he doesn't want none of this. I am worthy, like my mama always told me. I am here. I have fought all my life as a black man, to be respected, and I will still fight. I will fight a good fight and get in some good trouble, as the late John Lewis always said. John Lewis, who had just died four months prior, was one of his inspirations, motivators, and examples of what a black man should be.

The night went on, and Brandon was able to break away from his harem and mingle a bit more before leaving. He accomplished his goal of six new numbers to put in his phone and on his prospective pursuit list. He was not a cigar smoker, but Gabriella bought him a cigar when he doubled back around to his 'Angels', and at about 1 a.m., and he was smoking it like a boss!

The lounge started clearing out at about one thirty, and Brandon was ready to make a move. He sat back and just took it all in. The patio was still full of people of all ages, races, and cultures, but everyone seemed to be progressive, successful, and classy. This was not just a local bar; this was an upscale lounge, and he fit in well. Brandon scanned the group and had to strategize. He knew it wasn't necessary to worry about going home with any of the women he had gotten numbers from; that would be for another time.

It was time for him to decide if he was going to go home alone, if he was going to try to get any of Gabriella's friends' numbers, or if he was going to give in to the many advances Gabriella had made throughout the night. At first, he considered her to just be friendly, but she had made many subliminal messages that she was trying to have an afterparty that did not include her little clique. Brandon had no doubt about that in his mind. He also had to advise himself like a boxing coach when a fighter was in his corner, in between rounds.

Now, if you're going to go with her, she is not coming into your apartment; you'll be going into hers. And after you lay her out on her back, side, and stomach, you aren't spending the night. You won't have a stalker living in the same building, so make it clear before anything happens, you're just there to have fun and that's it. A lot of women want you to marry them after a one-night stand. You do need to get close to her and find out what this building is about, and if you can get in her panties, getting in her brain will be easy. He got up and executed his mission.

"Damn, ladies, are y'all gonna close out the lounge? Nobody has to work tomorrow?"

"Once every three months or so, if we're not all available on a weekend, we meet up on a Thursday night and take the next day off or go in late. We've been doing this for three years. Right, girls? Ever since we all worked together. Now we don't, but this is our ritual," Chavon explained. Brandon looked at her and knew he wouldn't mind going home with her another time. He looked at Rebecca and Selena and felt the same. He knew he couldn't rightfully mess with all of them or cause drama between them, but he also decided one of them other than Gabriella would get it at a later date.

He continued with the exit strategy. "Well, I'm gonna go. I must finish unpacking tomorrow before my kids come to stay with me for the weekend. Can I get each of my Angels' numbers so I can keep in touch with everyone?"

He passed his phone clockwise around the circle. Gabriella got the phone last and said, "I'll put my number in your phone when we get to my place," and laughed and passed his phone back. "I'm ready. You ready, Charlie?" She kissed each one of her girls and grabbed Brandon's hand again, leading him to the door and walking out and onto Bloomfield Avenue.

"I didn't know I was coming to your place. Who made that decision?" Brandon teased.

"Well, if you didn't, that only leaves one of us. I just want to continue the night and get to know you a little better privately. I won't hurt you. You don't have to be scared," Gabriella joked.

"Oh, I am a little scared. You're an aggressive girl. I don't know. You better not hurt me; I'm fragile."

"Oh please. Boy, bye. I don't believe that."

Brandon thought, No this white girl did not just say 'boy, bye.' He did like her ability to have fun, her confidence, and gift of gab.

"You're right. I ain't never scared, but I must be honest. I've never had a rendezvous with someone I just met and who lived in the same building. That's a little scary. I don't want to make a friend and an enemy at the same time."

Gabriella stopped in her tracks. "What do you mean? Why would we be enemies? Do you plan on doing something bad or wrong to me to violate me or my trust in some way?" He was startled by the word trust, so he stopped too.

"Trust? What is it that you are trusting me to do? I haven't made any promises, commitments, or agreements about anything, so how can you even trust me at all? You don't know me." They slowly started walking again.

"Oh my, you are scared." Gabriella laughed hysterically and Brandon joined in, not exactly sure what it was they were laughing about. She continued. "Let me be clear. I'm not a fatal attraction or stalker, and I doubt you're a killer—or at least I don't think you would be dumb or crazy enough to do something to harm me when I know where you live.

Well, not which apartment, but it would not be hard to find out if something bad was to happen. You seem like a person who's smart and has a good head. That's why I said I just want to get to know you. I'm not asking you to make any commitments or promises. Let's just go and have part two of your celebration and have fun."

Brandon was convinced and started strutting faster, pulling her by the hand. "Now we're talking, and I'm not scared; I'm excited! But seriously, I do thank you for making sure I had a good time. That was nice of you and your friends to adopt me on my first night out."

They walked into the lobby, got on the elevator, and stepped into the lush apartment 22S of the immaculate, extravagant, and upscale "Raven" high-rise building. Gabriella's place was lit. She had modern decor, expensive taste, and what seemed to be a peaceful existence. He felt comfortable there, like he could spend the night and not feel weird and once the door closed Gabriella didn't come across as desperate as she appeared to be at the lounge.

Brandon took his shoes off, at Gabriella's request, and he just knew his clothes would be coming off shortly thereafter. Brandon was more than tipsy, and he began to take off his shirt.

"Hold on, homey. I asked you to take off your shoes to not mess up my rug. Your shirt is fine. It can stay on."

Brandon, not believing she was serious, grabbed her, pulled her to him, and started kissing her. She broke from his grip, picked his shirt up off the floor, and put it back in his hands. That sobered him up and got his attention.

"What's wrong? I thought you weren't scared," he joked. He slowly put his shirt back on and took a seat while she explained.

"Oh no, I'm still not scared. I thought you might assume that I wanted to come back home to have sex with you, and I'm not necessarily saying that it wasn't a thought. I was drunk and you look good."

"Okay, so what's the problem? I'm drunk, and you look good too." Brandon wasn't thinking at all about his reservations about sleeping around where he sleeps. That concern went right out of the window when he got inside and realized how horny he was.

"Oh, it's no problem. I listened to what you said, and you might be right." Gabriella was playing her own game. She most certainly had planned to smash, but as she got closer to the building, she imagined what would happen the next day or the next time she might see him on the elevator, in the lobby, in the pool room, etc. Gabriella figured she would have a better chance at something that was more than sex if she didn't sleep with him right away. She had to cool her jets.

"What? What did I say? You mean I talked my own self out of the pussy? No way. I cock-blocked myself? I'm going to have to have a talk with me when I get home." They both laughed, and Gabriella, still very horny herself, sat down real close to Brandon and started playing in his dreads as he put his head back on the couch.

"Don't fret, honey. First, let me show you around. Then we can figure this thing out. I mean, I'm very much attracted to you. I just don't know if I want to be in the elevator with you and a woman you may be bringing home. I won't lie and say I've never had sex with anyone I worked with, which is really the same, but it turned out to be a disaster."

"So what is it that you expect? We already had this conversation, and you said that you really can't expect anything from me at this point. Right?"

"Right, and you can't expect anything from me. I may

have led you to believe that we were coming here to have sex, but I never said we were, and you never asked. So aren't we both in the same position and on the same page? Let's just see what happens. I think you're cool. I don't want to mess up our chances of being friends by doing some hoe shit on the first date. If I didn't care about getting to know you, I would fuck you all night." They both laughed. Gabriella setting him straight made him more attracted to her.

"First of all, you must hang with Chavon a lot because you sound like a black girl, but I get it. Second of all, I have been in situations like this where a woman will lead you on and then want to be ethical and moral after dry humping me at a club. But I won't hold it against you. You're right; let's both think about how we want to approach this friendship. I don't want to ruin my first friend at my new home either. I may need you, and I don't want you to feel like I used you and then began to ignore or ridicule you when you see me. Damn, my dick is mad that I'm talking like this right now. But he'll be okay; I'll take care of him later. Let's see the layout of this bachelorette pad you have. It looks like you're having way too much fun in here," Brandon teased.

"I'm not even gonna ask how you came to that conclusion because I sure do!"

Gabriella had an expensive taste and had traveled the world. Her home was like a museum, and she shared the photos and trinkets, which told of some of her excursions. It made Brandon more intrigued and interested. He didn't even care she had decided to play hard to get because he knew that would have affected how he viewed her, and now she seemed like an attractive phenom, as opposed to a loose lady. Brandon knew he would want to come back over and spend some more time with her. He knew they would eventually get it in too.

They both were hungry and wanting to combat alcohol with some food that would absorb it. After the tour, Gabriella made him a big breakfast, and they ate on her balcony and watched the sunrise. They fell asleep on her couch fully clothed, and when he awoke to the vibration of his alarm on his Apple watch, he didn't wake her. He left her a note on her whiteboard on the refrigerator that said, "Thanks for my welcome party and sweet afterparty. Talk to you soon."

Brandon quietly left Gabriella's apartment at 8 a.m. without waking her. He stepped onto the elevator and was ecstatic to see a black woman on it. She was a lady who also had dreadlocks and appeared to be in her mid- to late sixties.

"Good morning, Miss." Brandon greeted the lady, hoping she was a part of the movement and not a sellout since she lived in the building. Her dreads made him think she might be a soldier instead, but you never could tell. Looks were deceiving. He wanted to tell her how good he felt to see a sister there, but he decided to wait for her response.

"Good morning and God bless," she sang in an upbeat, excited tone. Brandon smiled, glad that she was pleasant and not snappy.

"I'm new here, and I am excited to see a relatable face and to hear that you're in such good spirits. My name is Brandon. Do you live here, ma'am?" He was mad his mind went to a stereotypical place, imagining she would be a maid and not a resident.

"Oh, Lord, please don't call me ma'am. My husband left me for a younger woman, so I already feel old. And yes, I do live here. Welcome to The Raven." Brandon was thrown off by her disclosure and wasn't sure what to say next. "And don't worry; I'm over him. She ended up having three kids and taking him straight to the bank for alimony and child support, and now she got a young stud that she's taking care of with his money. How about that? God sure knows how to be worse than karma." Brandon and the lady both laughed. "My name is Melinda."

Brandon wanted to ask her questions like he had with Gabriella, but they had reached his floor, and he didn't want to weird her out. However, he didn't know how or when he would see her again in this enormous complex, so he took a chance.

"Nice to meet you, Miss Melinda. I'm new to the area and just need to find someone friendly who can brief me on how things work. As a black man, even in 2020, I have to be very careful. They're still hanging us from trees." Brandon stood, holding the elevator open.

"Honey, I'm off to run some errands, and I'm running a little late. You want me to stop by? What's your apartment number?" Brandon nodded and told her 16M, which she repeated as the elevator doors closed.

He walked around the bend, looking ahead for the dirty detective to show up. Although the incident had only happened the day before, he felt like he could possibly be traumatized and scarred. He didn't want to be paralyzed or fearful, not being able to move freely. This was supposed to be his sanctuary, and it shouldn't just be inside of his door.

He walked inside and took a deep breath, again saying, "I did it. I really did it." The building complex had lots of amenities—pools, gyms, shopping, and even a small three-screen theater—so he was going to be able to play where he lived, and no one was going to interfere with that.

Not to mention the bars and lounges on the strip. Thinking about the night before at Fume made him smile. He had really had a good first night. I was the man last night. Well, I'm the man every day; they just made me feel like a star. He thought about the girls who catered to him, really making him feel like it was his welcome party. He went over the whole day up until leaving Fume with Gabriella.

He floated into the kitchen, sat on the white leather stool at his island, and turned on the news. So much was going on globally, but he was still intrigued by the afterparty with Gabriella. He realized she was just 'macking' and gaming him at the lounge and having fun with it. He thought she'd be all over him or want him to be all over her at her place, but she behaved like a human and not a jump-off.

Brandon had to fight the urge to go and crawl in his bed to get a few more hours of sleep; he had to finish unpacking before his kids came for the weekend. He didn't want their help in unpacking because he knew it wouldn't look the way he wanted it to. "When you want something done right, you've got to do it yourself. Let's go." He pushed himself. He didn't have much left to do because he wanted everything to be new. He didn't want to bring a lot of old baggage, so most of his belongings went to his storage unit.

He watched the news and the election travesty, with Donald Trump refusing to concede to Joe Biden. He had done his part to vote, but his trust was always in God. That's how he had been raised: not to trust in man or in this world.

* * *

Mark Stephens was walking past 16M, and he was smiling. He had gotten some information on Brandon, and although it wasn't much, it was a start. Mark put his ear to Brandon's door and heard the news. He kept walking and got on the elevator, ready to begin another day of running the world. His world consisted of the underworld, and he felt like a ruler of it. Mark had been a detective for ten years, and the power had made him insensitive, arrogant, and uncompromising. He was always on attack mode, and it seeped into his existence and interaction with his wife and kids. Not only was Mark always looking for a problem, but his attitude helped to create them.. Mark didn't care. He was in it for the thrill of bringing anyone he wanted to bring down, down, down...

Mark was excited about the new homicide investigation he was running with his partner, Paul Sirvillo. The twins, Terence and Tyrell whose street names were Slim and Slime, who were murdered were notorious, but "Not notorious enough," Mark teased and chuckled as he stepped off the elevator and into the parking garage. The street boys—or hot boys or dope boys as the hood called them—kept the boys in blue on their toes, always giving them something to do.

Mark met Paul at the fifth precinct in Newark on Clinton Street, and they proceeded to the neighborhood where the twins grew up and were known to frequent. Mark and Paul knew nothing of black culture, only of stereotypes, having both grown up in all-white neighborhoods. They had to start from the cradle and move to the grave to work on this case.

They knocked on Tyrell and Terence's door, and a man opened the door but not the screen. He knew what detectives looked like and understood why they were there.

"How can I help y'all?" the man asked through the torn screen door. He locked the screen, and the detectives began their routine speech.

"We're here to investigate the murder of Tyrell and Terence Black. We're looking for their mom, Adena. Is she available?" Paul, the good cop of the pair, asked politely and almost apologetically. Playing the good cop was his thing, but it wasn't his true nature. He liked the thrill and drama just as much as Mark did. He just knew how to hide his pompous attitude and character better than Mark did. Mark didn't care; he liked being and playing the bad cop.

"Yeah, she's here, but she's not feeling well. We just lost

our two sons," Mr. Black stated indignantly. He began to close the door on the officers of their own law, but they continued.

"Well, can we have a word with you, sir, as those were your sons as well? Mr. Black, is it?"

Terence Black, Sr. stopped and paused. He looked at the two men at his door and took a deep breath. "How may I help you?" He stepped back from the door, not opening it or unlocking it.

"May we come in? We won't be long," Paul gently urged.

"No. There is no reason for you to step foot in my house. Find out who killed my sons. Yes, they grew up with their father in the house."

"We'd like to do that, but we could use your help. Do you know of anyone who would want to kill your sons and why?" Paul took out a notepad and clicked his pen open.

Mr. Black crossed his arms and leaned back. With his head back, he looked up to the ceiling and scratched his head. "Now, where should I begin? Let's see. America, and that's Ameri-K-K-K-ah. Like yourself, police officers don't want to see young black men make it or have more than you. Um, a lot of white people. Should I continue?"

Mark became immediately agitated. "Mr. Black, we're trying to find out who killed your sons. Do you think this is a joke?" he said rudely.

"Mr. Detective, you would think I'm joking the day after my sons were murdered; it just proves my point. One, that you're oblivious to the fact that not only are you officers of your own law a big part of the problem, but that you're in denial... or you just don't give a damn. This country does not, has not, and probably never will want to see the black man prosper, make the money you make, have the houses you have, live in your neighborhoods, or drive the same cars."

"Mr. Black, if I may be honest, statistics show that your sons most likely were killed by someone they know, of the same race as them. Everybody is always complaining about the police, but your kind is killing themselves."

"I'm gonna say this—and I don't know why because it'll be a waste of my breath—if my sons were killed by someone who looks like them, that does not erase the systemic mental abuse that each person faces—like myself, my sons, and the millions of black boys and men who live in a country that wants to destroy us. They may have pulled the trigger, but this racist nation was the puppet master." Mr. Black shut the door.

Having no understanding of the man's perspective, Mark and Paul walked away, shaking their heads as if he had said something outlandish. It didn't matter whether they didn't understand or they didn't want to accept the truth, because the facts would never change. One thing was for sure: They were dead silent walking back to the car until they spotted Cheesy.

Cheesy was the neighborhood gossip king and crackhead. He was riding his bike in the middle of the street. Mark ran in the middle of the road to stop him. Cheesy tried to avoid him but was stopped when Mark grabbed his handlebars. Paul casually walked over to partake in their second interview.

"Hey, Cheesy. Where've you been, bro? I've been looking for you," Paul said, steering him over to the corner. Cheesy was unable to avoid the detainment.

"Listen, y'all. I don't know nothin'. Please don't bother me out here. The last time I talked to y'all, I almost ended up dead. Please let me go." Cheesy was nervous, looking around and behind his shoulders. He stepped off the bike and tried to walk away and leave it, but Mark grabbed him by the arm.

"Hey, man, where you going? Just act like we're giving

you a hard time. Who killed the twins? What's the word on the streets?"

"The word on the streets is that the Italian mob did it. That's all I know. Let me go."

"Listen, Cheesy, you owe us. Meet us at our meeting spot in one hour. We got something good for you. You know we always take care of you."

"I'll try." Cheesy got back on his bike and rode off.

"You better," Mark said.

There were the usual groups of unemployed and street-employed people hanging out. They watched as Mark and Paul approached the group on the stoop. Swazy, who was too familiar with the detectives, called out.

"I don't even know why y'all are coming this way. We don't fuck with y'all police. Y'all probably had somebody kill the twins." Mark approached Swazy, grabbed him, and patted him down. The small crowd started groaning and complaining.

"Yo, leave him the fuck alone. Y'all ain't got shit better to do than expect everyone to solve your cases for you!" They backed up and started walking to their car.

"At least we got jobs," Mark said, laughing.

"We got a thousand dollars for the person who will give up who killed Slim and Slime. Y'all know how to reach us. Some of y'all are always helping. We won't say no names, though," Paul said while getting in the car and slamming the door.

Let's go see their girlfriends. They have kids with two sisters. How convenient. They take twinning very seriously. Gotta fuck under the same roof too." The detectives laughed.

"It doesn't matter what anyone says; we have to handle

this situation before it gets out of hand," Mark said. "We can't be laughing until we sew this thing up and tie up loose ends."

"Of course, but we also have to find out what the people close to them know."

The two officers pulled up to the condominium building the sisters lived in, with adjacent apartments. Surprisingly, they found the address through the tracking of the brothers' cell phones. The twins' licenses were registered to their parents' home, which was what many people working in illegal businesses did so the police would have difficulty finding them.

The building was new and immaculate and in what some would call the "good" part of Newark. The officers buzzed the two apartment bells. One didn't respond. The other intercom was answered with a "Who's there?"

"Uh, this is Paul Sirvillo."

"For?"

"I'm a detective investigating the deaths of Terence and Tyrell Black. May my partner and I ask you a few questions?"

After a long pause, the response was, "Come on up."

On the way over, Mark and Paul had discussed their strategy on how they would get as much information as possible. Now it was time for their acting skills to come into play.

Two beautiful, seductive, and shapely women were standing in the hallway, talking, their doors ajar, when Mark and Paul exited the elevator on the seventh floor. The women sized them up as they approached. One of the women was visibly pregnant, and the other was holding an infant. There were other children playing inside of the apartments as well.

Mark went forward and held out his hand to introduce

himself. No one took his hand to shake it, so he put it back down. "Ladies, my name is Mark Stephens, and this is my partner, Paul Sirvillo. We're here to see if you have any information on the deaths of Terence and Tyrell. May we ask you a few questions? First, of course, starting with your names."

"May I ask why you don't offer us protection, especially knowing that if we talk to you, we're putting ourselves at risk for retaliation? What would really make me want to share what I know? You don't care what's gonna happen to my kids and me after you solve your case," the pregnant sister said, and the other nodded in agreement.

"That's an excellent question." Paul interjected in what seemed like a genuine response. They knew they would get nowhere being harsh and stern with the two women. They had to show compassion. "And I understand your concerns. It's about us working together. We can't protect you if we don't know who we should be protecting you from." The sister who was holding her infant shook her head.

"We're scared. We don't know what to do. We don't know who knows where we live. We don't know if the situation is over or not."

"What situation?" Mark inched closer, speaking softly and beginning to smile on the inside, feeling the two women would be easy to crack. The women looked at each other and asked to speak privately. They stepped into one of the apartments, closed the door, and came out a few minutes later.

"Ladies, this would be much more discreet if we went into one of your apartments. Can we do that?" They looked at each other again.

"We have a conference/community room at the end of

the hall. Let me see if someone's in there." The pregnant sister seemed to be the more dominant one.

Mark gave Paul the eye and gestured toward the quiet one.

"Can I at least have your name so I can address you properly?" Paul moved closer to her, and she felt him in her space and took a step back. "You don't have to be frightened. We aren't the bad guys."

"It doesn't matter that you have a badge. I know plenty of bad cops. And my name is Désiré."

"Désiré? Well, I don't want to say anything inappropriate, but I do understand why that's your name. Is that the real name that your mom gave you?" Paul grinned and Désiré blushed.

"Yes. My mom said she knew I would be a beautiful woman," she said, playing with the baby's fingers.

"Is this your baby? She's beautiful too. Is she by one of the twins?" Paul went to touch the baby, and Désiré moved back again. "I'm sorry. I mean no harm," he said charmingly.

Désiré's sister, Harmony, urgently walked back to the group.

"Listen, I'm not feeling well. My baby is kicking. Y'all got fifteen minutes. Follow me." Harmony turned around and led them down the hall. "Désiré, close our doors and tell the kids we'll be right back. Leave the baby in the apartment with—"

"Are there young kids in the apartment alone, ma'am?" Mark interrupted, although he was the least bit concerned.

"My name is Harmony, and my aunt is in there with them. Thank you."

All four walked into the lounge area on their floor and sat

across from each other, with the sisters and detectives sitting next to each other.

"How can we assist you, although you should be assisting us?" Harmony asked.

"Miss Harmony, we're just doing our job. We're trying to find out what led up to the murders of your boyfriends."

"Fiancés," Harmony corrected. "We were gonna get married next year. I know you're doing your job, but do you have any information?"

"We don't have much information. We're aware Slim and Slime both worked at the Boom Boom Room in Passaic, and they worked the night of this occurrence. Their car's location was in Newark on a street that's usually deserted and in a parking lot that's old and doesn't have cameras. We're looking at cameras on adjoining streets for any cars in the vicinity, but you have to understand that sometimes people can wait for hours until a target arrives. It seems to have been a well-thought-out plan. Someone could have walked up, or someone could have been on a roof. There are so many variables. Right now, we have no suspects, and we have nothing that stands out on the cameras. That's why we're asking for your help. We don't want it to be a case where the person remains on the loose and hurts someone else. Did they have any known enemies or altercations recently with anyone that you know of?"

"They had a problem with Escobar. Yeah, Escobar sent a threat to them through their cousin," Harmony said as if she had a change of heart and was eager to cooperate.

"Okay. What was the threat, and who is the cousin?" Mark asked, taking a notepad and pen from his suit jacket. The girls looked at each other. Désiré remained quiet while Harmony remained in control of the conversation.

"We don't want to put her in danger. Can you work on that lead first and see if anything comes up? I heard he was at the club that night too."

Mark and Paul gave each other a look, not knowing whether Harmony was just giving them anything or genuinely giving accurate information.

"Can you give us some information about who Escobar is? Since we know that it isn't Pablo himself," Mark said, holding back a chuckle.

"Yeah, he runs the twins' parents' block. He's the man out there. Now, is there anything else? We need to get back to the kids and the planning of this funeral."

"Oh, you have to plan the funeral? That's awful. So sad. You two seem like strong women. I hope everything works out well for you and your family. Did you have any insurance policies?"

Paul spoke up, interrupting Mark. "Mark, they're grieving. I don't think that's important right now. But, ladies, we have a trust fund that was started a few years back for children whose parents have been murdered. If you need anything, don't hesitate to call." Paul took out his card and gave it to Désiré. Mark gave his card to Harmony. Both their eyes brightened after hearing that they could receive financial assistance.

"It's been very hard. People always assume that because we live in a violent city, we're okay with it, like we're used to it or that we think it's normal. We don't. We didn't want our kids to have to grow up without their dads," Désiré spoke, on the verge of tears. Paul got up and walked over to console her. He rubbed her back as Harmony looked on in disgust.

"I understand. We see this too often, and people think the

same about us because we have a violent job, that we are not affected. Give me a call. I would like to help you."

Désiré wiped her tears and said okay. The officers thanked them and left the ladies in the room. They were on their way to meet Cheesy and see what he could tell them about this Escobar.

Brandon was awaiting the arrival of his children, twelve-year-old Malika and nine-year-old Major. He only had two loft beds set up in their room to partake in creating their second home together. Brandon missed living the family life but not the strife he and Ciara went through. He couldn't put his finger on why they had had so many issues. There were a lot of variables that contributed to their stressful and volatile union.

Brandon himself had been raised by his father, but his dad had died when he was fourteen, leaving him to become a man on his own. Although his mother had done a lot to try and make up for the void in his life, there were just some things about manhood he couldn't teach himself. Yes, a few men throughout his childhood tried to step in and rear him, but he never respected their approach. They acted like his dad, not his friend or mentor. He was an angry kid and had held a lot of his emotions in. He felt resentment toward his father for dying.

On the other hand, Ciara had been raised by her father, while her mother had abandoned the family. She was miserable too. She felt that she had never been taught how to be a woman, and the various women her father dated just didn't measure up for her. Her father eventually married when Ciara was seventeen and about to graduate high school and go to college. She had missed all of the nurturing and had begun a path of destruction early on that her father narrowly helped her escape. So there they were—two young adults having children and playing house, without a clue or rulebook on what to do to make it harmonious, positive, and emotionally healthy for themselves and their children.

The end result was a lot of fighting, breaking up, getting back together, and repeating the cycle. Brandon's doorbell rang, and he swung open the door after checking to make sure it wasn't the stalker down the hall. He had been in the building for two days, but it had felt like a week already with all that had transpired. He had moved in, been held at gunpoint, met a sexy neighbor, met a possible ally, unpacked, and reminisced, all while trying to figure out what his next move in life was going to be. He enjoyed his position at Love and War and was eager to get back to work on Monday, but there was just something missing.

"Heyyyyyyyyyyyyyyyy, there are my babies!" Brandon said as Malika and Major grabbed him and hugged him tightly. "Okay, group hug!"

"Mommy, come on," Malika said, opening her arm to invite her mom into the cipher. Ciara looked at Brandon and rolled her eyes while joining them. The kids started screaming as they dropped their bags and ran to check out the incredible view of New York from the living room.

"Hey, take y'all shoes off. You ain't gonna mess up this house like you do the other house! Come pick these bags up, put them in your room, and leave your shoes in there."

"Oh, the other house is what it is now, huh?" Ciara traipsed around the apartment as the children ran from room to room, yelling in excitement and awe. She looked out of the massive living room window and paused. Ciara looked at the beautiful view and, for a moment, imagined living there too. She had never thought she and Brandon wouldn't make it or wouldn't be able to work out their problems. Brandon joined the kids in their room, and they began discussing ideas about how they wanted their room to be.

"Daddy, I want a swinging chair to hang from the ceiling, and I want a beanbag chair for that corner, and I want—"

"Oh, Lord. I should have known there would be a thousand things. I should have just decorated the room myself," he joked, hugging Malika.

"Well, I want a basketball hoop and a new PS5. Can we have two different TVs in here?" Major added.

"Let me get out of here. Y'all make a list and we can go over it. Geesh!" Brandon pulled the door closed to their bedroom just in case he was bombarded by Ciara when he returned to the living room.

He walked back into the living room and found Ciara standing in the same spot, whimpering. He had a moment of remorse and compassion for her pain. Although he didn't want to deal with it, he knew that he had to, and not just for her, but so the kids wouldn't feel bad for being happy while their mom was feeling depressed. He did what most women say most men do all the time: he asked a stupid question.

"What's wrong?" He hadn't even gotten the word wrong off his lips when Ciara spun around and verbally attacked him.

"Really, Brandon? What's wrong? What the fuck do you think is wrong! I gave you eleven years of my life, I gave you two beautiful children, and you move on with your life like I'm nothing!"

The kids heard the commotion and stayed in their room. They weren't in the mood for the drama between their parents. Malika pulled Major by the arm, and they tiptoed into their father's room to watch TV. They tried to turn the volume up as loud as possible, but they could still hear their parents' loud voices, although they couldn't hear what they were saying.

"Ciara, how many times do we have to have this conversation? We weren't getting along! Our kids don't deserve to grow up in a volatile household. Do you always have to make every encounter about you? Can you ever think about them?"

"I gave my life to them too! You don't think enough about them to have done everything you could to keep their family together! I can't fucking stand you. You're a selfish son of a bitch, and you talk about me?" Ciara jumped across his all-white living room and punched Brandon in the chest. He grabbed her wrists and dragged her to the door, and as he was about to open the door and put her out, the doorbell rang.

They stopped dead in their tracks and looked at each other. Brandon, still clutching Ciara's wrists, leaned in to look through the peephole and was infuriated to see Mark at his door. He gave Ciara a look that said, "If you say a word, I will fuck you up." He swung open the door and startled Mark.

"Is everything okay in here, guy?" Mark asked, looking past Brandon and into Ciara's face, then the kids who came running to see who was at the door.

"Listen, man, move away from my door. I didn't ask for your help. We're fine."

"Are you okay, ma'am? I'm an officer who lives down the—"

"You're off duty and in my personal space and business," Brandon stated, cutting him off.

"You're a resident who's causing a commotion on my floor. We don't have incidents like this in this building. This is a safe building. I'm going to have to ask you to keep it down." Mark winked at Brandon and slowly walked away.

Brandon slammed the door and whispered in Ciara's face, "You are no longer welcome to come in here. From now on, I'll meet you downstairs and outside. Kids, come and say goodbye to your mother." Brandon didn't move away from her but stood there while Malika and Major gave Ciara a hug as she silently wept, not wanting to move.

"Malika, grab my pocketbook off of that chair, please." Malika did as she was told.

"Mommy, don't cry," Malika said, giving her a hug and walking back into the bedroom where Major had returned to watch TV.

Ciara looked at Brandon with disgust and walked out the door. Brandon shook his head. He knew he had to protect her. He opened his door and walked behind her. She turned around, saw him, and proceeded to the elevator. Brandon paused and watched as she stepped in, and the doors closed. He walked back to his door and paused, debating if he should go around the bend and find Mark, but he knew he couldn't do that. He would have knocked him out, so he decided to deal with his children instead.

"You guys all right? I'm sorry about me and your mom," Brandon said under his breath, tired of always having to apologize for his and Ciara's chaotic behavior.

"Dad, I'm used to it, but actually, it's rather counterproductive to the advancement of the black community," Major confessed and advised, shrugging his shoulders. At the same time, Malika shook her head after hearing her brother's answer. She looked at her dad with a bit of disdain.

"That's not even good, even though I'm glad that you

aren't upset. It should naturally have some effect on you; we are your parents." Brandon didn't even know what that was supposed to mean.

"Why can't y'all just love each other? If you loved each other before, you should love each other now. That's what I think, Dad, but you don't listen to me anyway because I'm a kid, so I don't matter," Major said sarcastically, then realized he could get reprimanded for talking to his father like that.

"Listen, man... I know you don't like the situation, and I feel bad for you, but you'll understand more when you become an adult. The black community has a lot of trauma, and unfortunately, our biggest ally is also our greatest adversary. Black women and men often dump their problems on each other instead of being each other's peace. I know it hurts. It hurts me too." Brandon sat at the foot of his bed, where his children were lying comfortably.

"Dad, I really don't want to talk about it. If you loved Mommy, you could have worked it out. I like your place, though," Malika stated matter-of-factly.

"Malika, you don't know what you're talking about. I have tried to work it out. I'll be in the living room. We're going to a restaurant down the street for dinner in a few hours." Brandon stormed out the room, unable to hide his frustration.

* * *

A sobbing Ciara entered the elevator and noticed an older black woman with dreads looking at her.

"Baby girl, you okay? Well, that was a dumb question. And I can't ask you what's wrong because that would be rude, so let me just pray for you. Oh, that might be offensive to you. I'm sorry. I just hate to see another black woman cry. Girl, we have cried oceans, haven't we?" Melinda joked, trying to lighten Ciara's spirit.

"We sure have. And I would love for you to pray for me. I need it." Ciara wiped her tears and looked at Melinda for some word that would help her gather herself. Melinda put out her hands and Ciara grabbed them.

"Lord, this young lady needs some healing and peace. This young lady needs you, Lord, because only You can ease her pain. Only You can cover her heart and mind. Give her a hedge that she may be protected from whatever is harming her, Lord. In Jesus' name, amen." Melinda squeezed Ciara's hands before letting go. They were unmoved by people getting on and off the elevator.

"Thank you so much, ma'am. I really appreciate that." Ciara wiped the last tear that was in her eyes. "Maybe it's working already."

"Please don't call me ma'am. My name is Melinda, and of course it's working. Everything with God is for your good. So if your tears are for someone who hurt you, then God removing them would be something to rejoice about. I know it's easier said than done, but you are a gorgeous girl. You got the curves and the face. You remind me of what's that girl's name? Cardi B's friend? They did that 'Wet Ass Pussy' song."

Ciara told her she was referring to Megan Thee Stallion, and Melinda said, "Yeah, her. If you got the smarts too, then you're a triple threat. Don't let no one steal your joy or make you feel unworthy of the best. But you've gotta believe that yourself first." The elevator doors opened at the lobby, and the two stepped off, still conversing.

"Do you have a minute? I'm going to the coffee shop right there. Do you need to talk?" Melinda pointed to the shop that was in the lobby mall. There were plenty of shops in the building, with various businesses catered to children and family activities. There was even a large indoor park in the basement, next to an astronomically large laundry room.

"Yes, I have a minute." Ciara sighed, realizing her initial plan of spending some time with her family had backfired because she had been unable to contain her emotions. She needed to talk to someone about her situation with Brandon, and her friends and family were all tapped out on their countless issues. They were well past the point of hearing about their years of unending drama.

"So would I be wrong to assume that those tears were male-inspired?" Melinda asked Ciara as they walked to a small table after ordering their beverages.

"No, not at all, unfortunately." Ciara sipped her extra-sweet French vanilla medium roast. She really wasn't a coffee drinker but needed an excuse to stay.

"Well, you can say 'unfortunately,' but it's better than having just found out that you had stage-four cancer, ain't it?"

Ciara thought about it and nodded in agreement. "It's just that my ex just moved away from me and my children after us being together for over ten years. I gave him all of me and had two children for him and—"

"Wait a minute, is his name Brandon?" Melinda realized Ciara had gotten on the elevator on the same floor the new resident she had met the other day had. She remembered him asking her to stop by. Ciara looked surprised and nodded.

"It's like I love him, but I hate him now. I have no way of coping with these feelings."

"Girl, I've been there and so have millions of other women. And that is definitely unfortunate. We have this idea of true love and a fairy tale, and it usually ends in tragedy and disaster."

"I know. My mom left my family, and I wanted a family of my own so bad. I was young. I made mistakes. I learned as we went, but so much damage has been done. Our kids are already twelve and nine. I don't even know where the time went. But I have to accept that there's no chance of us working it out. I mean, first, he moved in with his cousin Jarrod, and now he bought this place. He has clearly moved on, and I'm sitting here stuck."

"Girl, he seems like a nice guy." Ciara looked at Melinda with disgust. "I know, I know. They all pretend and portray themselves as these good guys, and behind closed doors, they're monsters. But he seems reasonable. I mean, he doesn't appear to be a total asshole. I actually met him in the elevator, like I met you. He asked me about the building, and I told him I would stop by and talk and give him the rundown. There's a lot of shit going on in this place."

"Have you been here long?" Ciara began to feel like maybe Melinda was going to try to help her in some way.

"Well, this building is only three years old, but I'm one of the first residents. And I know everything because I like to frequent with the super sometimes to get all the info, girl." The two women broke out in laughter. "He's a white guy, but he doesn't have family, and I'm like an auntie to him. He pays me to cook for him, clean, and run errands and stuff."

"That's nice of you," Ciara replied.

"Listen, I have an idea. I'm going to go and stop by and talk to Brandon. I'm going to tell him that I met you. I'm going to offer my babysitting services and see what information I can get. I'm all for the black family and our kids having both of their parents together. We have enough problems in this world. We've got to become allies with the black man, although it appears to be nearly impossible. But give me your number. I'll keep you posted." The new comrades exchanged numbers and hugged.

"Girl, I'm either going to help you get your family back, or we will figure out a plan B so that you can be happy. You're still young. Maybe we can find you a rich man in this building and see how he likes that. No, that's bad. I shouldn't be plotting against my neighbor. But I have to rock with the black woman first. He better act right because he doesn't want me on his bad side. Let's just see what happens. I may get up there, and this man will tell me that you're a crazy person."

"Don't they all say that about us women, that we are all crazy? They never take responsibility for their part in it, though. He probably will say something bad, but I don't feel crazy. I did. Now, I just feel like a clown for still crying over this man who doesn't even give a damn." Ciara shook her head and walked away as Melinda watched her with compassion.

Melinda had planned to do some shopping in the lobby, but she was compelled to see Brandon instead. She got on the elevator and was at his door, ringing the bell while thinking of her strategy. Brandon opened the door, a curious look on his face, and Melinda walked right in.

"Why are you looking all surprised, brother? You asked me to stop by, right?" Melinda walked past Brandon and was impressed by the all-white kitchen and living room she could see from the small corridor.

"Oh my, this is nice. Did you change your mind about me coming, or can I sit down at this nice counter and chat with you? I have a bone to pick with you." Brandon motioned for Melinda to sit down.

"Miss, I'm sorry, but I completely forgot your name. Yes, I did ask you to come, and—" They both turned as the kids ran into the living room.

"Daddy, who's that?" Major asked as Malika quietly stood by.

"Major, what is wrong with your manners? Miss..."

"Melinda. My name is Melinda Jackson, and if you don't speak to me properly, I'm going to put you over my knee. My grandson is about your age, and I was gonna say you could play with him, but you might be a bad influence, being all rude like that. When an adult enters the room, you say, 'Hello, how are you? May I help you? My name is Major, and

I will work for free.'" Major and Malika looked confused, and Melinda burst out laughing.

"Honeypies, relax. I'm only joking. I just met yo' mama on the elevator, and she seems like a woman who would teach her kids right, and I met yo' daddy here on the elevator the other day, and I thought he seemed like a pretty levelheaded gentleman too. Represent your parents. You know I would love to babysit you and straighten you out." Melinda put a fist up, and Major and Malika ran back to the room. Melinda and Brandon started laughing.

"You know I'm just messing with them. I do babysit, though, if you ever need me. I keep my grandkids all the time, so they can have playdates, but that's not what I'm here for. Before I tell you why I came, you can tell me why you invited me."

"You are hilarious. You know who you remind me of?"

"Jennifer Lewis. She's actually my cousin's cousin's cousin, and if you believe me, I have some land I'm selling from a flowerpot."

Brandon shook his head. "You should let me manage you and get you out on the comedy circuit. But on a serious note, I wanted to talk to you about a detective that lives in the building."

"Mark Stephens. He's a racist asshole. I would say stay away from him, but you live down the hall, so that's gonna be hard. You had a run-in with him already? Damn, how long have you been here?"

"This is my second day. Yesterday, when I was moving in, he pulled a gun on me."

"He did what! Did you report him to management?"

"Not yet. I wanted to figure out the best way to deal with it. What's his problem?"

"Besides probably having a little dick, he's like most other white boys in America who grew up thinking he was superior to everyone who didn't look like him. He had white privilege his whole life, and now he sees that other people are successful, and he can't stand it. I'll pay Jerry, the super, a visit and find out if there've been any antics or tactics yet. Mark likes to use him for information, and I like to use him for his money. No, I don't mean that; I mean that I enjoy the benefits of helping others. I gotta go and get to the bottom of this." Melinda got up and sat back down.

"Wait... Might I ask, why was your beautiful children's mother crying in the elevator?" Brandon paused and stood still. He didn't know where to begin.

"Listen, tell me another day. Take my number. I can see you'll need me, so let's just say I'll be your consultant on this matter of this asshole for now, and if I have to put in too many hours of private-eye work, then I will be charging you. I do want to talk about Ciara. She seems lovely. Text me your number. I want to hear about her." Melinda left swiftly on her mission to save a black man and a black man's family.

* * *

Brandon and the kids walked to Cuban Pete's, a well-known restaurant on the strip. The weather was good for November. As a family, they window-shopped and laughed and joked the whole way there. As soon as they sat, Brandon was ready for dialogue with them.

"So what y'all think about my place?" He looked intently between Malika and Major.

"Dad, I want us all to live there, Mommy too. We're a family." Major looked away as he finished his sentence, hoping not to be reprimanded by his father for telling his true feelings.

"Major, get it in your head. Our family is dead." Before Malika could say the next word, Brandon was nose-to-nose with Malika. She jerked her head back.

"Malika, don't you ever let me hear you say your family is dead again, do you hear me? You ain't grown, and you don't even sound intelligent," Brandon scolded.

"Dad, it's just a figure of speech. Of course the family is not dead... but the family is dead." Malika stared at her father who was speechless as he looked at his teenager and had to face the reality of her point.

"You never know," Brandon said, asking himself if he really meant that there was a possibility of reconciliation or if he was selfishly but unknowingly selling them a dream.

"So if you'll get back with Mommy, what's the purpose of all of this moving and everything? Mommy is beautiful. She deserves someone to love her and not break her heart."

Brandon slowly dropped back down into his seat, took a deep breath, and said, "Y'all have to understand that I'm human. I make mistakes. I've made mistakes with Mommy, but Mommy isn't perfect either. When two people love each other, they have to do the necessary things to make it work. One person can't do it. Now, I'd love to keep talking about your mother and me, but... no, I'm lying. I don't want to talk about it. I'm just as confused as you guys. Feel better now?"

"I don't want to even think about it anymore. It makes me feel bad." Major picked up a crayon and started coloring his menu.

Brandon wished he could say something that would fix the situation, but he didn't know the solution. He was just relieved to at least be honest. He couldn't pretend he had all of the answers. But he wanted them to know it affected him too.

“I’m sad too. Now, let’s have some fun.”

Brandon and his kids enjoyed the food and celebratory atmosphere and nearly couldn’t walk back from being so full. While they were out, Melinda was working on her own recipe.

Brandon, Malika, and Major arrived back at the building, and they were all lying in Brandon’s bed, watching TV, when the kids fell asleep.

Brandon moved out into the living room to relax and listen to some music. He called Melinda but got her voicemail. He went through his phone to see who to call and passed by Gabriella’s name. He figured he would see what Gabriella was up to. She answered on the first ring.

“Hey, Brandon, I didn’t think I’d hear from you so soon. How was your day?”

“Oh, it was good. My kids are here. We just went to Cuban Pete’s. That food is fire.”

“Yes, it is. That’s cool. Do the kids like your place?”

“They love it.” Brandon smiled, reminding himself of his major accomplishment.

“So when am I gonna be invited to see it?”

Brandon got up and tiptoed to the bedroom to see if the kids were still sleeping. He had a thought to invite her over and wrestled with it. “When did you want to?” He thought it would be nice to get some action. He was feeling tense with all of the drama between Mark and Ciara. He wondered if Gabriella would still play hard to get or if that was just her resisting the first-night stigma.

“Well, I’m not doing anything. I don’t know if you want to introduce me to the kiddies, but children actually really like me. I have a few nieces and nephews that wish I was their mom instead." They laughed and she admitted that she was only kidding.

"Let me see if you look presentable. FaceTime me back; I forgot what you look like," Brandon pressed the FaceTime button to merge from a regular call to video.

Gabriella's call came through and when he accepted, she was topless.

"Do I look presentable enough for you?" She winked. Gabriella had her hair up in a ponytail and had on shorts that barely covered her but showed her camel toe. Her crop top was pulled down to expose her supple breasts and a small heart tattoo over her real one.

"Oh yeah, real presentable. Why couldn't I see these pretty things last night? I know you've heard you have pretty titties." He was instantly erect and trying to decide if he should get some in his office since the kids were in his bedroom.

"Yes, I've heard, that I'm pretty and perky." Gabriella had clear skin and was toned. She wasn't too skinny or too thick for his liking; she was a model type with blonde hair and blue eyes. She looked like she liked to tan because she had a bronze glow.

"Let me see them jump." Brandon stuck his hands down his pants. He couldn't wait to bust a nut, so he decided to get it done virtually instead of killing the mood by telling her to stop and come over.

"Oh, so you want to get nasty over the phone, I see." Gabriella stood up and started dancing around to no music. She moved over to her laptop and put on "I Like It Like That" by Cardi B. as her song of choice. Gabriella placed the phone on the stand, moved away from the table, and danced and enticed Brandon even more. She sensually rubbed on her breasts and licked her fingers, looking into the screen intently at her audience of one. She turned back to let him watch her ass, pulling down her short shorts for his viewing pleasure. Brandon was impressed. Women come in all shapes and sizes, and he enjoyed the variety. He knew he would never marry any other woman but a black woman, but marriage was the furthest thing from his mind.

"So is this what you called me for?" Gabriella sat back on the couch with her legs up and spread open. She was confident, freaky, playful, and sexy. She controlled the room and loved the attention of one-on-one interaction more than the public. She was reserved at work and outside, except when partying with her girls, but was a dominatrix when it came to sexual encounters. She was never shy or scared.

"No, but I'm glad I did. This is a nice surprise." Brandon was stroking himself.

"I'll let you see the kitty if you let me see the snake." Gabriella put her hands in her panties and started rubbing on herself. Brandon pulled his tool out of his pants and let it stand up by itself.

"Damn, he's good looking too. I'm sure they would have great fun together." Gabriella pulled her panties off and threw them to the floor. She spread her lips open and slowly put her fingers in and out while gyrating her hips. Gabriella pretended it was Brandon's hands touching her. She imagined him being right there with her and was ready to allow herself to have multiple orgasms. She was whining and purring like a pussy cat.

Brandon stuck his tongue out, pretending he was licking her, but in his mind, he knew that would never happen. He didn't put his mouth on everyone.

Gabriella got up and grabbed the phone and put it close to her clit, while Brandon jerked hard and released faster than he would have liked. He didn't want to make her think he didn't have the stamina, but the past two days had been so stressful he couldn't wait to bust a nut.

"That looks like a good creamy shake; I would love to drink that one day," Gabriella teased.

"Oh yeah? Well, we can arrange that real soon. My kids will be leaving on Sunday. Let's hit the strip and then you're invited to come here after." Brandon stuck his thing back in his boxers and pulled up his sweatpants. He paused when he noticed Gabriella was cumming with damn near her whole fist inside of herself. Brandon's mouth dropped, and he almost wanted to laugh.

"Damn, you ain't playin', Snow White. Get that nut. You look pretty with the cum face." Brandon sat back down, leaned back, and put his head back while listening to her moan.

Melinda called Jerry on the way down to his apartment.

"Hey, Melinda, what are you up to, sweetie? I haven't seen you in, like, a month. You cheatin' on me behind my back?" Jerry joked.

"Yup, because you always cheat on me. I was gonna stop by just to check on you. You have any of your hoes or sluts around?"

"No, I'm all alone. You want to make me dinner for the next three days? Are you in the mood? I've been working double-time trying to get this building repaired and decorated for Thanksgiving, and I've already spent too much ordering out this month. You always give me a good price."

"Sure. I'll be down in a minute." Melinda was the auntie Jerry never had. He was brought up in foster homes, and she was a foster mom, and when they first met and shared that information with each other, they immediately formed a bond. Melinda felt most of his self-destructive behavior was caused by the void of not having a loving family during childhood. She had seen it too many times before, which is why she had to stop being a foster mom when her own children came of age. Melinda had become attached and too emotionally scarred from the knowledge of what some of her foster children had endured as innocent minors. Her profession was a social worker, and then she became the head director of Social Services in Newark before retiring and moving into The Raven.

Jerry trusted Melinda and would do anything for her because she had his back like no one in his life ever had. He had been in very loving black foster homes and very dysfunctional white ones, so he was not racist at all. He had black foster siblings, as well as other races.

Jerry trusted Melinda and would tell her about everything that went on in the building and would spill the beans even more if he was under the influence of narcotics.

Melinda stepped off the elevator and knocked on Jerry's door. He opened it up in nothing but his boxer shorts, as he usually did.

"Hey, cutie. Come on in." Jerry walked back to the living room and to his usual porno film.

"Okay, I'm here now. Do you need that on? I mean, I know I'm not perky and fluffy anymore, but right now, my ego can't take that." Melinda pointed at the porno on the screen.

"Melinda, you are the most beautiful woman I know; those girls just get my dick hard. You have my heart," Jerry confessed.

Jerry picked up a bill with white powder in it and sniffed it up into both nostrils.

"Jerry, you really need to get yourself together and off of the controlled dangerous substances. But you don't listen, so what's new? I see we have a lot of new people moving in," Melinda probed.

"That's always the case. People move in and people move out, nothing new about that."

"Yeah, and Mark spies on some and gets them kicked out. Dickhead, he is. I remember that nice girl that was a high-paid call girl, and he watched her place and started arresting all of her johns because she wouldn't fuck him for free."

"Yeah, he's a pain in my ass. He got me about to spy on some black guy that just moved in. I haven't met the guy yet, but he better be on the up and up because he lives on Mark's floor, poor guy. He doesn't know what evil is lurking down the hall." Jerry took another sniff.

"This guy. It's not enough that I'm sure he's harassing civilians while he's at work. He gotta throw his weight around when he's off duty. What he's doing is illegal, having you spy on people."

"Yeah, but I don't need any problems, so I have to stay on his good side. He got me off on a sexual harassment charge from one of the tenants here and helped some of my drug arrests disappear, so he thinks I owe him for life. One day I'm gonna use his own shit against him; when the time is right." Jerry took a swig of vodka straight.

"Yeah? What do you have on him?"

"Lots of stuff. Mark not only spies on black and Spanish guys because he feels they don't belong here, but he preys on the single women too. He's pushed himself on a lot of them."

"So why doesn't anyone report it?"

"There've been complaints, but he always manages to get out of it. He lets the management slide on things that other people would get arrested for. He does dirty favors, so he has people who owe him, and he pays off the rest. He's supplied the drugs for most of the parties that the higher-ups here have had in the empty or model apartments. He gets it from the evidence room or steals it from drug dealers. They let drug dealers come in with large parties and pay large amounts of money to rent out one of the penthouses and then bribe them when they find drugs the next morning."

"Well, every dog has his day. He's gonna mess with the

wrong person one day. What do you want me to make for you?" Melinda asked.

"Anything you feel like making. Just make me four dishes, and I'll give you a hundred dollars. I spent that in one day at DoorDash."

"Okay. I'll be cooking tomorrow, and I'll bring the food to you on Sunday. I need money for groceries." Jerry gave Melinda $200 for the food and for cooking it.

Melinda left and called Brandon to inform him that he needed to watch out for Mark, but didn't leave a message when he didn't answer, figuring he was still at dinner with the kids.

* * *

Désiré was sitting in a winter-white turtleneck, long-sleeved knit jumpsuit with a matching blazer bedazzled with yellow buttons. The buttons matched her canary-yellow three-carat diamond studs and four-carat pear-shaped diamond engagement ring. Her makeup was perfect, and her honey-colored skin was clear and matched her brown eyes. Her blonde hair was pulled up on the top of her head with a long ponytail that reached down to her perfectly round derriere. She finished her look with champagne-colored Michael Kors knee-high boots that were five inches high.

"So, Paul, what made you ask me out to this beautiful restaurant? I'm so flattered." Désiré blushed as Paul listened, but his eyes were stuck on her bulging breasts that could not be contained, even by a knit turtleneck.

"I really felt compassion for what you're going through. I just felt an instant connection with you for some reason. I mean, I don't do this often. You just seem to have a pure heart, and that's rare in the world today. I want to get to know you." Paul was a fit and handsome white guy, a single ladies' man.

"I just thought you were cute, but I didn't think I gave you the eye. Did you see me looking at you?" Désiré flirted.

"I sure did. I knew that you were going to call me when I gave you my card. I just didn't think so soon." Paul looked down at the menu of the expensive restaurant. Unbeknownst to Désiré, the restaurant was owned by the owners of the strip club that her man and his brother were bodyguards at. He was supposed to be working, so he figured he would kill two birds with one stone and case the restaurant. It would also be a plus if she recognized anyone who could help the case.

Paul's phone interrupted their conversation, and he excused himself and stepped away when he saw it was Mark calling.

"Yeah, why are you calling me, dude?" Paul whispered, walking behind the bar to be out of earshot from Désiré, but still keep an eye on her.

"I'm making sure you're on schedule. Is she at the restaurant with you?"

"Of course she is. I get the job done; stop supervising me, dude." Paul hung up, and his phone rang again, Mark's name appearing on the screen.

"Come on, guy. What is it?"

"I found Escobar. I'm trailing him now. Did Tony see the chick yet?

"No, and I'm not answering this phone again. We'll exchange notes tomorrow. Do your work, and I'll do mine."

Désiré looked up as Paul returned to the table and touched her hair before sitting back down across from her.

Désiré didn't know why she was there except for the fact that she followed her inner urge to call him, while questioning the other bad choices she had made in her life. She thought that maybe the look that he had given her at her condo was out of sincere concern for her and the baby. She also wanted to know about the fundraiser money he had told her and Harmony about.

"So does your sister know that you agreed to have dinner with me?" Paul probed, trying to cross his T's and dot his I's.

"No, she would have fucked me up," Désiré said, half joking. "Pregnant and all." They both laughed. Paul looked up as one of the managers of the restaurant approached their table. Paul stood up and sucked up.

"Here's the man of the hour, Mr. Tony DeSilva. This is my beautiful date, Désiré Robinson." Tony took Désiré's hand and kissed it.

"I see why that's your name. Your mother named you that?" Désiré nodded and blushed.

"Tony's one of the managers here." Tony looked intently at Paul, warning him not to talk so much, and made a quick exit.

* * *

Mark turned on to the dead-end block that Escobar's 2019 E-class Benz had turned down when he suddenly noticed two cars were tailing him. Escobar's car stopped abruptly, and he jumped out and held his hands up for Mark to stop. The two cars behind Mark's stopped and waited. When they didn't beep, Mark realized that they're working with Escobar. He put his hand on his gun and stopped his car.

"Yo, I don't care if you a cop or not. Why are you following me?" Escobar approached the driver's side, and Mark rolled down the window, his gun pointed at Escobar's chest.

"You ain't gotta shoot me. Why are you following me? You need something, Detective Stephens? You think I don't remember you? You framed my brother for murder. Are you trying to do that same thing to me now?"

"Step back. I'm getting out of the car." Mark, gun in hand, got out of his vehicle and shut the door. "I'm not putting this gun down; you have me surrounded on a dead-end street with your goons blocking me in. I could just shoot you right now and claim that I felt threatened."

"What do you want? I'm not doing anything wrong. There's no reason for you to be following me."

"Where were you the night the twins got shot?" Mark pried.

"Fucking my bitch," Escobar said. "And I will go down to the department with my lawyer if you want me to, but we ain't gon' do this out here on this street so you can make up an excuse to kill me. Rondo, you got the video recording, right?" Escobar yelled to one of his friends, who was recording the incident on his phone.

Rondo yelled, "Yup, I got all of it!"

Mark leaned in close to Escobar and said in a low tone, "I know how to get what I need to get done, cameras or no cameras." He got back in his car and made a three-point turn to get from between the cars in front of and behind him. He put a peace sign up to the camera as he passed Escobar's partner Rondo. Rondo kept recording until Mark's vehicle was out of sight.

Mark had one more stop to make before heading home. He pulled into the parking lot of a hotel on Route 46 in

Garfield, about twenty minutes from Newark. He waited until a male in his late twenties, looking frail and like he needed a fix walked up and got in his car. He gave Mark a gun and about ten shell casings that were in a plastic bag. They said not a word to each other. Mark passed him a wad of cash, and the meth addict couldn't run fast enough back into his hotel room to make the call for his drugs to be delivered. Mark pulled off and headed home.

As he got off the elevator on his and Brandon's floor, Mark leaned in and put his ear to Brandon's door. He didn't hear any commotion, just some music playing. He laughed to himself as he contemplated knocking and creating a false dilemma, but he decided to go home and work on his other project.

As soon as he put the key in the door, his children, Peter and Rebecca, ran up to greet him.

"Hey, here are my two favorite people in the whole world!" He hugged his kids and brushed past them. Grace stood beaming with a bright smile as she watched her family.

"You're home early. Great! Dinner isn't ready yet, though. Would you like a beer or something while I finish cooking?" She lost a bit of the spark in her eyes when Mark forgot to kiss her on his way to the fridge.

"Damn, I'm starving. Yeah, I'll take a cold beer." He opened up a plastic container that had tuna fish in it, grabbed a spoon, and took a few spoonfuls out of the container. Grace walked up behind him and wrapped her arms around his waist.

"I know you're hungry, but I'm starving for some affection and attention. Remember me, the lady who loves you? Maybe I can get a kiss when you come through the door if that's not too much to ask for."

Mark turned around and gave Grace a peck on her lips and went into his office. He locked the door and took out the gun and shell casings, locking them in his safe. He sat down at his desk, took out his phone, went to PornHub, and proceeded to jerk off to beautiful black women.

Bang! Bang! Bang! That was all Mark heard as he jumped up out of his sleep, still in his chair, his pants down to his ankles. Porsche the Pearl had given him such a climax that his lights went out before he could even lift his pants back up.

"What the fuck! Who's banging like that?" His pants were up and buttoned in two seconds flat.

"Dad, Mom said come and eat. I was knocking, but you didn't answer!" Peter ran back to the dining room and sat down.

Mark checked himself, went to the bathroom to wash his hands, and joined his family for dinner.

"Mark, the children would be so ecstatic if you joined us tomorrow at The Raven's Roar," Grace stated gently.

"What time are you guys going?" Mark stuffed a piece of meatloaf in his mouth and followed it with an overflowed fork of mashed potatoes. "This is great food, honey."

"We want to go early, Dad, because you'll probably have to leave to go to work," Rebecca whined.

"Okay, we can do that. We're going at ten, when it first opens. And if you're not ready, I'll be leaving to go to work. Grace, I need another plate of this food. It is really delicious, sweetheart." Grace jumped up and hurriedly prepared another plate for Mark.

"It's gonna be so fun! We haven't been there in so long!" Peter jumped up and down and knocked his juice on the floor. He froze and looked at Mark as he grabbed him by the collar and put him down to his knees.

"Now you see what you did, asshole?"

"Mark, stop it! Don't talk to him like that! Please let go of him!"

"Father, please let him go." Rebecca grabbed her father's hand, and he let go of Peter.

"Stop babying him, Grace. You're gonna make him a punk." Mark returned to his seat and grabbed a bunch of napkins and threw them at his son.

"Look at the damned rug. I told you to get a darker rug, but, no, you don't listen to me because I don't know what I am talking about."

Grace wiped her tears so the children wouldn't see them. "Mark, please not tonight. Rebecca and Peter want us to have a family day tomorrow. Let's not fight. And he can't wipe the juice off of a rug with napkins." Grace got the handheld wet vac and cleaned the rug.

"See, all clean." She excused the kids from the table and suggested they go in the living room and watch TV while their parents talked. Their heads were down; it was their way of showing that they weren't jovial, and Mark wasn't remorseful or apologetic.

"Mark, what's going on with you? You're always agitated, you never have time, and you've been so cold to me. I can't take this anymore."

"Oh yeah? What's that supposed to mean? You want a divorce?"

"Do you want a divorce? Because I meant I need you to fix it." Grace looked at her husband and wasn't even sure she knew who he was any longer.

"You need to lighten up on me. My job is stressful, then I have to come home, and I can't get any time to myself. I bust my chops to make sure you guys are happy and you're not."

"Listen, Mark, I try. I can't keep this marriage together by myself. This has been going on for years now. One day you're happy and then the next, you're not. It feels like we're drifting farther and farther apart."

"Didn't I just say it's my job? What do you want from me?"

"Time, compassion, affection, emotional support. I need love and how come you don't understand that?" Grace walked out of the room, and Mark slept on the loveseat in his office.

Saturday morning, Mark woke up to Peter banging on the door again. Rebecca went into her parents' bedroom and woke her mom up.

"Mommy, come on. We have to get to Raven's Roar. I want to get there before it gets too crowded. I'm meeting some of my friends there."

Grace cooked breakfast and didn't say a word when Mark came out in his clothes from the day before. Usually, she would have complained that he didn't come to bed, but she was tired. She was fed up, and she was uninterested.

After Mark and his family ate breakfast, they got dressed and left for their excursion. The Raven had a few kid- and family-friendly attractions in the enormous complex basement, which was almost totally self-sufficient, barring its own school. Raven's Roar was an indoor amusement park and arcade.

As Mark and Grace approached the elevator, they saw Brandon with his two children, who were close in age. The kids sized each other up but didn't say a word. Brandon, acting as if he'd never seen Mark before, blocked him out and proceeded with the conversation that he was having with his kids.

"So give me three words that mean the same as... arrogance."

Brandon quietly counted backward from ten as Major blurted out, "Boastful."

"Yup. You have two points. Malika, what you got?"

"Haughtiness, conceit, egotism, disdain. Need I say more?"

Malika stuck her tongue out at Major, who said, "Scorn, presumption, and loftiness. Now what?"

"Okay, okay, it's a tie, with eight points each. Do you want eight dollars cash or sixteen dollars in your bank accounts?"

"I'll take my eight dollars." Malika held out her hand.

"I'll take a deposit," Major decided.

"Major, that's smart."

"No, it ain't because I want money to use for Raven's Roar."

Grace and Mark looked at each other. Peter and Rebecca were in awe of the intellectual but fun game that Brandon and his family were playing and a bit jealous that their dad lacked in that area. Mark didn't do much with his children besides scolding and avoiding.

The elevator opened, and Brandon didn't move until Mark and his crew stepped off. He hung back to put space between them on the line.

There were three other families that Brandon let go before him, and he hoped that he didn't run into his tormentor detective inside the place. That was a hopeful yet unfulfilled prophecy because when Malika pointed at the

Wavy Wagon, he could see Mark's kids on the line, Mark and his wife were standing on the side waiting. He took a deep breath and walked with pride and stride, his head held high. He walked past his stalker again and treated him like a ghost.

When they were in the line, Brandon walked to the other side to wait. He wouldn't give Mark any energy, but he also knew better than to tempt him or himself by giving Mark a chance to pick at him.

He waited and watched as his kids and Mark's ended up sitting next to each other on the simulated hayride, which had twists and turns that would make the passengers feel like they would fall out or off. The kids laughed and screamed, but he didn't notice any verbal involvement between the four. That changed when they got to the Maze-Alicious obstacle course. It seemed that the quad had planned to meet up there.

He strolled slowly as the kids ran together. This time Mark and Grace trailed behind him, and he could feel the gamma rays from their eyes on his back. He thought for a second what it would be like if he and Ciara were still together. She would have whispered quietly in his ear. "Babe, don't let them see you sweat. So what if their kids become friends with our kids? I'll deal with their mother. I don't want you having any interaction with him so he can have an excuse to frame you for something. At least he showed us his true colors from the beginning."

Brandon smiled. It was hard sometimes to have good thoughts about Ciara, but there were some good memories. He just felt like they had tried enough times and that the outcome was always the same: dysfunction and toxicity. But for some reason, he always thought about her and the quality times, when everything was harmonious. Ciara was the one woman who loved him more than any other woman he ever dealt with. She was the one who tried to understand him and his challenges of just being a man, let alone a black man. Ciara never gave up on him.

The gang was officially traveling together as they ran again to the Raven's Wrecks bumper cars. Damn, bumper cars are always a way to make friends with strangers as you're crashing into them. Now, the parents were facing each other as they were facing each other on opposite benches.

Brandon needed a distraction, but looking at his phone and hoping it would ring didn't make it ring. He wanted a distraction to take him away from the tenseness that he was feeling. Brandon and Mark didn't make eye contact, but Brandon also noticed that the couple didn't interact with each other either.

See, that's why that marriage shit ain't it, he thought. I wasn't trying to be like that with Ciara. What sense would it have been to say I do when I wanted to say goodbye? I don't care how long we were together or what everyone said we should have done by that point because we had children. I was tired of her thinking I owed her that and that I had to marry her. Let me stop lying to myself. If there was anyone that I would have made my wife, it was Ciara. She was my rib, and she always had my back. Damn, why did relationships have to be so hard?

Brandon noticed Mark and Grace talking, and Grace looked at her husband with no sparkle in her eye.

He better not mess with me, or I may end up bending his wife over to give her some sexual healing and me some valuable ammunition. Brandon laughed out loud and looked up to see them watching him with a confused look, wondering what he was chuckling about. He smiled and winked at Mark. Mark looked away.

Yeah, nigga, you don't want your own medicine. Okay, that's a mental note. He can dish it, but he can't take it. Nice.

Brandon smiled, and Grace was still looking as Mark was on his phone. He decided not to wink at her, but he caught her eye in his and gave an extra-long look to let her know that he could see her misery and would gladly help to relieve her pain.

Man, quit enticing Becky. He cracked himself up and quickly turned away so they wouldn't think that he really was insane.

"Daddy, can we go to play basketball with them? They live on our floor." Major pointed over to Peter and Rebecca, as Peter was talking to his dad and pointing at Malika and Major.

For what seemed like eternity, Mark and Brandon looked at each other with a blank stare, both probably thinking the same dreaded thing about their kids wanting to be friends.

"Sure, Major, are you guys going outside?" Major jumped up and down, screaming, "No, Dad! It's in here, but it's ten dollars each. We have to pay so it can just be us on the court. Can we have money for snacks? You don't have to come in; it's right there! Peter said it's a bouncy court, with, like, a trampoline, and we can jump up and down while we—"

"Son, I get it. Here." Brandon reached into his pocket, pulled out two twenty-dollar bills, handing one each to Major and Malika. Major grabbed the money and ran to Peter to show him as Grace and Mark slowly got up. They wanted to cry at the thought of having to deal with Brandon and possibly plan playdates. Brandon wanted to cry too, but the vision of their dismay brightened his day. He was sure that this was way more traumatic for Mark than it would be for him. Touché!

The sound of Melinda's phone ringing startled her. She looked at the phone and saw Jerry's number. She had been up late cooking and listening to her oldies but goodies.

"Hey, what you doin' up at ten o'clock on a Sunday? You're supposed to have a hangover." Melinda sat up on her bed and put her slippers on. "Here's your menu." She walked into the kitchen. She opened the refrigerator and started taking out Jerry's food.

"Okay, you have some turkey wings, collard greens, mac and cheese, meatloaf, candied yams, white rice, ziti, and an apple pie. You should be good for a week. You don't have to thank me, you paid me... but then again, you're welcome. I made sure I picked at everything to make sure it was just right; it's delicious." Melinda cackled.

"Shouldn't I get some money back for that, though?"

"Hell no. That's called taste-testing to make sure it's perfect. I was thinking about keeping it for myself and telling you that I got robbed of the money on my way into the store. But I didn't have a police report in case you didn't believe me."

"You're something else. It's okay, as long as you didn't pick your nose while you were tasting," Jerry retorted.

"Oops!"

"Melinda!"

"Only kidding, only kidding. I'll be down there with your food after I pick my nose, take a shit, and wipe my ass. I'll take a shower first too." Melinda hung up the phone and made two plates of Jerry's food and put it in the refrigerator for later.

As she was dressing and listening to The Whispers' "If You Just Say Yes," her phone rang again. "Damn, I'm popular today. I hope it's a booty call. I wish." She shook her head.

"Hellooooo," she sang, not recognizing the number and trying to sound upbeat.

"Miss Melinda?"

"This is she. And who do you beeeee?"

"This is Ciara, Brandon's ex... from your building... I met you Friday."

"Oh, yes, baby. How are you feeling? Are you feeling any better? I've been looking for a handsome man in the building for you. Do you prefer black, or are you open to any color or hue? You know I got you." Melinda moved to the music while moving around and gathering her belongings.

"I am a little. But I don't want to meet anyone in that building. That wouldn't be a good idea if I really want Brandon back. Even though we aren't together, it would still be a violation."

"Whoop-de-do! Girl, you passed the first test. That shows me you ain't no hoochie mama. I had my fingers crossed, girl. If you had said it was a go, I would've been so upset. Okay, now we're in business." Ciara looked at the phone and put it back to her ear, shocked that this older lady had tried to play her.

"Miss Melinda, you are something else. You remind me of my aunt Jackie," Ciara said, giggling.

"Girl, every black person has one aunt like me who is a former or undercover crackhead, but I promise you I ain't no crackhead. I'm just crazy like one. So what's up, girl? Have you spoken to Brandon?

"No. I texted my daughter that I would be outside to pick them up at five. I wondered if you could ask Brandon if I could come up and have a moment to talk to him with you there? So that way, you can kind of be a mediator. I just want to express a few things."

"Girl, I will if he says yeah, but let me tell you something: Don't express anything. Turn your expression into a question."

Ciara looked at the phone again. This lady, she thought.

"And what makes you say that, Miss Melinda?" Ciara figured Miss Melinda was probably a control freak who had to be in charge all the time.

"Well, Miss Ciara, since you disagree, do you want to hear why? I will tell you." Miss Melinda chuckled and then got serious again. "Men think we talk too much. They want us to just shut the fuck up and be pretty and stupid. As soon as we open our mouths, if it ain't to suck their dick, they want us to close it right on back up, honey. So I'm saying that to say, he doesn't want to hear shit, but he doesn't know shit either. None of them know shit. Men are so goddamn dumb. Ooh, I'm sorry. I digress. Woosah. That just gave me a hot flash." Miss Melinda started fanning herself with her free hand.

"Okay, let me try this again. What you do to trick these dummies is ask them a question first, like, 'What can we do to work this out?', and he won't have the answer. Then you can say, 'Well, would you be open for counseling?' instead of saying, 'We need to go to counseling.' You're still leading the conversation, but you're letting him go first. Get it?" Miss Melinda went into her living room to sit on the couch and look at the serene view outside her window. It was her calming spot.

"I get what you're saying, Miss Melinda, but what if he says no? He can say he doesn't want to go. Then what?" Ciara paced back and forth in her living room.

"Honey, what are you doing, jogging? Why are you breathing like that? Relax. Sit down. Take a deep breath. It's going to be okay." Miss Melinda shook her head. "I feel your pain, girl, but at the end of the day, all you can do is try. So I'll call him. And to answer your question, if he says no, have your questions already prepared, and you may not win the battle, but it's the war you want to win. You see what happens and then strategize from that point. I'll let you know what he says. I'll call you back after I speak to him, okay?"

Ciara was silent. She didn't even want to get off the phone. She was sitting in front of her dresser mirror, tears streaming down her eyes. She looked at her reflection and couldn't speak; she could hardly breathe. Her love for Brandon was all she had, besides her love for her children, which was created by her passion for their dad. She didn't understand why she couldn't have both, why she had to sacrifice what mostly every woman wanted. Her own, complete family. She struggled to say, "Thank you, Miss Melinda. Okay." She hung up the phone, and it dropped to the floor. Her strength was gone.

Ciara lay on the floor in a fetal position for about a half-hour. Her stomach tightened as she moaned and howled like a wounded animal, like a mink caught in a trap. She knew she was beautiful, but she wanted Brandon to find her attractive. She wanted him to adore her. No one else mattered. Nothing mattered to her but her family, and nothing would compare. She stared at the white ceiling, as if she were waiting for words to display some sort of explanation. The wall remained blank. Tears fell into her ears, and her throat felt like it was closing in on her. Gagging on her saliva, she barely made it to the bathroom as saliva and white foam came through her fingers that were covering her mouth and she nosedived into the toilet. Gagging and trying not to choke on her own spit was a tug-of-war of hacking and spitting. She slid down onto the floor, her face in the toilet bowl as if she had drunk too much liquor. She had an empty stomach, so nothing was coming up, but something was asphyxiating her.

"Why? Why, Brandon? Why? I'm not good enough? I've given you everything! No other woman will ever love you like I do! I can't stand you! What did I do not to deserve happiness and love?"

Her anger kicked in, and she jumped up, looked in the mirror, wiped her mouth with the back of her hand, and, with the phlegm dripping from her hand, she yelled at her reflection in the mirror, "Bitch! This ain't love! How can you think this is love? Fuck him! He got it coming today and that's it! Today! If he doesn't stop showing his fuckin' ass, you're going to say deuces! Deuces, muthafucka! Fuck that nigga! He wouldn't be where he is today without you!"

Ciara studied her reflection. She looked into her eyes and said, "Now, calm down." She transitioned from the sobbing to the madness to calm. She breathed deeper and wouldn't look away.

"You're an awesome woman. You are loving; you are supportive. You have so much to be proud of yourself for. You do not harm anyone. You do right by your kids, and you did right by that man. If he doesn't know it, you'd better. Now, take a warm, hot bath, soak, and get back your power. You are beautiful, smart, sexy, and you are fearfully and wonderfully made."

* * *

Melinda got on the elevator to take the food to Jerry, greeting any and everyone who got on the elevator. She was a God-fearing, warm spirit who had been through a multitude of ups and downs in her life but would not let it break her. She had been hurt before and got tired of being abused and mistreated by those she loved. She vowed to be a light wherever she went.

A white woman and man in their thirties got on the elevator and were talking about Donald Trump. "They are going to steal the election, these socialists. They want to take our freedom." As the white male spoke, the woman nodded in agreement. Melinda shook her head in disgust. It wasn't surprising that they would talk about such nonsense in front of her because she was invisible to people like them. They didn't mind speaking their mind because she didn't matter enough for them to even pardon their language.

Melinda exited the elevator and was banging on Jerry's door with an echo that raced through the corridor.

Jerry opened the door, looking worn out.

"Jerry, you look horrible. I was banging on the door. I was scared you were in a drunken stupor and not hear the doorbell. Melinda cackled. You better stop drinking, drugging, and sexing yourself to death. I keep telling you. I'm at least thirty years older than you, and you're starting to look like my daddy. Well, if my daddy was white, but you know what I mean; you get the picture. As a matter of fact, I should take a picture of you right now and use it for bribery if I need to. You look like a broken-down pimp who got addicted to his own supply."

"Damn, Melinda, just make me feel worse than I already feel and look. I know I look obliterated. These women don't want to do anything else but come over here, use my stuff, halfway fuck, and leave with all my bucks."

"Ha-ha-ha-ha, I must be rubbing off on you. You talkin' real slick. You need some of this food to bring you back from the dead. And if you die of an overdose, don't ever say I didn't warn you."

Jerry froze as he was removing his food containers from the recyclable grocery bags. "Melinda, please. That's not nice to say; I thought we were buddies. You're wishing death on me, like Fifty Cent said?" He continued to unpack as Melinda grabbed each dish that he didn't want and rearranged his refrigerator to make room for them. She turned her nose up.

"First of all, I'm not trying to be nice. I wish life and rehab on yo' ass, and you may be alive, but something died in this damn fridge. Damn, this shit stinks. I'm throwing this stuff out."

"Be my guest. It hasn't been cleaned out since you did it three months ago. And I know, I know. I'll give you forty dollars to do it. This food looks amazing, as always. Turkey wings, mac and cheese, and collard greens, I love me some soul food."

Melinda's phone rang, and when she saw it was Ciara, she excused herself and went into his living room. "Hey, hon, you on your way over to get the kids? I called and asked him, and he said you have a half hour, which means an hour in black people's time. So come on. Call me when you get in the lobby, and I'll meet you."

Melinda joined Jerry back in the kitchen, made a plate of food, and wrapped it in foil. "Okay, step-great-nephew, I gotta run and go save another soul. Thanks for sharing!" She held up her covered plate, grabbed a plastic grocery bag, sealed the plate, and walked toward the door.

"I know you made yourself at least two plates already before you came down with the food," Jerry joked.

"I may have, but it tastes better on your paper plates."

Melinda rode the elevator up to the lobby and grabbed a table in the Food Court, where various television sets played multiple programs. Melinda sat by the CNN corner and began eating. She watched as Chris Cuomo and Don Lemon talked about Trump's latest antics. Trump was on the campaign trail, telling everyone that the country would try and steal the election from him. Melinda became agitated and began speaking in a heightened tone to the television.

"This man cannot be re-elected. He is the most arrogant, egotistical, narcissistic, delusional, immature, selfish, ignorant—"

"Man like most every other man." Ciara walked up, looking beautiful and glowing with a brand-new outfit on, looking like she was about to go on a first date. Melinda's eyes popped out of her head.

"Now that's how you look when you're trying to get your man to realize what he fucked up. Go ahead, girl. You have either been resting since you dropped the children off, or you been doing something you ain't supposed to be doing, girl. But either way, I won't tell, and I'm ecstatic that you came to conquer. Now, please, please, please make sure you don't lose your emotions, says the woman who was just arguing at the television. I ought to shut my mouth and just watch your work. You ready?"

"As ready as I'm gon' be." Ciara stood and waited for Melinda to clear her table and empty her garbage. The elevator trip felt like forever as Ciara rode quietly, listening to Melinda pray.

"Father God, give this woman, this mother, this black queen the comfort to know that everything will be okay. Let her know that she should give You the desires of her heart. She must also trust that You know best and ask that Your will be done because Your will is perfect, and we cannot lean on our own understanding. In You, Lord, there is peace. There is love. In You, everything happens in Your perfect time. Let Ciara find a solution or an answer today so that she can continue with purpose. Amen."

"Amen." Ciara squeezed Melinda's hand, and they stepped off the elevator and proceeded to 16M.

"Please, God, give me the strength." Ciara rang the bell and tried to push her nerves out of the way and let her confidence come from her attire, which said "phenomenal woman." She didn't look like she was going to the club, but like she was going to a business dinner.

Brandon opened the door looking and smelling good. He had on comfortable loungewear; clean sweat shorts, a T-shirt that read "Straight Outta My Momma," and clean socks. Ciara remembered how Brandon was always particular about having clean socks.

"Ladies." Brandon stepped aside and let Ciara and Melinda walk past. He stepped out and looked up and down the hallway. That had become a habit for him since the first day, and it was the one major thorn in his side from his move to The Raven: living on the same floor as a racist cop. Brandon walked into the living room and sat on his loveseat. Ciara sat across from him on another plush chair, and Melinda sat on the couch in between them, facing the windows.

Brandon looked intently at Ciara. He didn't want to give away that his mind was undressing her. Damn, if she would just let me hit it, things could get back to normal. He knew he shouldn't be thinking nasty thoughts, as he was supposed to be a good boy and on his best behavior. The children had been given strict instructions to stay in the room until they were done. He hated that Ciara exposed them to too much information, and he felt that it swayed their opinions to her side. No one said a word, but all eyes were on Ciara to start the conversation.

"Brandon, I really want to know why we're here. Why did everything you told me turn into a lie?"

"A lie? You tell me? What did I lie about?"

Ciara told herself to calm down when she began to feel like jumping up and slapping him.

"Brandon, one thing you shouldn't do is ask her a question when she just asked you one," Melinda said calmly. "That's very condescending. I believe you know what she's referring to. Don't you?" Melinda looked at Brandon with the eyes she had when she was young and in Ciara's shoes.

"Okay. Why are we here? We're here because we couldn't make it together. So now we're apart." Brandon looked down at his carpet, thinking, now these two are gonna try to tag-team me. Why did I sign up for this nonsense?

"Brandon, you don't understand. I never turned my back on you. I never treated you like you were nothing. I never played with your heart. I never took you for granted."

"Now, that's a lie. You may not have turned your back on me physically, but you think you're gonna talk to me any kind of way? You think you're gonna disrespect me like I'm some lay-down nigga? You thought it was cute to listen to your girlfriends and show your ass?"

"Brandon, I know you just said ass. And I know that ass isn't really a curse because it's a donkey and it technically isn't a four-letter word, but can we keep this respectful? That is a queen sitting right there... the Mother Earth. This is a woman who laid on a table and risked her life to bring your heirs to the throne. She is the vessel by which you have your legacy. Don't take that lightly. Kamala Harris is about to be the first black woman president, and she's no better than this black woman who was also just like Kamala: fearfully and wonderfully made by God. See, you can't revere Kamala Harris or Michelle Obama or even Queen Bey, Beyoncé, but then look at this woman—who's all of those women to you—and treat her like trash. She's no different than them, except that her struggle is coming from her King not acting like he is her King, if you really want to be honest."

"Melinda, no disrespect, but Ciara doesn't always carry herself like a queen. She wants to be the man. She wants to tell me what to do, how to do it, when and why to do it." Brandon was feeling the heat of the accountability that Melinda was throwing at him, but he wasn't ready to submit or humble himself.

"Brandon, don't get defensive. I'm not on anyone's side, but the side of the black family. And we gotta do better. I don't know the ins and outs of your relationship, and I don't have to. What I do know is that you both have been given a job by God to raise those kids, and a part of that responsibility is in you, Brandon, being the man that you're supposed to be so that she can be the woman that she's supposed to be. And that might sound unfair, but being a competent leader means that your flock, if you will, who is your family—the family that was assigned by God to you—will want to follow. Only if you're doing your job correctly."

"Okay, so, Melinda? Ciara should not conduct herself with respect to her King?"

"I didn't say she shouldn't. I asked if you are or were conducting yourself like a King for her to respect you as one. I'm just asking and don't answer; think about it and let her finish, because you've made your point. I think you're trying to tell her that because she did not conduct herself a certain way, you no longer strived to be her King. Is that right?" Brandon nodded with enthusiasm, feeling glad that his point was heard.

"Ciara, can you tell us why that is or was?"

"Because he didn't value me. He treated me like nothing. Like I didn't matter." Ciara stared at Brandon.

"Okay, so do you two see that you've just played ping-pong? Each person has basically said the same thing about the other, that each lacks respect for the other. So you two are even in that regard. And respect is a big thing. But it's not like trust. It's not hard to just start treating someone with respect. Respect is also earned, though, so if someone didn't respect you, oftentimes, —not always—the person did something to show that person that they didn't respect themselves or that person doesn't give it because they feel disrespected. Wait. What did I just say? Did that make any sense?" Brandon and Ciara both chuckled. Remaining serious was hard when listening to Melinda talk. They each agreed that she had made sense.

"I get it. I don't get how Brandon deals with issues by running, but he wants to be listened to. You can't show someone that what they say or feel doesn't matter, but when you have something to say or gripe about, now everyone is supposed to be open to listen and alter their behavior for you when you won't?" Ciara spoke calmly, maintaining her cool.

"You think someone wants to say the same thing over and over again? I left other times and came back to the same bullshit, Ciara. Oh, excuse me, Miss Melinda. I mean come back to the same stuff, nothing changing. She's a know-it-all," Brandon explained.

"Okay, hold on. So both of you are saying that the other doesn't listen or alter their behavior. Sounds like to me, again, each person is doing the same thing to the other. First, it was disrespect and then not listening, which, technically, is disrespectful, but also now one is walking out. Brandon, if you walk out and come back, and even if you talk about it but if there are no set solutions or strategies to avoid the pitfalls of this happening forever and ever, then it's going to happen forever and ever. Until both of you stop it; it doesn't just stop. But guess who has the power to stop it? Now, everybody on the count of three repeat after me: I do. One, two, three..."

Melinda said, "You do," as Brandon and Ciara both said, "I do," at the same time.

"See, you both just said, 'I do.' Wouldn't it have been nice if you two had said 'I do' in front of your families and friends and your children, if not before them? So let's get to that. How come you two never got married?"

"Well, you just said if not before the children were born. I was too young even to become a father, let alone a husband. I think it's good that we didn't get married because there would have been infidelities in our marriage, and that would blemish it," Brandon admitted.

"So both of you have cheated?" Melinda asked.

"No, just me. She dated other men during our breakups." Brandon, disappointed, looked at Ciara as if she were guilty.

"Yes, we were broken up. And he still tries to bring stuff like that up, but I should just forget the cheating. He almost brought another kid into the world, but the girl decided at the last minute to get rid of it. Had I gotten pregnant by another man, I probably wouldn't have lived to talk about it."

"Ciara, did you think that you two would get back together those times? And if so, why didn't you just wait? You're a queen, as I said, and in a man's mind, his woman should never lay down with another man because, in his eyes, you're still his woman." Melinda looked apologetically at Ciara and hoped that she wouldn't think that Melinda had just thrown shit in the game.

"Thank you! Finally! A woman who can woman up!" Brandon jumped up and clapped his hands.

Melinda stood up and pointed her finger at Brandon and clapped her hand one loud time. "If you don't sit your behind down. I didn't finish. For one, it's twenty-twenty, and she didn't cheat! And who's to say she slept with any of them? Ciara, unfortunately, there is a double standard. You could certainly not have another man's baby and think that he would come back. But, Brandon, in Ciara's defense, we ain't back in the day. Men are supposed to be able to forgive nowadays. This ain't medieval times. You shouldn't have cheated. Again, this comes back to the head. You are the head. Two wrongs don't make a right, but you're out here leaving the home, the nest. You allowed another bird to swarm around your nest and swoop in on Mother Hen! Shut your mouth because you allowed that!" Melinda sat down as Malika approached timidly, with Major in tow.

"Mother, may I say something?" Malika asked, her hands up to her chest, clasping her hands like she was about to pray.

Ciara looked at Brandon and nodded.

"Daddy, our family needs you. And I know you're here like you always say. But you're not there; you're here. And it makes a big difference in our lives. Major isn't the man of the house. You are. I didn't like you and Mommy arguing, but I would rather that than this."

Melinda walked over to Malika and hugged her while her parents sat speechless, looking from Malika to Major, then to each other.

Mark Stephens sat in his Impala with his gun on his lap, waiting. He had on a baseball cap and dark shades. He was watching his favorite black girl on her OnlyFans page. She was fingering herself as he was rubbing himself. He jumped at the loud knock on his driver's side window.

"Aaaaaaaaaaaaaayooooooooooooo! You like them black girls, huh? I hear you. Black girls rock, man. They got that magic!" Mark closed the site on his phone and motioned for Cheesy to get in the car with an arm movement that showed he wasn't only agitated, but embarrassed.

"Get in the car, nigga." Mark started the car, and Cheesy froze in place, his mouth wide open, jaw almost to the ground.

"Oh, hold up there, dude. We ain't doin' the N word. We just had a black president four years ago. Did you forget? I may be many things, but I'm not one who'll let a white man call me out of my name. Actually, now you can call me Rick. That's my real name. You don't get to call me Cheesy anymore. That's for my friends."

"Rick, can you get in before somebody sees you with me and wants to kill you? I got a weapon, a badge, and I don't live in the hood. And you ain't getting witness protection or Secret Service or any protection, for that matter. So are you ready to roll or what?"

"Yeah, I need some paper. Some bread. Some cream. Some cheddar. That's why my name is Cheesy: because

I used to get all the money back in my day. Until I let this drug take a hold of my life. Let's go; enough about me. Now, listen. When you go in there, there's gonna be three of 'em; one at the door and Escobar and his right-hand man, Rondo. Escobar usually doesn't get his hands dirty, but one of his lieutenants just got a lot of time, so he's trying to find someone else he can trust to put in that position." Mark held his hand up for Cheesy to be quiet, and he dialed a number and put the phone on speaker.

"Repeat that so my wrecking crew can hear you." Mark put the phone down in the middle of the front seat. He was going to tell Cheesy to sit in the back, but he didn't trust him.

Cheesy continued with the plot. "Okay, so y'all gon' knock on the door, and there'll be three in there. You better know what you're doing because they're the body crew. They've buried plenty of bodies."

Mark raised his eyebrows. He thought of a plan on how to dig up those cases to send Escobar away. He didn't want to have to worry about what was about to go down.

The two cars pulled up to the motel parking lot, their lights turned off. Cheesy pointed out all of the cars that belonged to Escobar and his crew. Mark took pictures of the license plates for future use.

Mark parked at the beginning of the lot and called the motel office.

"Yes, this is Detective Burns from the East Orange Police Department. I spoke to you yesterday to let you know I'd be conducting some official police business. Again, I'm warning you not to interfere with this investigation or report any of this activity. As agreed, we won't further investigate the illegal practices that you're allowing to go on in your motel. I know that you're not responsible for what your guests do, so there's no need to call the police. We're already outside in unmarked cars."

"Man, you boys in blue don't play no games. Y'all got it all on lock. Okay, so when do I get my cut?" Cheesy opened his hand and let his palm face up to the sky.

"As soon as my team scores and makes it around the block. They'll wait for you while you buy your drugs, distracting them. Take this two hundred and get your feel-good medicine. Call them when you're done. They'll take you back home and break you off a nice piece of change. I don't want you out here in danger." Mark wasn't the least bit concerned if Cheesy became a casualty if Escobar and his crew became suspicious of him showing up right after a robbery, with the opp outside. He was just buying Cheesy's loyalty and slavery.

"Okay, I hope it's a nice piece, or you can lose my number, homey." Cheesy laughed.

"Hey, be quiet. It's goin' down. I need to be focused." Mark and Cheesy waited patiently.

Mark's crew—two men and a woman—tapped on the hotel-room door.

"Yeah, who is it?"

"Hey, I'm staying across the parking lot, and I need to get something," the girl said as the two men waited outside the view of the peephole. Rondo looked out and saw a white chick who looked like a drug fiend on a mission. She was shaking, twitching, and moving from side to side.

"Who invited you over here? You ain't got no business randomly knocking on somebody's door. That's how a bitch gets killed out here."

"Listen, I been staying here for a week. I'm from Michigan. I don't know nobody. This guy got me out here, and he must have a wife or some shit because he ain't been back in two days. He's not answering my calls. I have money. I just don't know where to score. Actually, this couple last night let me party with them..."

Rondo wanted to get the chick from in front of the door. He looked to Escobar for the okay. Escobar nodded and the second the knob was turned and the door unlocked, the whole crew bum-rushed the door. The girl stayed at the door, peeking out to make sure no one was approaching while the two men stunned the drug kings with stun guns and rendered them defenseless. The white men had on the classic black knit "hold-up" hats that had eyes, nose, and mouth slits in them. Their faces were unable to be seen and would never be identified. The girl stayed with her back to the men who were incapacitated and disoriented. The robbery was quick and easy. Uneventful.

They grabbed all of the money and drugs that were visible and pulled out drawers to confiscate the rest. They even removed the expensive jewelry from the men, who looked like they had been knocked out in a boxing match. They filled the backpacks that they each had on their backs and the one that the girl, Chrissy, had thrown to one of them at their command. The trio calmly walked out of the room, pulled the door closed and locked it.

Once in the car, they immediately called Mark to tell him they were pulling out so he could follow them, and they could get Cheesy his drugs and money. Cheesy was listening intently and wondered if they had killed Escobar and his crew. Mark hung up and pulled slowly behind the car when it pulled out and made a right out of the motel parking lot. Cheesy was instantly panic-stricken.

"Hey, wait, I thought I was going to cop the drugs. What happened? Why did the plans change?" He began perspiring.

"Calm down. They handled it. I knew you weren't going in. I just wanted to see if you were 'bout it, like your people say." Mark cracked up laughing, and Cheesy remained silent, having a bad feeling about something. He just didn't know what it was.

"Stop shittin' in your pants, man. You really thought it was a good idea to go cop from some dealers who had just got robbed? You ain't thinkin' right. You got that drug overriding your common sense, man. They got everything for you. I'll call you tomorrow. Or should I still lose your number?" Mark grabbed Cheesy by the back of his neck.

"Hey, we got more work to do. Don't you worry. Now, go 'head. They'll drop you off." Cheesy got out of Mark's car and dragged his feet while walking to get in a car full of strangers. He told himself to stop being nervous. He got in and watched Mark drive off.

"Hey, man, here's a thousand dollars and a whole super rock for you to cook up, sniff up, shoot up, shit, whatever you wanna do, man. Thanks for getting us this score."

"Oh yeah, I'm going to have fun tonight with some honeys, money, and this get right. Yeah, it's gonna be a gooooooooood night!"

* * *

Mark drove to an apartment building about twenty minutes from the robbery scene and rang the bell for apartment 12C and was let in.

The desk clerk from his department, Camilla Strong, answered her door in nude-colored lingerie ensemble and a glass of champagne in hand. She was nowhere near as pretty or sexy as his wife Grace. She was built like a man in a woman's body, and more athletic than feminine. She was just another pawn in Mark's games. Camilla stepped to the side and let Mark enter.

He put his gun on the foyer table and turned around, taking the glass that she handed to him. Mark took a sip and pulled her to him. He wrapped his arm around her waist and landed his hand on her ass cheek, squeezing it hard. He walked to the couch and sat on it, picked up the remote, and started changing the channels.

"Hey, hunky, you okay? You seem a little stressed. What do you need, honey?"

"You know what I need. It's not a clothes-off moment—I am sure to be getting a call soon—so loosen me up. Maybe I will come back after my work is done. I can say I had to work a homicide all night."

Camilla crawled on her knees in between Mark's legs and started rubbing on his penis through his pants. The immediate erection led to her unzipping his pants and bringing out Mark's monster. She spoke to it by saying hello and then swallowed it into her mouth. She wasted no time getting Mark on the edge of his seat and thrusting upward into her mouth. She did her tricks and twists and turns while he was in her oral water cave. He was doing reverse push-ups off the couch and aiming toward the field goal of her throat.

Mark's phone started ringing, but he ignored it. When it rang again, he leaned over to look at it, but did not stop her from giving him her tongue and saliva lashing. He was enjoying every minute of it. He looked at the call from Paul and sent him an already created call-you-right-back text and leaned forward. Pushing Camilla on her back and without removing himself from her mouth, he landed on his knees, plugging her like he was a jackhammer. He lay flat on top of her, his stomach on her face, while he ejaculated down her throat. He gyrated for a half-minute, until he had released everything.

Mark jumped up and called Paul back, who told him to come to the Heritage Motel.

"Gotta go. I may be back," he said as he walked toward the door, still fixing his clothes and tucking his shirt back in.

"Call me if you're coming," she said as he went through the door.

Before it closed, Mark replied, "For what?"

Mark pulled up close to the grassy field next to the motel where there were about five different police and detective cars. It was Paul and the homicide unit. There was a white girl named Chrissy giving the police an account of what she walked up on. Mark approached and listened as she described walking to the 7-Eleven across the street and seeing a dead body in the grass on her way back.

Chrissy said she immediately called the police because she had seen the same guy a few minutes before, coming from the motel room across the parking lot from her room. She agreed to be escorted to the station to give a statement. She also added that she had seen three black men and a lot of traffic in and out of the room all day. Mark walked her to a police cruiser and advised that she be taken back to the station and held in waiting to give a statement to him when he arrived.

Mark and Paul then gave instructions for CSI to gather all of the evidence properly, as they would be going to interrogate the three black men, who'd been arrested about a half hour before by narcotics detectives, based on Chrissy's statement of a lot of traffic in and out of their room.

Paul drove behind Mark as they were going to the station. When they got there, they spoke to the two narcotics detectives who had confiscated large amounts of drugs and weapons from the motel room. Mark and Paul were there to question the trio about the murder that had occurred nearly a block away from the motel.

Paul went into the room to prepare the three for a line-up for Chrissy to identify whether they were the three she had seen in the room the dead guy was coming out of. She positively identified all three. The three men were separated and taken into three different interrogation rooms.

Paul went to question Escobar while Mark went to talk with Darren Davis, and Manny questioned Rondo Rollingson.

Paul walked in and sat down and offered Escobar something to drink. He refused.

"Listen, buddy, we can make this easy or we can make it hard. Either way, it's gonna be cake for me and possible death for you. You never know." Paul smiled and winked at Escobar.

"Listen, Officer, I'm not your buddy, and I have nothing to say without my lawyer. You wanna tell me why I was arrested? Either let me go or charge me. Let me call my lawyer."

"Mr. Briggs, I would be nice to me if I were you." Paul leaned in. "You never know when you might need someone's assistance."

"Officer, I repeat. What was I arrested for?"

"Well, I am a homicide detective. I'm here to question you about a body that was found by the hotel where you were dealing. Someone saw the same gentleman come out of your room. Now he's dead a few hundred yards away. So I'm here to ask what you have to do with that."

"Now, what makes you think I had something to do with that? I was in my room all day, and I wasn't dealing shit."

"Well, it sure looks like a lot of shit in evidence. But that's between you and the arresting officers. Like I said, I'm here on a murder investigation."

"A lot of shit? Bullshit. I ain't have shit in my room. I had got robbed... You know what? I think I'm pretty sure about what's going on here. Lawyer! That's all I have to say." Escobar leaned back in the chair and started thinking. He backtracked the events of the day leading up to the arrest. Shit was just too weird and coincidental, but he couldn't figure it out just yet.

"Suit yourself. Have a good day... if you make it back out today." Paul walked out of the room.

Mark walked into the room with Darren Davis, whose street name was Rugged, ready to play bad cop. That was his favorite role. He shut the door and immediately jumped right in Rugged's face, getting so close that their noses almost touched. Rugged didn't flinch a bit and stared directly back in his eyes.

"Listen, I'm tired, and I wanna leave here and go fuck my girlfriend, then go home to my wife, so I ain't got no time to be bullshittin' with you."

"All three of you are in big shit. You got drugs, guns, and a dead body. Which story are you giving? Or would you like to tell the truth and make it easier for us all?"

"Officer, that was impressive. I need to call my lawyer." Darren put his head down on the table. Mark walked out of the room.

Manny Martinez, one of the detectives, was the next to go and speak with Rondo to try and crack the last nut.

"Yo, man, y'all got a lot of dope. Did you know someone got shot, and they had just came from your motel room?" Manny questioned.

"Listen, man. I been doing this a long time. I ain't shoot nobody, and I ain't have shit. Are you charging me?"

"I don't know. I'm just asking if you know what's going on out there? Are you sure you don't wanna speak for yourself? You never know what's going on in those other rooms where your friends are." Manny sat down with his chair turned backward, resting his elbows on the top of the chair.

"Those ain't my friends, man." Rondo looked right back in his face.

"Well, I'm glad you know that, man. There's no honor among thieves. Now, what do you know?"

"I know that those are my brothers. I need a lawyer. You calling me a man should tell you I ain't rollin' over like no dog. Now, what do you know?"

"I know that you can play hardball, but we own the ball," Manny replied, standing up, "and I know that I ask all the questions around here. You want your lawyer?"

"Yup," Rondo said and winked.

Grace woke up in the middle of the night, unable to sleep. Mark hadn't yet arrived home, and although that was nothing strange, her woman's intuition told her that he wasn't still working. He hadn't even texted her that he was still working, which made her feel uneasy. She called his cell phone, and it went to voicemail. She left him a message.

"Mark, if you were still at work, you would answer. I'm getting tired of this neglect. I'm tired of being mistreated. I'm going to have to decide whether I still want this marriage, because it seems that you don't."

Grace hung up the phone and sobbed silent tears until she fell back to sleep. When she woke up to get the children ready for school, Mark still hadn't come home. She decided against calling the station. She wasn't ready to hear that he was okay and hadn't been harmed because that would mean that he was doing something that he shouldn't be. An officer's wife's worst nightmare is having her husband killed in the line of duty and a wife's worst nightmare is having her husband cheat.

She didn't wish bad on Mark but knew that if she called and he hadn't been in any emergent situation, it would confirm that he was spending the night with someone else. He could always lie and say that there was a homicide investigation, but her gut told her that wasn't the case last night.

Grace was overly agitated and defeated. The kids weren't being cooperative either, fighting with each other throughout breakfast. She tried to remain calm, thinking that they, too, were probably stressed out over their father's absence, his constant inattention, and emotional neglect. She fought back tears and quickly wiped the ones that fell before the children noticed.

"Let's go! You're gonna be late. Get your coats on." Grace, who was always fashionable and well put together, didn't care about her appearance that morning. She had on a Pink brand sweatsuit, with pink Pumas, her blonde hair in a ponytail. She grabbed her Prada bag and rushed Peter and Rebecca out and into the hallway.

The two took off running down the hall while Grace quickly locked the door and yelled for them to stop running. They were around the bend and out of her site, and she began walking quickly. As she came around the bend, she saw Peter bump into Brandon as he was locking his door.

"Peter!" Peter and Rebecca stopped in their tracks and waited for their mom to catch up while she chimed, "I'm so sorry!" Brandon turned around, noticing the stress and angst in her face.

"No, it's okay. They're just being kids," Brandon answered.

"Sorry," Peter said under his breath.

"Yes, 'Sorry I'm stupid'," Rebecca teased, and Peter took his backpack and swung it around, hitting her in her nose, which immediately shot out blood in different directions.

"Oh my God!" Grace ran to Rebecca and began looking in her pocketbook for something to cover her nose with while reprimanding Peter and holding Rebecca's head back while the blood ran down her face.

"Miss, hold on. I'll get some paper towels." Brandon rushed inside his apartment and brought back a whole roll of paper towels and gave it to Grace, who was stunned at his rush to assist them.

"Thank you. I-I mean, you didn't have to. I am sorry; they're just a little rambunctious this morning." Grace rolled the paper towels and, still holding Rebecca's head back, put the folded paper towels on her face to control and contain the bleeding.

"Are you okay?" Brandon asked as he began to walk to the elevator. He was taking public transportation to his job for the first time since moving into The Raven. For a moment, Grace thought that Brandon was talking to her and not her and Rebecca, but that he had seen in her eyes that something was wrong. She imagined that he saw through her eyes, to her soul, and was concerned about her pain. She was shocked at the thought and quickly brushed it out of her mind. She then realized that she hadn't answered him and began daydreaming but snapped out of it to not give herself away.

"Oh, yes, thank you. I appreciate it. Sorry again." Rebecca began to hold her own paper towel with her mom's prompting, and Grace and the kids began to walk behind Brandon toward the elevator.

"No need to apologize. You saw my two; they're the same way. I get it. Really."

The four of them stepped onto the elevator and became extremely quiet. No one said a word. The kids were captivated as always by the outside view in the elevator, and Grace's mind was everywhere. She was thinking about Mark and what had just happened. She secretly glanced at Brandon, who was on the opposite side of the elevator, looking out the window.

The elevator began to fill up on the way down, with other people leaving for work, some with kids and some without, everyone filing out at the lobby. Grace and the kids went their way and Brandon went his. Brandon rode into the city, enjoying the commute—the sights, his new adventure in getting to work—without a second thought about what had transpired before that.

Grace dropped the children off to school and went to start her day. She had given up her career to become a housewife and mother. Mark was wrapped up in his position, and she was wrapped up in him; and he didn't care anymore. Grace had been a schoolteacher and loved it but quit when she had Peter.

All throughout her day, Grace's mind wandered to Brandon. She caught herself as she replayed him saying 'Are you okay' and him zeroing in on the frown behind her smile. Initially, she was programmed by Mark to not like Brandon, when Mark came into the house ranting about Brandon when he first moved onto their floor. She thought he was just another drug dealer who would come with lots of company and loud music to disrupt their building. She remembered how surprised she was seeing him in the elevator, quizzing his children about vocabulary, and how he had quietly chaperoned them around Raven's Roar that day.

Was he ever married to their mother? What does he do for a living? Where is he from? Stop it. You can't like a black guy, she told herself. And then lied to herself, you have had black friends before. You aren't racist. But you can't like a black guy and be thinking about him. You're married. But you're miserable. Grace shook her head and was startled out of her thoughts.

"Miss Grace!" Her pedicurist was waiting for her to confirm the color that she was going to put on her toes.

"Black," Grace blurted out.

"Black?" Chi Lyn repeated.

"Yes, black, please. And please hurry, Chi Lyn; I have a hair appointment too."

Grace made sure to have a busy day and stay away from home, as that would only make her think about the fact that Mark hadn't come home the night before. She left the nail salon with black fingers and toes, and she didn't even know why.

* * *

When Brandon arrived at his office after his time off to move, it was filled with cards, balloons, and gifts that read "Congratulations" and "Best Wishes." There were some house gifts from mostly the ladies in the office. He felt an enormous feeling of accomplishment. He had some wins and losses in his life, like everyone else, but this was the first time that he had attained something like this, solely on his own, and it felt amazing.

Ciara had always reminded him of how much he needed her and wouldn't be able to make it without her. It seemed that she was eating her own words, being the one trying to get back with him. "Yeah, now you want me. But I was worthless, right?" Brandon again tried to shake the thought of Ciara out of his mind. He knew that he had provided for his family, but he also knew that she had been his rib, his backbone, his supporter, his rock. She had done what a woman was supposed to, uplift her man, and that was more than money could buy. It was just her inner demons and his that kept them at war with each other. Maybe they both had some inner demons.

The day she came with Melinda ended up in the air after their daughter expressed her dismay at their separation and constant discord. They all had left after that, and Brandon had spent the rest of the day relaxing, continuing to unpack, and having another sexcapade on FaceTime with Gabriela. They had a date planned for Wednesday, where they would go out together for the first time to a "Sweet T's", a new soul food restaurant on Bloomfield Avenue.

Brandon wasn't really interested in anything serious with anyone. Going out with a woman that you're about to have sex with was just a part of the game. He didn't mind taking her out before bringing her to see his place. They knew what their sexts were leading up to. He just planned to reiterate to her that if things didn't develop, he would appreciate her not making any scenes in the building where they both resided. He hoped that there would be no drama. He had enough of that dealing with Mr. Dirty Detective.

Kayla, Brandon's assistant, came into his office to announce his first appointment for the day. He was meeting with a client who was promoting his new charity. It was a famous football player whose son had been diagnosed with a seizure disorder. He created a charity for epileptic disorders and wanted to do fundraisers to raise awareness and funds for research. Brandon had created a three-month ad campaign with an itinerary of events that involved other celebrities. It would take place in the major metropolitan cities across the country. He knew that Johan Meltin would be impressed and be willing to pay the $75,000.00 fee to Brandon. Brandon would only have to give his firm 10 percent because he was one of the top five earners there.

Johan walked into the office with his lawyer. The men shook hands and sat down to discuss the strategy that Brandon had created.

"Wow, man, when did you get married?" Johan asked Brandon after noticing all of the balloons and gifts. Brandon looked confused and then realized what he was talking about.

"What? Man, you scared me for a minute. Nah, I just bought a condo, moved into my dream building. I had my eye on it for a few years. It's a whole complex, a resort almost."

“That’s good, man. That’s a good feeling when you accomplish your goals. You’re scared of marriage, huh?” Johan laughed.

“Man, I ain’t ready,” Brandon said, laughing. “How long have you been married?”

“I’ve been married for five years. But you definitely have to be ready. If you ain’t, you’ll ruin it.” Johan looked through the portfolio, raising his eyebrow at some of the offerings Brandon had detailed. He smiled and gestured for his lawyer to look at a particular page.

“I don’t know if I’ll ever be ready for a woman to own me. I have so many things I still wanna do. I love my freedom too much.” Brandon walked around to his desk to begin the overview of the proposal.

“Man, ‘own’ you? That ain’t what marriage is about at all. If you find the right woman, you want her to hold you down and keep you together. I guess if you look at it, you do own each other. You own each other’s happiness, each other’s pain, everything.”

“Yeah. I’m good on my own. I got me.” Brandon sat.

“I feel you. I was there too until I realized that I can’t get nowhere with a bunch of women who don’t matter. I love my freedom too, but I share my freedom with my partner. I don’t want to be free to travel, experience the world, go through struggles or hard times without mine. I guess you just ain’t come across the one yet who makes you feel like nothing matters but you and her and your family. So, dude, I like this layout. This looks good. Real good. I appreciate the other celebs that are willing to be a part of this movement without really asking for too much. That’s cool.”

“Yeah, when it comes to charities for kids, people are

always supportive. I mean, not everyone, but most. So are the numbers okay with you too?"

"This is perfect. You're under the budget, so I am going to think of anything that I want before we finalize it," Johan said, swiveling back and forth in the camel-colored leather chair that he was lounging in.

"Okay, cool, man. I was actually thinking the same thing, what we can add. We'll go over everything and take your ideas and come back with another package. You can just give me another installment of thirty thousand."

"I'll give you the balance of fifty and then whatever's extra after we decide on that as long as my guy right here approves everything in the agreement. What do you think about everything? Are the insurance and security enough?" Johan asked Brandon.

"Yes, we always partner with either Tuff Peeps or Safe Side Security. They travel, they outsource, they always provide the best security. They treat every client like the POTUS, so we'll do each event once a month. We have a whole year lined up, so in six months, if you're satisfied with how everything is going, we can sit down for the second-year itinerary. The great thing is that you only need to appear at half of the events, so you can do every other month, or you can pick the cities you'll participate in."

"So people won't be offended if I'm not present?"

"I mean, they would love to see you, but we have other celebrities so that you aren't obligated. Plus, you probably have other responsibilities and events. You can do videos for the ones you can't attend. We have enough people lined up, and if your wife wants to do some appearances with your son without you, we can do that too."

"Well, I'm trying to do every one, and me and my wife

will do it together with my son. But you're right; once the season starts, I may have to miss some."

"Okay, I hear you, brother. It's dope. Don't even stress it. I got you."

"This isn't about money for me; it's just responsibility. My son is gonna be able to bring light to this disorder and help others, and I'm glad that I'm a public figure who can guarantee that. When you're blessed, you're to be a blessing."

"I appreciate you using me to create your vision and make it come to life. I'm glad you can make all the events with your family. And it's even better that you want to pay in full. Mr. Venable, is everything to your approval?" Brandon asked the lawyer.

"From what I can see. I'll review again after this meeting and get back to you with any requested changes within forty-eight hours."

Brandon presented the whole portfolio to Johan and his lawyer, Ron Venable. He saw three more clients and made another $75,000 that day. He was so excited that he invited the office to his house after work the following Friday to have an impromptu happy hour and housewarming. Love and War was a small, yet successful, agency with twenty-five employees, and out of that twenty-five, about ten coworkers had agreed to jump on the Path train to New Jersey with him on Friday.

* * *

Wednesday morning came fast, and when Brandon stepped onto the elevator, he ran into no other than Gabriella, who was looking like a professional whore, like a female CEO who stripped at night. She had on a too-tight skirt that rose above the knee, no stockings, and her commuter sneakers.

He knew she had some fuck-me pumps in her bag. Gabriella made Brandon salivate.

"Well, what a nice surprise," Gabriella said, walking up to him and standing directly in front of him. The elevator was a bit crowded, so it did not seem odd.

"Yes, it is. I get to get a sneak peek of what I am going to see tonight." Brandon looked her up and down, smiling.

"Well, you know I won't be wearing this." Gabriella swung her hair and turned around so that Brandon could eye her ass.

"Oh yeah, you're a woman. You've gotta have two to three costume changes a day." Brandon whispered in Gabriella's ear. She giggled and then he blew in her ear, which made her shiver.

The elevator reached the lobby, and the two got off and began walking to the exit, continuing their small talk.

As they were going out, Grace was coming in. Gabriella stopped to talk.

"Hiiiii, Grace! Oh my God, it's been, like, three months since I saw you. How are you? The kids?"

Grace barely smiled. She looked down when she answered. "They're good. I just dropped them to school early for a program." Grace's eyes looked up and landed on Brandon's, who was looking at Gabriella's ass again. He looked up and noticed that Grace had caught him.

"Oh, I see you've met my neighbor. He saved Rebecca on Monday. Hello." Grace gave Brandon the look that came from her soul and then turned away.

"Oh, it was nothing," Brandon said, then asked himself if Grace had just given him the eye.

"Okay, Grace, call me sometime; gotta get to the train!"

Gabriella took off with Brandon by her side, sprinting to make it to their trains. Gabriella worked at a downtown law firm. Brandon wondered if he was going to be seeing her every morning or frequently and if he was going to feel obligated to walk with her to the train. He hoped not.

Brandon's day started as any other day would. He went over his schedule with Kayla and saw three clients before lunch. Just as he was walking back to his building after enjoying the Midtown bustle and going down to the corner for a chicken gyro, he got a phone call. He didn't recognize the number.

"Hello? Good afternoon, Brandon Phillips here. How may I help you?" He didn't trip about people having his number. If they called with nonsense, he would just block them after. He always got referrals from current or former clients, so answering all calls was good practice.

"Hey, Brandon, it's Chavon." He looked at the phone to try to remember who Chavon was. His silence let her know he didn't know who she was.

"Gabriella's friend. Gabriella, who lives in your building. The black girl that was with them the night at the cigar bar..." She paused. "You still don't know who I am?"

"I knew after you said Gabriella." Brandon laughed. "How are you?"

"I'm good. I was just calling to see how everything was going with your new place. I remember you were talking about a neighbor that was bothering you or something. I actually was going through my phone looking for a number and came across your name, so I figured I would just reach out and say hi, if that's okay." Chavon didn't want to sound desperate. She knew that he should be calling her first, but he didn't.

"That's fine. Thanks for calling and asking. I haven't had any incidents with him in a few days, but I am having a few coworkers over on Friday. I'm hoping he will be somewhere else; I'm crossing my fingers." Brandon wanted to know what the call was really about. He didn't have time for small talk.

"So do you want to go out or something? Get to know each other? I mean, do you want to? I don't know. I guess I'm kind of asking you out, but I know I'm not supposed to." Chavon felt stupid.

"It's okay. Just don't propose to me and we'll be good. There's nothing wrong with making the first move. It's what you do after that that can mess you up," Brandon said, laughing.

"Really? Oh, so you want to put me up on game?" Chavon laughed back.

"Nah, I can't break the man code. I gave you enough. No proposing and don't be pushy after the first call; that's it. You gotta figure the rest out. I'm going back into my office, though, so I'll give you a call soon."

"Okay, so..." Brandon hung up. He didn't know if it was a setup by Gabriella. There would be no reason for her to do that because we aren't even a couple, but females play so many games, you never know, he thought. I mean, she was probably calling for herself, but, obviously, Gabriella didn't share that we're going out tonight. Or she did and Chavon didn't care. I don't know and I don't care. I can do what and who I want to do. Brandon smiled and entered his office. He made his rounds, making sure everyone was okay, as a supervisor should, and went back into his office to continue his day. He was meeting Gabriella in the lobby at eight so they could go to Sweet T's early. He didn't know if taking a white girl to a soul food restaurant would be comfortable or not, but he just wanted someone to try the food with. He didn't care what people may think. He had never been on a real date with a white girl before. He had slept with his share, but never took any of them out.

Brandon left the office at five o'clock and was home by six thirty. He took a shower and was dressed by eight. He called Gabriella and told her to meet him in fifteen minutes. He rolled a blunt and smoked in his apartment for the first time. He was feeling good and relaxed and didn't want to be overthinking anything.

Brandon was casually dressed in jeans, Timberland boots, and an Eddie Bauer fur-lined parka with fur. Gabriella had on a three-quarter chinchilla fur with matching headband. She had on jeans and a tight cardigan sweater. The fur was overkill as far as he was concerned, but he knew women were extra. Brandon felt that Gabriella would bring too much attention to them, and it was overkill.

They took an Uber instead of walking down Bloomfield Avenue to Sweet T's, which was owned by his hometown barber, Dre Perrin, and his girlfriend, Tonza Houston.

The host seated them, and Brandon instantly knew, judging by the looks he got from the black waitress, the dinner would be challenging. He didn't want to bring it up, but Gabriella did it for him. "Looks like we have a bitter waitress. Is she your baby mama or friends with her or something?" Gabriella broke a piece of bread and spread the butter on it.

Brandon waited to see if she was serious or joking and to see if she was going to butter him a piece of bread the way Ciara had always done. What are you thinking about Ciara for? he asked himself. She did not. He reached over and buttered his own bread. Strike one.

"I was hoping that you were playing, but you didn't laugh." Brandon took a bite and waited patiently for her response.

"Playing about what?" Gabriella took a sip of her water.

"Never mind." He looked at the menu. "Do you like soul food?"

"Oh, I was saying that she had an attitude, so you never know. I love soul food. Whenever I go to Chavon's house to eat, I bring take home containers." Gabriella joked and looked at her own menu.

"You never know if that could be my baby mama?" He didn't even like how that sounded. "What do you like?"

"I like short ribs of beef, mac and cheese, and collard greens, and, ooh, I love deviled eggs. And look, they have Kool-Aid! That's funny. And you know what it is, like I do. You're a black man in a soul food restaurant with a white woman."

"Yeah, I guess I didn't think this through. I get it, though. Do you?" It was time to pick her brain and see what she was made of.

"Of course I get it. There aren't enough black men to go around, so I'm stealing a black woman's opportunity,"

Gabriella said in a cavalier manner as matter-of-factly as she could. The impact of what she said hit Brandon hard.

"So how do you feel about it? Do you think that I owe it to my community not to deal with a white woman? I'm just asking because you're my first date." Brandon looked up and saw his waitress had returned with their beverages.

"Do you know what you want yet?" The girl whose name tag read Blair waited.

"Yes, we know what we want. Do you have any recommendations, Blair? That's a nice name." Brandon wanted to change her energy.

"Everything is good." It seemed Blair wasn't going to let him make her smile.

"Okay, so we'll have two orders of deviled eggs; the lady will have an order of short ribs with the mac and cheese and collard greens; and I'll have crispy catfish, candied yams, and collard greens. How are you today?"

"I'm a little down because my grandmother died and the funeral is in a few days, so I'm sorry if I don't seem too friendly today." Brandon and Gabriella looked at each other, and Blair walked away after repeating their order.

"See? That's how women overthink things. You had her all wrong, and I jumped on the bandwagon with you to throw that poor girl under the bus. You should be ashamed of yourself for calling that girl a racist." Brandon shook his head. Gabriella got offended and was about to tell him how wrong he was when he smiled.

"Oh, you were about to get told off. I never said she was racist." Gabriella told herself to relax.

"No, but you said she was mad because I was with you, and you had me about to get her fired for her attitude," Brandon scolded Gabriella again.

"Stop, that's not funny," Gabriella whined.

Brandon felt bad. "Okay, let me stop messing with you. I'm just playing. We were both wrong. And right at the same time, though. Some people do have a problem with it. And I understand. I mean, yes, we're all individuals and can be with whoever we want to, but we have to look at what's bigger than us sometimes too. It doesn't make it wrong, but, especially, when kids are involved, we just have a responsibility to try to think of more than just what you want, but who you're affecting with your actions." Brandon was shocked to hear those words come out of his own mouth. "I mean, sometimes things don't work out, and you deserve to be happy. What two people share, only they know."

"Now you're talking. Damn, I felt like I was about to be in a history class. And listen... honestly, if I didn't understand, how would I have black friends or, really, would I be here?"

Brandon laughed. "You know, they always say that white people will always say they have black friends to not be seen as racist—and I don't consider you to be racist, or I wouldn't be here either—but it's more about understanding than ignoring or being oblivious to the plight of someone you call a friend or even spouse."

Gabriella looked at Brandon as if she was waiting for him to elaborate. He continued. "Not you, because I don't know you that well. I'm saying, in general, some people can be around you and not try to understand your plight, and that doesn't just apply to race relations. That applies to health issues and family problems too. Some people just are self-absorbed or lack empathy." Brandon sipped his juice. He was impressed with himself but not haughty.

"Oh wow, you know some big words for a black guy," Gabriella said and lifted her glass. "Cheers. You are an exception to the rule." Gabriella sipped her Kool-Aid.

"Wait a minute, what did you just say?" Brandon pushed his chair back from the table, about to get up to go ask for the meal to be put in to-go bags when Gabriella stopped him.

"I said I got you. How you like me now? Ha-ha. You fell for it." They both cracked up laughing.

"I respect and am amazed at people, all people and people of color. All types of people, but people of color have a different..." Gabriella tapped her manicured coffin nails on the table to find the word she was looking for, and Brandon finished her sentence for her.

"Swag, sweetie. The word is swag." Brandon dusted his shoulders off while Gabriella encouraged him.

"Yes, that's it, swag. You guys are super strong. White people would kill themselves if they had to endure the same shit."

"Ding, ding, ding! You got it... Now you won. You get to get the ding, ding, ding! tonight. It was all a test, and you just passed."

Gabriella almost choked on her punch from laughing.

* * *

Gabriella was on her stomach, hanging off the side of the bed, while Brandon was thrusting as much of himself—all of himself—into her from behind. He grabbed her waist and lifted her up for the doggy-style switch and then came into the condom for the third time in a half hour. He was taking out all of his frustrations, fantasies, and lust on Gabriella, and they both enjoyed it. They had enjoyed the conversation at dinner and couldn't get in Brandon's condo fast enough. They were ripping their clothes off as he led her straight to the bedroom. His last joke had her eager to find out just what that ding, ding, ding! felt like, and she was not surprised that it was all that she had imagined and masturbated to since meeting Brandon.

As Brandon went to the kitchen to get a bottle of champagne to enjoy while they recharged in bed, he had a thought. I cannot let her spend the night. She'll get the wrong impression. He paused to rethink that thought and stopped to gaze out of the huge living room window, admiring the New York skyline on the horizon.

Mark was walking past Brandon's condo and took his usual pause to put his ear to the door. He heard Brandon yelling at someone, "Do you want orange juice for your champagne?"

Mark's eyebrows raised as he wondered who his neighbor had over and if there was a way to interrupt their fun. He shook his head and walked slowly to the door. He was dreading going home because he knew there was going to be tension, if not trouble. Ever since he stayed out Sunday night, things were even more strained than they had been. When he turned the key to go in, it was awfully quiet.

Grace was sitting on the couch reading A Woman Scorned by Ericka Williams. She looked up and looked back down at the book. She was at the part where the main character had just killed her husband. Grace smiled.

"Hey, honey, where're the kids?" Mark asked nervously.

"At my mom's. They're staying for the rest of the week, until Sunday."

Mark became more confused. "For what? And why didn't you ask me?"

"Oh, I don't know, maybe you were missing." Grace was tired of being the submissive fool. She was always the good wife, and she got nothing in return.

"Look, Grace, I told you I had a homicide to work. You

know my job," Mark barked, then noticed her newly painted fingernails and toes. "What the hell do you have black nail polish on for?"

Grace put the book on her lap, looked at her feet and turned her hand to look at her nails. She smiled and looked up at him with a smirk. "Oh, nice of you to notice something about me. They are black because black is beautiful." She picked the book up and continued reading.

"What the fuck has gotten into you? And I heard about the nigger down the hall who helped my daughter. If you were doing your job as a mother, Peter wouldn't have thought it was okay to bloody her nose."

"And if you were doing your job as a father, your kids would behave because they would know that you care. And if you were doing your job as a husband, my nails wouldn't be black." Grace knew that that statement would make his blood boil, but she didn't care.

Mark walked over to Grace and raised his hand, but something about the look in her eye made him pause before smacking the shit out of her. He had never seen her look so unbothered before. "Don't let me see you talking to that nigger, and if something else happens that you need his help, tell him you don't need his help. Do you hear me?"

Grace did not look up from the book, but answered, "I sure do."

Mark walked out of the living room to his office. He had the rest of the drugs from the robbery that they hadn't turned into evidence, and he, the two narcs, and the girl had split the confiscated money four ways, turning in $30,000 and keeping $5,000 each. Mark's partner, Paul, was unaware of his side dealings and illegal activities. He didn't know that Mark was setting up drug dealers, robbing some, and framing others.

"So you worked all night Sunday?" Grace yelled, still not believing Mark. She had asked him numerous times already but asked again to see just how many times he was going to lie.

Mark peeked into the living room and answered, "Yes. I was working all night Sunday." He lied through his teeth like it was nothing.

The next morning, Brandon woke up at 6 a.m. and realized that Gabriella was still in his bed. He shook his head and thought, you weren't supposed to let her stay.

He woke her up. "Gabriella, I gotta get ready for work."

"Well, good morning to you too. I gotta get ready for work too." She got dressed and left while Brandon was in the shower, not saying goodbye. When he came out and saw she was gone, he smiled, but then said to himself, "Damn, she do got some good pussy, though. I'll definitely be hanging out with her again." Brandon laughed at himself. "Damn, bro, you're back! Bachelor life, tenth edition! I'm ready for this adventure! New crib, new pussy. I'm about to call her friend Chavon tonight and see what's up with her too. Ain't nobody tying me down."

Brandon was running late and decided to take an Uber into the city. He hoped not to run into Gabriella and his prayer was answered when she was nowhere to be seen on his way out the building. He looked at Instagram the whole ride to work, mostly watching half-naked women showing off their assets. His workday was a breeze, and before he knew it, the day was done, and it seemed like he had only been at work for a couple of hours. When he reached The Raven, he decided he'd better take his car to the grocery store to get his snacks and finger foods for his first gathering with his coworkers. He jetted in his 2019 super tricked-out all-black Audi A5 coupe down Bloomfield Avenue to the Stop & Shop down the street. He loved that everything he needed was right there on his block. As he was shopping, Brandon realized that he didn't have a date for his own party. Even though he didn't need one, he wanted one.

After getting home and putting his groceries away, Brandon went through his phone in search of someone to help him "host" the next day's festivities. He came across Chavon's number and paused, contemplating how that might play out. Gabriella was a friend and neighbor. They just happened to be sexual; there were no intentions there. Chavon was her friend, but if they were that close, Gabriella would have told her that they were kickin' it, and Chavon wouldn't even interfere with that. And if she told her and she don't care, they both hoes, and I'm gon' have my fun. Brandon dialed Chavon's number.

"Hey, Brandon," she sang out, excited and blushing.

"What's good, lady? What you up to?" Brandon smiled after hearing her thirst.

"Nothing, sitting here watching Basketball Wives." Chavon turned the TV down to better hear every word coming out of Brandon's mouth, waiting for, "Can I see you?" to ring in her ear. Yes, Handsome, ask me out.

"Drama." Brandon shook his head. "Don't tell me you're a drama queen." He opened some chips, sat at his island, and turned on his living room TV to watch the news.

"Everybody loves drama; that's why these shows are hits." Chavon looked in the mirror and puckered up her lips, stuck her tongue out of her mouth, and started simulating fellatio while imagining she was doing it to Brandon.

"Nah, I don't. I mean, yeah, on TV, but not in my life. I just need a good sports event, great pussy and head, a full stomach, a fat wallet, my kids, and God. And I didn't put God last; I just went backward. In that opposite order, like Scrap's mother, Momma Dee, says." He laughed.

"Oh, so you do watch reality television." Chavon sat down, placed her phone on the end table near her couch, put one hand down her pants and the other back and forth between her breasts and started rubbing herself. She wanted Brandon. Just the sound of his voice turned her on.

"Sometimes just to get a laugh every now and then. If I were to watch it religiously, I'd get mad at the ignorant shit. Plus, I'm a man."

"Shit, it's a lot of ignorant niggas and bitches." Chavon's voice almost quivered as she began to climax on her last word. She thrust her hand deep into her vagina and ended up on her knees unbeknownst to Brandon. Brandon looked at the phone, wondering why her words had suddenly slurred a bit.

"You over there drinking? Why your words starting to slur?"

"Oh, no, my phone had slid off the arm of the couch, and I tried to catch it. I'm good." Chavon jumped up and back on the couch like she had been found out. She was just glad that she got the nut before he interrupted her.

"Yeah, don't be lying. I called to invite you to a get-together I'm having with my coworkers tomorrow. I guess you can say you would be my date. You know, even though I'm single, if I don't have a hoe waiting on me in my own spot, that's not a good look. And I ain't calling you no hoe; it's just a figure of speech, if you know what I'm trying to say." Brandon was testing her, and she ain't even know it.

"Nah, I get what you sayin'. I mean, I was about to say, like, 'Are you calling me a hoe?' but then I was like, 'Why would he call me a hoe to my face like that and mean it'?"

Brandon looked at the phone and shook his head and

thought, this is exactly why I'm single; these chicks ain't got a clue.

"So call me tomorrow, and we'll decide what time you should come. Okay, cutie?"

"No, you call me early and tell me, so I'll be ready," she ordered.

"Okay. I like a woman who takes charge. Are you gonna tell Gabriella that you're coming here?" Brandon didn't want any surprises.

"I wasn't planning on it. I'm my own person. I don't have to answer to anyone and especially not a girl who wants you when I do." Chavon was Gabriella's friend, but this was a black man, and she felt that she was entitled to him more than Gabriella was.

"That's what I'm talking about. This ain't high school. See you tomorrow."

Brandon started setting up his serving bowls, silverware, and sodas for the next day so that all he'd have to do is tell Chavon what to do when she got there. He planned to have everyone come around 8:30. He was going to try to get it in with Chavon before and after the get-together. He'd let her stay if she was good; if not, he'd send her walking... in an Uber. Brandon got in the bed early so that he'd be rested up for the next night, which would be long.

* * *

The next morning, Brandon ran into Grace at the elevator. She was alone. He felt awkward because he couldn't help feeling that her desperation was deafening even though she didn't say a word. Her eyes told it all.

"Good morning, Grace." He kept his distance so as not to cause a stir in her or her husband if he was lurking, which he always seemed to be.

"Good morning, Brandon. That's a nice suit you have on." Grace knew Mark would kill her for complimenting another man; especially—a black man—but she didn't care. Mark hadn't touched her in months, which told her that he was touching someone else. She liked how Brandon looked in that suit and undressed him in her mind, hoping he would be a dog and try her. She just didn't know what she would do if he did. She knew what she wanted but had no clue how to get it. Just one night with him; just one, she thought to herself. Brandon tried to keep his attention elsewhere, but there was nowhere else to attend to; they were the only ones standing there in the hallway.

"This elevator is taking a mighty long time," he joked, trying to break the massive tension. He knew it was sexual tension on Grace's part, but that wasn't his problem, nor was he trying to find a solution for it.

"Yeah, this is rush hour. And to think that three elevators would be enough in here. But it's not." Grace blushed as she caught his eye. Brandon smiled on the inside. I bet her panties are creaming right now. The elevator reached their floor and the door opened. Brandon was relieved that there were people on it. He went to one side of the glass to overlook the scenery while she went to the other.

Brandon rushed through the lobby and made it to the train without seeing Gabriella again. Whew, he thought as he got on the train to Penn Station.

His train ride was quick, and the whole day went well. He made another $50,000 and felt like the mack because the usual office flirts were trying to put their dibs in to be his after-party date, which made him glad that he had called

Chavon. One thing he never did was mess around with coworkers, as that was always a recipe for disaster because his attention span was short, and he always remembered his father telling him to never shit where you eat, and that was one life lesson that he always followed.

Brandon made sure that he left work early to divert the group that was supposed to ride the train with him to Jersey, making the excuse that he had to get his house ready for their arrival.

He thought of more fond memories of good times that had been shared with his father and his brother. He wished that he had a sister so that he'd be able to consult with her about the women that he dealt with.

"Dad, when did you know that you were in love with Mom?" Brandon asked his father at eleven years old, when he thought that he was in love with a classmate named Dana.

"I knew when she tried to tell me about hanging out with my friends instead of looking for a better job and I listened. I was saying to myself, who does she think she is telling me what I should be doing? but I wanted to do whatever she said. It was so weird. No other woman could ever get me to obey her. When I made that revelation and admitted that to myself, I honestly became scared of the power she had over me. Scared because she was the real deal. I just had to surrender, and my life got so much better. I mean it; she made me complete. Men, we fight it, but it's the best thing when you find the right girl. She makes you want to be a good man and want to treat her like she's the best gift that you ever received."

* * *

Brandon spoke to Chavon earlier in the day, and they agreed to meet at his house at six o'clock.

By 6:15, Brandon was standing at his massive living room window, looking over the city of Montclair, his dick in Chavon's mouth. He was in awe of himself and how he had achieved that accomplishment. He didn't need to have sex with her at that point. He was good until after the party.

She walked in, and when she asked what he needed her to do first, he said, "Suck my dick," not knowing whether she would oblige or not, but was tickled when she did. He looked down at her bobbing her head back and forth while he and his dick stood at attention.

"Damn, girl, that is just what I needed," he said and thought, and just what's gonna have me not calling you again or maybe just for this, because this feels great. Why would I not let you do this again?

He knew that he didn't want his cum on his new carpet, so he was hoping that she wasn't an amateur who didn't swallow. She swallowed and got up like it was nothing. He popped a bottle of Bartenura, and they toasted and sipped on a glass.

"Now what do you need me to do?" Chavon joked as Brandon tried to gain his composure.

"Damn, girl. I didn't know you was gonna try and win the championship. Now my knees are weak." They both laughed. "I need you to set this party up nicely. Give it a woman's touch."

Brandon went and lay down in his room to watch TV and relax. He woke up to another round of being swallowed up by Chavon. He pushed her off him and onto her back.

He got off the bed and dropped the shorts that he was lounging in along with his boxers, and Chavon pulled her leggings off to reveal that she wasn't wearing any underwear. Brandon smiled and winked at her.

"So you was ready, huh? How'd you know that I'd give you some?"

"I wish that was a funny joke, but you bombed on that one. You know that if you gave Gabriella some, I wasn't gonna miss out." Chavon got back on the bed with nothing, her chocolate body naturally glistening and glowing. She went back on her elbows and opened her legs.

Her kitty-kat was shaved just right, and she had one tattooed inside her thigh. It was a sexy Hello Kitty. He knew that at least one man had said "Hello, Kitty" out loud to her after seeing it, and he wasn't going to be corny along with them. Instead, he crawled up in between her legs and kissed the tattoo. He kissed her thighs and put his nose close and took a sniff. He had to decide if he was going in or if he was just going to put it in. Nigga, you buggin'; get a rubber and have a safe one. He talked himself out of being impulsive and doing something that he would regret later. Shit, you don't know if this will be a one-night stand or a recurrence. Relax.

He got up and went to his dresser drawer and pulled a rubber out, put it on, and dove into a pleasantly wet, wet ride. She felt right, tight, and he wasn't being polite. He took charge and gave her all of his dick, with long strokes, putting his back in it. He wanted to see how she'd react to him being a beast, and she loved it, with added moans, whispers, and grabbing his back to pull him in even more.

He glanced over at the clock, which read 7:30. They had a half hour before people would begin to show up, so he unapologetically advised her, "You better get yours because I'm about to get mine. People are about to come. I will maaaaake it uuuuuuup to youuuuuuuuu... uhhhhhhh, daaaaaaaaaamn. Yeah, that was a gooooood one."

He was about to lift up out of her, and she said, "Hoooooooooold uuuuuuuuuuuuuuup. I'm cummmmmmmmmming." He felt her walls pulsating and he smiled.

"Okay, I'm glad you got one. You good?" he asked her, and she smiled and nodded her head, looking like she was in ecstasy.

"Yup, I'm actually still cumming. You should have stayed in." She closed her eyes and leaned her head back on the pillow and put her hands in between her legs.

"I gotta jump in the shower."

Brandon jumped up and took a quick shower and got presentably dressed for his guests. He looked in the mirror and winked at himself. "You a bad mutha—shut your mouth." He started laughing.

Chavon walked in on him and joked, "Oh, you feelin' yourself, huh?" As she walked naked toward him, he admired her voluptuous body. It sure had Gabriella's body beat. Chavon may have just put the nail in Gabriella's coffin, because he sure wasn't going to mess with two friends. He was past ménage à trois; they always ended messy.

Brandon put on green Adidas sweatpants with a white Adidas tee and his Adidas slides. He felt fresh and looked it. He was excited to show off his new place to the people that he spent most of his days with. The whole crew came in together. They brought bottles and small gifts and cheer. After their calm beginning and a few emptied bottles, the get-together turned into a turnt-up party. Everyone was in awe of the beautiful living room view, standing in front of the window, which was a glass wall that stretched the entire width of the living room.

The dancing began, the music got louder, the laughs and

language were boisterous, and Chavon was making sure that everyone was comfortable, enjoying themselves, and had red cups that stayed full.

At about midnight, a series of loud pounds was heard at the door. Brandon knew who it probably was. He told everyone to relax, turned down the music, and was shocked to see three police officers on the other side of the door when he opened it. His blood immediately began to boil. Chavon walked up behind him to assist if he was to blow his top because she could see in his eyes that he was two seconds from exploding.

"May I ask why you officers are pounding on my door?" The small group of about twenty people quietly and subtly began sitting on couches and chairs as if they'd gotten reprimanded by a schoolteacher.

"We have a warrant to search the premises of this apartment. Please step aside, sir." Brandon blocked the door.

"A fucking warrant for what? I'm having a housewarming party. I'm not breaking any laws. You're not going to taunt my guests. And who called for a warrant? Mark Stephens!"

"Yes, sir, Mr. Stephens advised us that he attempted to knock on your door over an hour ago to request that the music be turned down and smelled drugs coming into the hallway."

"Drugs! I don't do drugs! Nobody in this house has done one drug! These are my coworkers. Where is that muthafucka? Come down the hall, man!"

"Sir, I'm going to advise you to calm down. We're going to execute the warrant, and if there are no drugs on the premises, then no one will have a problem. Please step aside."

"I ain't steppin' shit!" The two white officers behind the Hispanic officer who was talking to Brandon put their hands on their guns and took a step forward.

Chavon stepped in. "Officers, this man just bought this condo. He's having a nice party. There's no need for this, and now you're putting hands on your guns? Are you in danger? You have guns; we don't. Why are you feeling the need to touch your firearms?" A few brave people in the apartment walked up and a few of them took out their phones and started recording. The officers stayed silent but didn't remove their hands.

"Ma'am, do you live here?" The talking officer inquired of Chavon, who had gently pushed Brandon behind her while stepping in between him and the first officer.

"And what does that matter? We can turn the music down, but we aren't doing anything wr-," Chavon said as Brandon cut her off midsentence.

"You cannot search anyone in my home. You don't have a warrant for them."

The officers remained insistent. "We didn't say we were going to search your guests, but we are going to search your home." Mark Stephens slowly walked down the corridor. He had on an overcoat, which seemed strange as he was approaching the apartment.

"You'd better go back to your apartment," Brandon said in a calm yet volatile tone.

"Are you threatening me, sir?" Mark asked politely.

"Listen, officers, may I speak with him for one second? Can we step right over here? I just need to speak to Mr. Phillups momentarily." Chavon was peaceful and persuasive.

"Go ahead, but if you close the door, we will get it open."

"We sure will," Mark teased.

"You ain't gon' do shit. You better hope you pull this off, whatever you trying to do!"

"Excuse us, officers." Chavon pulled Brandon to the side.

"Look, do you have anything illegal in your house?"

"Hell the fuck no. I ain't into illegal shit; I work for everything I have."

"So you might as well let them execute the warrant, because they're gonna do it one way or the other, and we don't need this to escalate to a dangerous situation, Brandon. We did nothing wrong. I mean, you did nothing wrong, and we—meaning, your guests—did nothing wrong, so..."

"I know what you meant, and okay, but I'm telling you, this muthafucker is up to something. This is the asshole I was talking to Gabriella about that night." Brandon was fuming.

"Listen, y'all sit tight, okay? I apologize. Y'all all can go have a seat," Brandon said to his guests and walked back to the door to get to the bottom of the dilemma.

"What is the warrant for?" Brandon asked.

"Here you go, sir. Now, please step aside." The officer passed Brandon the warrant and he went to the island in the kitchen and began to read it.

He yelled, "Drugs and firearms? This is bullshit!" One of the officers walked over to Brandon and stood by him.

"Chavon, close my fucking door!"

"Officer, may I close the door?"

"Yes," the officer responded without looking at Chavon. She caught a bad vibe.

"Good night, neighbor," Mark sang as he laughed and began to walk back to his apartment.

Brandon began to yell, but the officer shook his head no to Brandon, who looked, breathing heavily.

"Are you okay? You need some water?" Chavon asked Brandon, and he nodded yes without looking up.

Some of the guests asked the officer if they could leave after about a half hour of the other two officers still searching Brandon's cabinets and closets.

After an hour, more people apologetically left as Brandon was then in a subdued, shocked, and overwhelmed state at the thought of what was going on in his dream home. Chavon sat quietly next to him as the officer stood, stone-faced.

After two hours passed, only Chavon, Brandon, and Tori, the owner of Brandon's agency, were left. One of the officers came out of Brandon's walk-in closet and out of his room, holding a pistol.

Brandon's eyes popped out of his head when he saw the gun held up, and the officer asked, "Sir, is this a registered firearm?"

"Oh, hell no! He planted a weapon in my house? Oh, hell no!"

"Sir, if you don't have a license, we're going to have to take you down to the station for having an unregistered pistol. So do you have the license for this?"

Brandon had felt this defeated in his lifetime before, being harassed and discriminated against by cops on several occasions. It was an experience that many black, Hispanic, minority, and indigenous people—mostly men—had experienced many times in their lives, but this time was different. He had never felt so humiliated. His employees—the people he supervised—had been there to see it. He had envisioned himself residing in this building for at least three years, and it was feeling like the worst nightmare had come true, not the best dream. He shook his head.

What happened next was more of a blur. Brandon woke up the next morning with not only a slight hangover but feeling more despair. He was in a jail cell alone. How the fuck did that gun get in my fucking house? he had asked himself about a thousand times, knowing the answer, but not knowing how to prove it.

Mark had this done. There were no ifs, ands, or buts about it. He knew that Mark did it, but he also knew that Mark had the building management in his pocket. He knew it was time for him to turn the tables on Mark. He just had to figure out how.

Brandon sat in a jail cell until Monday morning. He called his mother, Raquelle, on Saturday, who told him that his boss, Tori Tavvin, was going to get him out. Brandon's mom prayed with him.

"Lord, we know that you have us covered. You know that my son is not a man that will do something to get himself in legal trouble. Bind up the enemy, Lord. Make a mockery out of Satan and his followers who are trying to destroy my child. This child that you gave me, I need him, Lord. You have blessed me tremendously with such a loving, comforting, supportive, and sympathetic son. I just ask you to keep him safe and exonerate him, Lord, so that we can give you all of the glory. Amen," his mom said confidently and peacefully.

Brandon smiled. "Amen." He loved when his mother prayed. He felt the power of the Holy Spirit when she spoke to and about God.

Raquelle reassured him that he would be fine, as she always did. There was never a time that his mother lost her calm. She had been through a lot in her life, like most, but what set her apart was her unwavering faith. Although Brandon had never given her many problems growing up, his brother made up for it after their father died by being in and out of juvenile detention centers, jails, and eventually prison. Bruce was actually nearing the end of a three-year prison sentence for credit card fraud. Every time another incident happened, Raquelle showed reserve and dignity. He made himself promise to go see his brother soon. Two days in jail was nerve-wracking; he couldn't imagine what Bruce's life was like behind prison walls.

Brandon adored his mother and never wanted to give her more stress than she already had, and he was glad that he had adopted her positive outlook on life. He was not nearly as willing to forgive as she was, though. Mark was going to pay.

Brandon was grateful to have a boss who was very fair and not racist. Tori was a Jewish man, and although Jews and blacks had their own challenging relationship as a whole, he did respect the Jewish community for their own unity and discipline. Although they were persecuted against, as many minorities are, they had managed to keep more of their culture, customs, and history—most likely because they knew where they had come from, as opposed to African Americans, who had no idea what country, tribe, or clan they had originated from due to the diaspora of the slave trade.

"Mommy, look, I don't want you to worry. I know you'll put it in God's hands, but I know you're still concerned. I promise you: I will come out of this victorious."

"I know you will, Brandon. You're a champion. Champions just have setbacks. They never really lose anything. A champion and a man of God. That's unconquerable. I'll be there when you walk out of those doors. I told Tori I'd get you out, but he insisted. He has a lawyer already lined up to represent you too. See, things are not always black-and-white. All white people are not racist, and all black people are not useless."

They talked a little while longer, and then Brandon got off the phone. He slept the rest of the time, so that he could get to Monday morning faster.

"Phillips!" He heard his name called at 7 a.m. on Monday morning. He was feeling drained and not himself. He had had some nightmares that he had gotten stuck behind bars and had to serve a lot of time, as well as seeing his daughter get married, and he wasn't able to be there. He couldn't fathom what would make people choose a life of crime, which greatly diminished their chance to live. He was taken to a van, shackled on his feet, handcuffed, and transported to the courthouse, feeling like a loser and a criminal, although he knew he was neither.

He waited in a bullpen with other people who were awaiting arraignment on various charges, and the conversations he heard were aggravating and ignorant to say the least. He realized why he hadn't made it a habit to visit his brother, often because of his limited mindset. Many people who go in and out of prison become institutionalized and out of touch with the outside world. They talk about the same things or the past, when they were "outside," and as quickly as the world continues to change, they get left behind, unable to relate to current issues and conversations.

"Man, my girl is asking me to get her a new iPhone. I told her she don't need no iPhone. She can't FaceTime me, so what she wanna FaceTime somebody else for? I ain't slow," one of the men in the holding cell expressed to someone that he knew.

"Listen, don't trust her, man. She FaceTimin' somebody. These chicks ain't shit, man. They all good when you bringin' in that illegal money, but soon as you get popped, they on to the next man." They both shook their heads, and Brandon shook his head too, but his thoughts were different than theirs.

These brothers are lost. They're worried about phones they can't buy, women they can't keep; meanwhile, they made a choice to do crime and now want to blame it on the women who are probably tired of their mess. Damn, I'm glad I'm not messed up in the game like that.

Another brother spoke and sounded like he had a bit more sense than the other two.

"Man, don't blame your women. They gotta be tired of y'all. I know my lady is tired. I don't know if y'all have been in and out of prison, but I'm sure if you have a good woman like I do, she has nagged you about doing right. My woman tried to leave me plenty of times. I promised even more times that I would stop selling drugs, robbing people, running scams, but I didn't. Yeah, she stayed because she loved me, and, yeah, she took any money I gave her because we have bills and kids. But that don't mean she wanted me out here risking my freedom. That's what I chose to do. And I'm risking losing her every time I get knocked. Shit, she deserves better. If she finds someone while I'm in here that is willing to be a real man and not only provide but make sure he doesn't do anything that will take him away from her, it'll be my fault and my fault only." The two other men were speechless.

Brandon immediately got a revelation. Damn, I know Ciara is tired of me too. She's on the verge of hating me. What's my problem? Do I have issues within myself? Why am I not satisfied with my wonderful family? he wondered. Yeah, she can be a headache, but what am I really looking for that she doesn't have? Am I just being immature and not being able to discipline myself, control my urges, and blaming her for it?

"Phillips!" Brandon was startled to hear his name called for his first meeting with the judge. He prayed as he shuffled in, the shackles on his ankles making him feel like Kunta Kinte from Roots. Lord, please help me today. I can't imagine being put in prison for something I didn't do.

Brandon was brought to the defendant's table to stand and take an oath of honesty before the judge, who introduced himself as Judge Richard Kaukason, spoke. At first, Brandon felt at ease, as the judge seemed to speak to him with respect and lack of judgment because, after all, he is supposed to be innocent until proven guilty. However, things became very serious when his charges were read, and again, he was stunned by the system and how so many of his black brothers are subjected to this travesty of law throughout the majority of their lifetimes.

Some of us have been powerless, of course, and it's of no doing of our own, but others, who use the poor excuse that there's no other opportunity for them in America than a life of crime and criminal injustice, must know that this is due to their own choices and stagnation. Yes, America has been racist, and America has many successful black people in it. At some point, we have to save ourselves and not expect our oppressor to assist us in succeeding. We must know our enemy's tactics and use the tenacity of our ancestors to win. I've got to win this fight.

"Mr. Phillips, you have taken an oath. It's time for me to read your charges. We've run ballistics on the weapon that was found in your possession and unfortunately, there are two deceased twin brothers who were murdered with that gun."

Brandon felt a paralyzing weight come over him. He looked behind him and saw his mom looking on along with Tori, whose face was as shocked as Brandon's body felt. He turned back around to hear the rest of the accusations against him.

"Mr. Phillips, you are being charged with unlawful possession of a handgun, unlawful possession of hollow-tip bullets, conspiracy to commit murder, conspiracy to aid and abet a homicide."

"That gun was planted in my apartment by my neighbor, who's a detective." Brandon was more shocked that those words came out of his mouth. He knew that he had been advised by the lawyer sitting next to him and retained by Tori—Riegel Rosenbaum—to wait until he got proof to make such an accusation. They didn't want to let on that he knew what was going on because he knew that Mark probably had someone sitting in to report the proceedings back to him. The first thing his lawyer was going to do after the arraignment—and after Brandon secured the $50,000 that he had to give him—was to subpoena the surveillance footage from the building. Due to the winding, round corridors, Brandon was unsure if there was a camera view of his apartment door. He had to pay $75,000 to defend himself, and he was innocent. He was furious about that but knew that he was in a fight for his life and knew the old saying "You get what you pay for."

"Mr. Phillips, did you just accuse a detective of planting the weapon in your home?" the judge questioned with a doubtful tone, then leaned back arrogantly and took his glasses off, as if that would assist him in hearing Brandon's answer better.

"Your Honor, I am innocent, and it will be proven, so I am not going to do my lawyer's job, as law is not my forte. I just want to go on record that it is unfortunate that black men are guilty until proven innocent."

Mr. Rosenbaum gave Brandon a look that said, "Please don't."

"Mr. Phillips, you're going to have the opportunity to prove your innocence, just as the prosecution has the responsibility of proving their case. Let us not play any race cards. Officers have a job to do, and they do their job in keeping illegal guns off the street. A gun that was unregistered by you was found in your possession. There have been lives taken with that weapon. If you're innocent, you have nothing to worry about." Brandon looked at Rosenbaum and then back at his mom, who nodded at him to speak as he must.

"Your Honor, the gun was found in my condo, not in my possession, and with all due respect, I have to now pay money that I thankfully have to fight for my freedom. I would beg to lastly state that as the trial of George Floyd approaches, let's bear in mind that more black men are murdered who have no arms, no weapons, while many mass shooters who are white have been taken into custody without a hair being touched on their bodies. I'm here because of the color of my skin, and as long as we continue to ignore the inequalities of the American justice system, the more George Floyds there will be. I have a son. I don't want my son to be killed, and I don't want my son to be falsely accused, as I'm being right now." Brandon sat down.

"Mr. Phillips, stand up. You're going to respect the court. Now, your charges have been read. How do you wish to plead, with the advisement of your attorney and without pressure or undue duress?"

"I am black, and I am innocent," Brandon said as he stood.

"Mr. Rosenbaum, what's your request of the Court pertaining to your client?" the judge, who seemed to be uneasy and no longer powerful, asked in a weakened tone. Brandon knew that although the judge, the lawyer, or most of the white people in attendance didn't want to hear what he had expressed, it was his duty to say it, especially for all of the black people who had died over hundreds of years solely for being black.

"I ask that you release my client on his own recognizance, Your Honor. He has no prior criminal record, and he isn't a flight risk. His employer, Mr. Tavvin, is here to vouch for him, Your Honor. He has retained me, and I will also put my reputation on the line. As you heard Mr. Phillips—and as we know it to be true—our country has some improvements to make on the equal treatment of all, so I ask that you be a change agent and show mercy and understanding, Your Honor. Please let Mr. Phillips go home without the need to try to gather more money to be able to go home. Let him go, as he is truly innocent, and that I will prove."

The judge sat back and again removed his glasses while intently looking at Brandon and around the room. He rocked back and forth and wiped the sweat from his forehead. He looked at the white bailiff and the white officers standing in the back of the room as if pleading for help with his eyes. He let out a long sigh.

"Mr. Phillips, you may go without bail. I hope you're able to prove what you've said, as you've made accusations as well. I'll see you in a month." Judge Kaukason then hit his gavel and got up. "I will need a few moments in my chambers before we proceed." He walked into the back with his head down and an air of defeat.

Brandon let out a big sigh and shook his lawyer's hand, then thanked him. He felt someone hug him tightly from behind. He knew it was his mom, and he turned around and gave her a tight squeeze and extended his hand to shake Tori's.

"Listen, man, Tori, I can't thank you enough..."

"Listen, man, not everyone is oblivious to or unconcerned about the struggles that your people go through. My people were and still are persecuted, so I understand, but it's still different. We aren't being murdered on the streets, even being unarmed; it's a travesty. Let's go and have lunch on Love and War's expense account. You've made us a lot of money. I owe you." Tori patted Brandon on the back.

Brandon let Tori and Reigel walk ahead and out of the courthouse, and he stayed back and walked hand in hand with his mom.

"Ma, did I say too much?" Brandon looked in his mother's eyes as she walked with her head high and pride to match.

"No, sir. If we continue to be silenced, we may as well lay down and die. Brandon, I've always taught you that you don't have to be Rosa Parks, Malcolm X, or Martin Luther King to take a stand and change the world. You have to change the world that's at your fingertips. The world that you touch. It's the ripple effect. There is another black man—well, plenty of black men—in courtrooms all across this racist nation this morning. Every day. Some of them are guilty as charged, but it really doesn't matter if they aren't being treated justly. Two wrongs don't make inhumanity right. Nothing matters when the people who are supposed to uphold the law don't respect that very law or think that it only applies to some and not them. Nothing matters when black lives don't matter. They'll see that their very treatment will not only affect us, but they shouldn't have peace or peace of mind while killing and locking up innocent or guilty people because they think they're superior. Not their money, not their power or influence. God will have the final say, and know that He will protect you while you do the right thing, which is fight for your rights and against these preposterous injustices. They cannot kill us all. Now, go and talk with your attorney and Tori. I'll see you soon. I'll come by and see your new castle this weekend, since I had to invite myself." Raquelle grabbed Brandon's face and kissed both sides of his cheeks and then his lips and told her son that she loves him and is proud of him, as she always did.

"You sure, Mom? You don't want to come and sit with us? I'm sure you can give some great insight. And you know you're always invited wherever I am. I just didn't want you to come and try to help out, like I knew you would try to do. I wanted to set it up so you can come and put your feet up and look out of my massive living room windows and relax and exhale."

"Boy, I am not 'waiting to exhale'; I'm trying to be like Stella and get my groove back!" Brandon shook his head as he walked away from his mom and went to join Tori and Reigel, who were waiting for him.

Brandon went to lunch but couldn't eat. He tried to listen to the two non-black men who seemed very genuinely concerned about Brandon's situation and case. Brandon knew that Reigel would only be as enthusiastic as he was being paid, but, either way, Brandon felt better having counsel than having to handle everything on his own.

"So, Brandon, what's making you so sure that this cop has something to do with your case? I'm going to ask hard questions, but in no way does it mean that I don't believe you. I must think like the prosecution and ask you what they'll ask you before they do. Do you understand?"

"Of course, we have to be proactive. I'm still in shock that this is even happening, and, Tori, had you not been there, you wouldn't have been able to grasp how humiliating it was. I mean, my mom would have called you this morning to tell you why I wasn't going to be able to make it in to work, and even if she had disclosed to you what happened, you just had to be there to understand."

"Oh, no doubt. I was humiliated for you. It was terrible. It was as if they were celebrating their favorite team winning a championship or something. These officers are high off their fake power, and it really is dangerous for your people to have to come into contact with law enforcement. They have no respect for certain people."

"Because they don't see us as people. But, Reigel, to answer your question, Mark Stephens has been harassing me since I moved into that building. He lives on my floor, and

I haven't had any other negative encounters with anyone in that complex except him."

"I understand, but do you feel that his motive is strictly because you're black? Is he targeting you for some other reason?" Brandon stopped himself from being offended. He had to remember that Reigel was just trying to ask the questions that would be asked by the prosecution.

"I know that he pulled a gun out on me the day I moved in, and I should have reported it to the police. He acts like he's on duty in our building, and he isn't even an officer in that jurisdiction. I reported it to the building, and nothing was done."

"Okay, so we'll be looking into that. We'll subpoena his work record as well."

All he heard were faint sounds in his ear as his mind began to wander. The scene was vivid as Brandon flashed back to a time that his father was harassed by the police. His bones almost trembled like they did that late night on a dark street in North Carolina.

The lights and siren were so bright and loud that it woke Brandon and his brother, Bruce, up. They popped up, turned around on their knees, and watched the cop car tailing his father's car so close that he hoped his father didn't put his brakes on, because the patrol car would have rear-ended them. The fear was almost suffocating. His eyes were as bright as the blinding lights, and he nearly peed his pants. His father screamed at the boys to sit down the right way. "Before I get a ticket for that and whatever the hell he is pulling me over for!" The boys slid down and turned around. Brandon's legs wouldn't stop shaking, and Bruce began to cry.

Their father slowly pulled over. His mother began to pray, and Billy Phillips screamed at her to shut "the fuck" up.

Brandon was shocked to hear his father speak to his mother that way, but rightfully assumed that it was only because of his father's own panic. Brandon, frozen in place, saw the officers approach out of his peripheral.

The officers got on each side of the car. Billy rolled down the window and said not a word.

"License and registration," the officer on Billy's side said with aggression and rudeness.

"Officer, I'm traveling to see family in North Carolina. Why am I being pulled over?"

"I ask the questions here, boy, so let's go with the paperwork."

"I'm a man, not a boy. I have my boys in the back. They're pretty traumatized; I just want to know why I'm being delayed." Billy's hands shook as he opened the glove compartment to get his registration and insurance cards. Brandon knew that his father was distraught because his hands would shake when he was about to blow his top. Brandon's tears began to fall, and he whimpered quietly.

"You're in my state. I call you what I choose. I hope you haven't got any warrants, because your family will be traveling without you." The officer walked back to the patrol car while the other officer stood by. Billy leaned over his wife and persisted.

"Sir, can you let me know what I'm being detained for?" He looked up at a stone-faced officer who didn't even give him the respect to acknowledge his question. He slammed his hand on the steering wheel. "Dammit! There's nothing worse than racist cops looking for someone to harass."

The officer grabbed his gun and pointed it through the window and screamed, "Get out the car and on the ground now!" His partner ran up with his gun, and Brandon's mom started screaming.

The officer ran up, swung the door open, and grabbed Billy out of the car and put on the ground. He handcuffed him.

"Officer, please! I'm pregnant, and my husband hasn't done anything wrong. Please give him a ticket, and we'll be on our way. Please, my boys are in the back, petrified. Please don't hurt my husband!"

The officer ignored Raquelle, and Billy was lifted up and walked to the squad car and put in the back. The officer, still at Raquelle's window, leaned in and looked at Brandon and Bruce, who were now huddled together and both sobbing. He looked at Raquelle and walked back to the car.

"Lord, Jesus, please cover him with your blood. Lord, I plead the blood over my husband. Don't let them kill my husband." The more their mother prayed, the louder she got, and the only thing that began to drown out her words were her sons' cries. Raquelle didn't stop crying out to the Lord until her husband came and opened the door. He got in and sat, stunned and defeated. His hands shook uncontrollably, and Raquelle took his hands in hers and began to caress them. She embraced her husband with a calming peace. She rubbed his back as he buried his face in her chest. The police car pulled alongside them, and the officer in the passenger seat rolled down the window and said, "Y'all move on if you don't want no trouble."

From that day forward, Brandon changed his mind about the police. Before that, he had admired officers and thought he might possibly be one someday, because they protected people. He now saw them as agitators, dictators, and inhumane abusers. After about fifteen minutes of their mother praying over their father and thanking God that Billy had returned to the car safely, Billy finally sat up and looked forward, his head up and arms steady and extended to the steering wheel, and pulled back onto the dark road.

"I'm so sorry. I'm so, so, so sorry. I let my family down" Billy expressed his disappointment with himself because it was the only thing that would help him release the extremely humiliating ordeal without committing a crime. Raquelle wasn't sure if she should say something to make him feel better or just listen. He continued, thanking them and God, and his calmness began to come back as he continued to profess his anguish. Raquelle rubbed his neck and asked the boys if they were okay. They were still frozen and in shock.

"Pull over, babe. I need to get in the back with the boys."

As soon as Brandon's mom moved to the back seat, they lost their composure, each grabbing onto her as tightly as they could while she cradled them. His mom ended up losing the baby, which would have been his baby sister, the next day. Raquelle believed it was due to the stressful encounter.

"Hey, dude, you there?" Reigel startled Brandon.

"No, not at all. My life is on the line. I have to go. Can I call you with any questions or concerns—well, hell, my concerns are endless right now. I just ordered a car to pick me up."

"Sure, guy, don't worry. Call me. Any questions, okay? We got this."

Brandon excused himself and walked out. He got in the chauffeur driven private car and ordered the driver to go to the cemetery before going home and getting some much-needed rest. He was drained and wanted nothing more than to have a good night's sleep after having been surrounded by nothing but mental illness and drama, in a cage. He had to turn off the radio and put on some music from his phone, because the multiple stories of police brutality and racism since the death of George Floyd were disturbing.

Brandon pulled up to his father's plot and got out of the car. He needed to visit his dad and talk with his spirit. He was still wearing his suit from court, but it didn't stop him from sitting on the ground. He felt like a lost little boy. He read the tombstone and the dates numerous times. Fourteen was too young to lose his father. He sat quietly, not knowing what to say, but trying to feel his dad's presence and comfort.

"I just got the chills. Dad, is that you?" Brandon shivered a bit. "I need to know what I should do. I need to know how to keep going and not give up. I feel like I'm such a confused man, but Mom always tells me that a double-minded man is unstable in all of his ways. I want to be a family man, but it's so much easier to just worry about myself. I have a lot of conflicting thoughts. Oh man." Brandon sighed, feeling overwhelmed. He had so many thoughts racing through his mind.

"I wish I could just cry like women cry and release my stress, but I'm numb. I wish I could crawl back on to Mommy's lap and start all over. Then maybe you'd still be here.

Did you have other women behind mom's back? Did you have the same struggles and temptations that men have? Did you feel trapped by having a family and then feel guilty about it? Damn, I wish you could talk to me. Why can't you just talk to me!?" Brandon got up and walked back to the car that was awaiting him.

"You don't have to be strong, man," the white male driver said to Brandon, who considered telling him to mind his business. He decided to listen.

"Do I really have a choice?" Brandon asked.

"Sure you do. You can cop out. You can get on drugs or kill yourself like my dad did. He left five kids behind like a coward. I was eleven years old. I had no idea what life was about. I had no blueprint on what to do to become a man." Brandon felt weird.

"How did you know I was visiting my dad?"

"I didn't know who you were visiting. I just know you are upset, and I understand. That's all. I didn't mean to offend you." Brandon knew that this man had done nothing to him and that he should appreciate him trying to make him feel understood.

"I'm sorry, guy. I am not offended, and thank you for letting me know that I'm not alone. As men, we get tired of trying to be Superman while everything seems to be kryptonite. Women have no idea what we go through."

"Yes, you are right, and being white doesn't mean your life is all right either, just for the record." The driver paused and continued.

"And we don't know what women go through either. We just don't know how to not take our pain out on each other, the closest ones to you." Brandon nodded his head in agreement. He thanked the driver again as he got out of the car.

Brandon made it home and off the elevator, running into Grace as soon as he stepped off. She looked at him with sorrow in her eyes, and he was disgusted. Brandon didn't acknowledge her and walked straight to his door without looking back. As soon as he closed the door, there was a knock on it. Brandon peeked out of the peephole and as he was about to curse her and tell her to leave from his door, he got an idea. He knew that what he was about to do was risky, but he had to follow his gut instinct. He opened the door and rushed her inside. Grace stepped in and looked around in awe at how nice his home was.

"Please help me. I need your help." He sat at the kitchen island and put his hands on his head.

"I wish I could help you; I do. I don't know what to do." Grace stood over Brandon and wanted to touch him.

"You can. I know you know that your husband has been harassing me. He's been trying me since the very first day I moved in. How can you be with a racist? Are you racist too?" Brandon was laying on the reverse psychology real thick. He looked up at Grace with a genuine concern, all the while strategizing.

"I'm not racist. I just don't know many black people and I just... I don't know. I don't think protecting your race is racist."

"Protecting your race from what? Because the history of this country has shown that black people are the ones being erased, killed, murdered, and railroaded, like me. Your husband is trying to ruin my life, and for what other reason could it be than the fact that I am black? That's the first thing he saw when he pulled that gun on me."

Grace looked stunned. "You didn't know that, right? From the moment I stepped foot on this property, your husband has had it out for me. I was moving in. My moving truck hadn't even arrived yet, and I was told to put my hands up, and it was your husband who thought it was funny to pull a prank to try and scare the shit out of me. Intimidate me. Now, what else could he have seen except me?"

Grace looked at the floor. A tear fell from her eye and rolled down her cheek. "I'm sorry. I don't know what else to say." Brandon cheered for himself. He was appealing to her and finding a way in.

"So why are you here? And can you help me?"

"Brandon, I don't know. I am not supposed to be here, and I know that, but there's something about you that I can't ignore. I can't stop thinking about you."

"Grace, you're married and not just to any man, but a man who is trying to destroy me. Is it because of you? Does he know that you've been constantly thinking of me? Are you the cause of this?"

"No. I would never tell him that, but he is jealous, and he doesn't want me to communicate with you or plan playdates with our kids."

"So he's racist, right? I need your help. I know this is your husband, but I'm innocent. I can't be taken away from my kids. I need your help; please help me." Brandon was intense and serious.

Grace shook her head in disbelief. "What can I do? There's nothing that I can do. Nothing. Nothing." Grace began to sob, and Brandon embraced her. Her crying made Brandon even more curious about what she was becoming so distraught about. Brandon gently moved Grace back and looked into her eyes.

"Is he abusive to you? Is he harming you? If so, what are you going to do? Are you going to let him eventually kill you and ruin your children's lives?"

"He's more emotionally and mentally abusive. I mean, he has put his hands on me on a few different occasions, but I'm not fearful for my life."

"Why not? He's a ticking time bomb. I know he's controlling, and you can't take something like this lightly. You never know when he's going to go too far." Grace slid down to the floor and continued her meltdown. Brandon didn't feel as much compassion for her as he normally would have for someone else because he felt she was partly to blame. Mark probably could sense that her wandering eye was for Brandon, and he didn't want to be the focus of Mark's insecurity or revenge. Someone like Mark had an ego that would not allow any kind of embarrassment or humiliation, although he knew how to use those things to abuse his power and his rationale.

"I don't know what I'm gonna do. I... actually, I cannot stand him. I despise him. I wish he would just go away." Brandon needed to think of the best way to get Grace to work with him against her husband. He needed more information.

"Listen, I don't want to blame you. When I saw it was you at the door, I wanted to tell you to leave, but my problem isn't with you. Maybe we can be there for each other. What's going on? When I saw your family at the indoor park, you seemed fine. Is this something new?"

"No, this isn't new. Things have gotten progressively worse. I know his job is stressful but..."

Brandon took her hand and walked her to the couch. He put his finger on his lips to motion for her to wait before continuing.

"Hold on. Sit down and relax. Do you want a glass of wine? Wait, is Mark at work? Do you know when he'll be home? I really want my life, so this is a big risk."

"He comes home late just about every night. He's consumed and obsessed with work, with meeting quotas, with making arrests that turn into convictions." Grace paused and looked Brandon in his chestnut-colored eyes.

"What's his problem, and how did you not know about it?"

"I always felt that he was just all talk. I never really believed that he could be that arrogant or that mean or that obnoxious. But he is. I guess I ignored the red flags until they were glaring and beyond repair. I guess I was in denial. I try to ask myself what I ever saw in him, and I think it was because he was always funny. He'd make me laugh all the time with his antics, but I thought they were fake. Now his antics are disrespectful, painful, and detrimental."

"Detrimental?" That was the keyword Brandon needed to expound upon.

"Damaging to my future, to my fantasy, to my reality. My reality is way worse than the fantasy, but now I can't ignore it anymore." Brandon didn't feel sympathy, just desperation.

"Listen, you're young and you're beautiful. You can make another life for yourself. You don't have to live for others; you deserve to be happy. Do you want your marriage?"

Grace looked at Brandon and then looked out of the massive window that resembled hers on the other side of the building. She stared and the tears rolled.

"Wait. I shouldn't even be prying like that. I see that you're going through something. It isn't right for me to be questioning you about your personal life. I apologize." Grace didn't say a word. She was in denial, and she was confused. "I just really want to know what made you come here, though, seriously. I feel like although it's a surprise, it's kind of a pleasant one. If anyone has answers, it should be you." Brandon wanted to let up on her, but he just couldn't.

"I came because I feel bad. I don't know how I fell in love and had kids with such a monster. I just don't know what to do. I feel almost like I'm not myself, like I'm watching myself, and I don't know, I..."

Brandon excused himself and went into his room. He closed his door and went to the window and looked out of it. He had to think of the next move. He knew that he was going to have to risk dealing with Grace in order to beat Mark at his own game. But how?

Mark rushed into The Raven and pressed the down button on the elevator pad instead of up. He had just gotten off a stressful day at work and prearranged for Jerry to have a party waiting for him. It was earlier than usual, 7 p.m., so he had a few hours to play with before he was expected home. The funny thing was, Grace hadn't been the least concerned about him coming home lately. He didn't care either way.

Mark got off the elevator and banged on Jerry's door. Jerry swung open the door, eyes wide and sweaty.

"What the hell are you banging on the door like that for? You almost gave me a heart attack."

"I told you that I was on my way. Tell me that you got the girls for me."

"Well, yeah. I got two new girls. I never met them before."

"Where did you find them?"

"I went into the city, and they were at the bus station, and they asked me if I wanted to have a double good time. I couldn't refuse. I couldn't reach Candy and Sunshine, so they'll have to do." The two men walked through the corridor to the living room, where the girls sat half-dressed. Mark sized them up and looked them over.

"Hey, girls. Y'all like to party I'm sure," Mark said, cracking open a beer that was on the table.

"Who doesn't?" one of the girls joked.

"Oh, believe me, plenty of people don't. They're too good; too perfect. I don't like people like that. Like my wife."

"Yeah, we hear it all the time. Husbands who can't stand their wives. That's what we're here for: to make people happy." They both giggled while the two guys smiled and looked at each other as if they were done with the small talk.

"So, as my favorite theme song to my favorite show, The Partridge Family, says, 'Come on, get happy!' I'm ready for some happiness. Who's gonna volunteer to take me to my happy place?" They all started laughing at Mark's silliness.

One of the girls, wearing a fiery-red wig, pulled out a bill and opened it up. She used a folded match book and scooped up a combination of cocaine and heroin and snorted it up her nose. She walked it over to Mark, who looked at it cautiously. He was a cop who breaks the law, but he also had a sixth sense.

"What's in there? What is it?" he asked her.

"It's just coke," Redhead lied.

"Nothing else?" Mark took the bill and looked the girl intently in her eyes, as if he could make her tell the truth.

"No, that's it."

Mark took four servings into his nostrils and told her to make him a drink.

Jerry was in the back bedroom with Redhead's friend, having their own party.

The girl went into Jerry's adjoining kitchen and took a red cup out of her liquor-store bag. She opened a bottle of vodka and filled the cup halfway. She took some powdered GHB out of her pocket and poured it in Mark's drink. She put orange juice in his drink and stirred it before taking his drink back out and handing it to him. Mark finished his drink in two gulps. The girl, wearing a mini dress and heels, put on some rock music and began to dance around.

She took the bill out again, used and passed, and Mark participated again. She knew that it would be a few short minutes before he was passed out on the couch. She quickly made him another drink even though he was already looking woozy and pretty out of it.

"Hey, stop stalling and come over here and get naked." Mark grabbed at her wrist after taking the cup with his other hand. "Sit down." He pulled on her arm, and she sat. She slowly began to take her stilettos off and then her dress. She was sitting in her underwear, stalling, pretending to get ready to perform a sex act on Mark, when he passed out cold. He was leaned back, his mouth wide open. The ruthless girl got dressed and dug through Mark's pants. She pulled out a thousand dollars and a badge. When she realized Mark was a detective, she smiled. She pulled his penis out of his pants and took a selfie with her mouth on it. She took the drugs out of her pocket and put the bill on his lap and took a picture of that too. She took his phone and called her number and put it back, gathered her belongings, and left.

About four hours later, at 2 a.m., Mark was awakened by Jerry. "What the hell happened? Where's the bitches at? Did they leave? Did they rob us? What the fuck? Did she slip me a mickey? I don't feel right? I feel sick. Who were those cunts?"

Mark tried to get up and couldn't. He started throwing up all over Jerry's floor. Jerry turned around and went back in the room, screaming, "Dammit, you're throwing up all over my place! Go home to your wife. Fuck!"

Mark stumbled into his apartment at 4 a.m., throwing up all over the bathroom, then passing out on the bed. Grace looked at her husband, whose clothes had vomit on them, and had it been a year prior, she would have undressed him and cleaned him up and even made him some soup or tea. Now, she was disgusted and repulsed by him. She tried to pinpoint when things had begun to fall apart. When they got married, Mark wasn't even an officer, but he always wanted to follow in his grandfather's and father's footsteps and become a cop. Although his father died before they were married, Grace now recognized and remembered that her father-in-law was actually very racist.

Mark became more and more arrogant and narcissistic as his career in law enforcement blossomed. He had been promoted consistently, and ever since becoming a homicide detective, he had become more and more unbearable. Grace had a thought. She had never done it before, but she wanted to see what was really going on with Mark. She looked at his phone on the nightstand and slid out of the bed. She walked around and stood over him.

Grace was scared, but she kept thinking about her meeting with Brandon, wondering if she could do anything to help him. She really wondered how she could help herself. She just didn't think there was anything left of their marriage and often wondered if he was cheating. She probably never looked because she didn't think that she would be able to handle the truth. Now, the truth may be the very thing to set her free and to free an innocent man from bogus charges. She didn't know how Mark had done what he did to Brandon, but her gut let her know he had something to do with it. Her mind replayed the night that Brandon got arrested. Mark had come in bragging that he "got his ass now." She never asked Mark what he was talking about, but now she needed to know as much as she could.

Grace stood there, scared. Move, her mind told her, and she went into her own detective mode. She went into his office and opened his phone. There were three unread messages; two were from an unsaved number. As soon as

Grace opened the message, she saw a picture that made her eyes nearly pop out of her head. She nearly dropped his phone. She fell into his swivel chair and buried her head in her hands. Again, her mind told her to hurry up.

Grace looked at the other picture and read the message. "Detective Stephens, you need to call me. I doubt if you want your precinct or wife to see what you were doing last night." Grace could hardly breathe. Her heart pounded, and her hands trembled. She forwarded the text to her phone and grabbed a Post-it note and wrote the number down. She erased the messages out of Mark's phone and blocked the number so he wouldn't get any calls or texts from whoever the girl was. She would be hearing from Grace after she figured out how to get this girl to help her.

Grace then looked at the next message that was saved as Desk Clerk. When Grace opened the message, she was shocked again to see Mark's coworker lying in her bed, nude. Grace also forwarded that message to her phone. She searched the name and saw many messages between the two that clearly incriminated both of them for having an affair, and something that Grace caught made her look at Mark's wall safe. At that very moment, Grace realized that there was no turning back from here. She was about to uncover more than she had even imagined. She knew that her marriage was over.

Grace didn't want to, but she had to. It was now or never. It was 5 a.m., and she had two more hours before she would have to wake the kids up for school. She was glad it was Friday because she was going to pack up for the weekend and go to her mother's and figure out her next steps. Mark would be leaving for work around 10 a.m. An unexplainable strength had pushed her to the safe. A force had her operating as if she were outside of herself. She had someone with her. The little girl who had never stood up for herself had finally had enough. The woman she put on hold to be a wife was giving her the courage to take the next step. Grace went to the safe, which was conveniently already open. Mark had gotten that comfortable in his wrongdoing, not even bothering to cover his tracks.

"Our life together is over." Grace saw stacks of money. There were about ten stacks of hundreds, which she would eventually count to be $100,000. She knew that the money wasn't from his job, because his checks went straight into their checking and savings accounts. She was going to have to act as if she knew nothing until she was ready to execute her game plan. That would be easy because their intimacy was nonexistent, and now she knew why.

Grace saw drugs and shell casings in multiple sandwich bags. She counted at least six in each of the three bags. She took one out of each bag and put it in her bathrobe pocket. She took a picture of the inside of the safe and closed it, leaving it how it was.

Grace, now done with her mission, became extremely nervous. How could she have not known that Mark was involved in illegal activity and also cheating and doing drugs himself?

She ignored the fact that he had indulged at different times because she had found drugs in his pockets a few times when she did laundry, but she dismissed it from her mind, not knowing how to handle it because it wasn't frequent. She could no longer live in denial. The truth was smacking her in the face. Grace knew that Mark drank a lot, but she always remained quiet to avoid an argument. Nothing Grace ever said to Mark mattered to him. It was his way always.

Grace put her phone in her bathrobe pocket and lay down on the couch. She stared at the ceiling, hundreds of thoughts going through her head. She replayed her whole relationship with Mark and felt numb. She didn't feel like she was wrong. He had betrayed her, his position, and his family. He was the opposite of everything that he was supposed to stand for. He wasn't the man that she fell in love with, and he was robbing her of truth. He was having unprotected sex with random women, and although it had only been months since they slept together, she didn't know how long these things had been going on. She could have gotten an STD. At this point, she was too fed up to even shed tears.

She had cried many tears on many nights that he hadn't come home or didn't touch her when he was home, but she thought it was just him being stressed out from work, which his constant being on edge, snappy, and rude accounted for as well. She had been doing part-time work from home and had her own money, including taking her own allowance from their accounts. She knew that if they ever divorced, it would be nasty, so she had built her own nest egg, which was something every woman in her family had always told her to do no matter what.

Before she knew it, the alarm was going off and she jumped up. Grace robotically went through her morning routine. She made breakfast, got the kids out of the house and to the bus stop, and went back up to give Mark his breakfast. He was still in bed. She hoped that he wasn't taking off work.

"Mark, are you going to work?" She had to work hard to keep her voice normal and to hide the disdain that she had for him from her eyes. What she really wanted was to take a bat to him.

"I feel like I was hit with a bat. I went out for drinks after work, and I think somebody slipped something in my drink or something."

"What, like a woman?"

"What? No, like a dickhead who might know I'm a cop

and might want to try to set me up or something and tell my job something." Grace wanted to laugh in his face and had to force herself to keep a straight face. Hmmm, you're making a premonition on your future without knowing it. She shook her head.

"No way! You think someone would just do that to you? That's awful, honey." You asshole.

"Wow, you haven't called me honey in a minute. I just called in sick. Can you take care of me?" Her heart dropped.

"Yeah, but I'll have to run to the grocery store." Grace threw on some workout gear and quickly left the apartment.

* * *

The ringing of his phone woke Brandon up. He looked and it was Ciara. "Hey." He was hoping she wasn't calling to start with him about his arrest.

"Hey, you okay?" Her voice sounded sexy to him.

"I will be. This some bullshit, as usual. A white man don't want a black man in his building and especially not down the hall from him."

"Yeah, but how could he get in your apartment?" She sounded genuinely concerned.

"The super had to have something to do with it. I just have to prove it because the cameras are gonna be compromised by the time my lawyer even gets to subpoena them. I know that's not going to work at all. So how do I prove it? I have a plan; trust me. How are the kids?"

"They're good, but they want to see you. Can I bring them and stay with them?" She figured why not ask. He needed some family love, and she knew it. Brandon looked at the phone, then put his ear back to it.

"Yeah, y'all come on." He hung up and wondered why he hoped that Grace didn't see Ciara staying for the weekend. It was weird, but probably just because he needed to have her emotionally attached to him for now, and anything that might have her think twice about helping him would not be good. But he was not going to let Mark or Grace control his life too.

His phone rang again, and it was Grace. "Hello?" He wasn't in the mood to talk to her, but hoped she had some information for him.

"Hey, I need to meet with you," Grace whispered into the phone.

"When?" Brandon had a good feeling that she had some good news for him, and he figured he'd better meet with her before Ciara and the kids arrived.

"Meet me in the gym and dress like you're there to work out. Get there in fifteen minutes, and I'll come in after that. Go to a bike that has an empty bike on both sides." Grace hung up the phone.

Brandon jumped up and threw on sweats, a Nike T-shirt, and his Jordans and got on the elevator. He knew she was making sure they weren't seen on the elevator together or walking into the gym at the same time. He walked in and was glad that it was rather empty.

He got on the bike, and within five minutes, Grace was getting on the bike next to him. "I have to make this fast. Mark is upstairs. I looked in his phone, and some girl that he was with last night took pictures of him with drugs and with his sausage in her mouth. He's also messing with a female officer from his department; and he has drugs, money, and empty shell casings in his safe. What do I do?"

"Did you take pictures of everything?" Brandon was jumping for joy inside.

"Yes, and I took three of the casings. I wasn't able to get a sample of the drugs because I have to wait until he's out of the house to see if it's already opened. But what do I do? I erased the message from the girl because I want to contact her myself, and he never opened it. It was unread and I blocked her so she can't reach out to him again. He won't even be aware that she's trying to bribe him."

Brandon laughed. "You're good. Damn, I'm shocked. I guess his detectiveness rubbed off on you," Brandon joked.

"I've never heard that before, 'detectiveness'. But, yeah, I don't know what happened to me. I just became a CSI investigator or something. I just went on autopilot. So what do I do? I have to go. I'm sure he'll be able to go to work tomorrow, so we can meet again. He had a bad hangover, and he claimed someone slipped him a mickey. The crazy thing is that he was actually telling the truth. He just doesn't know it or that I know it." She shook her head while Brandon thought of what to tell her to do to hold her over.

"Call the girl. Offer her some money. Tell her more will be coming. Have her call the precinct and accuse him of threatening her and tell them to take a drug test, which will prove that he was partying with her. Then have her drop the casings off with Internal Affairs." Brandon paused. "Are you really ready for this? Your husband may end up doing some time. You know this, right?"

Grace looked away and looked back at Brandon. "Yes."

She seemed sure to him. "Okay, so I'll let my lawyer know and see what he advises." Brandon knew this was nothing but God.

"Okay. I gotta go. See you tomorrow?" Brandon thought for a minute and responded to Grace.

"Take the kids to the park tomorrow, outside at three o'clock. They can play and that will give us an excuse to talk." Grace nodded in agreement and got off the bike and began to walk away.

"Grace?" Grace turned around to hear what Brandon had to say, and he said, "Thank you so much. You're gonna help save my life."

"Maybe I'll get something special for it." Grace blushed and turned around and walked away.

Brandon stayed in the gym for an hour and a half, and the workout was a much-needed release of stress. He thought of what his father used to tell him. He would say, "Nothing worth having comes easy, son. The blessing comes after the struggle and the sacrifice." Brandon was beginning to see exactly what the late Billy Phillips meant by that statement.

He felt optimistic. He went back to his new place, which he still felt ecstatic about, and called Melinda.

"Hey, man. I heard what happened to you. Are you okay?"

"I will be. Who told you?"

"Who else? Jerry."

"Yeah, well, I'm sure Jerry planted the gun in my place for Mark."

"Wait a minute, you think that? Oh, I thought it was your gun. He said that Mark called the cops on you for having a loud party and they found a gun."

"Yeah, a gun that isn't mine. He planted it. I don't own a gun, and I don't know how he knew that I was having a party, if he did know. But I know that either way, he knew that he was going to call the cops on me. I need you to grill Jerry, please. I have to pay over fifty thousand dollars for a lawyer if this thing goes to trial. For nothing more than being a black man moving on the same floor as a crooked, racist cop."

"Yeah, I'll see what I can get out of him, but it would be his word against mine. And believe me, I have a close relationship with Jerry, but I won't allow something like this to happen, and I choose the other side. Right is right and wrong is wrong. So how are the wife and kids?"

Brandon shook his head. Melinda was something else. "The kids are good, and their mother is bringing them here today." Brandon wasn't sharing any extra information, and it wasn't that he didn't trust Melinda, but he just had to keep everyone separate so that he could find out as much as he could without anyone knowing who his resources were. That way, he would get firsthand information that wasn't passed down before getting to him. He wasn't going to tell Melinda about Grace and vice versa, nor was he going to tell Ciara what Grace was doing for him. Sometimes women are too catty to understand the different relationships that men have with various women. Every relationship is not sexual just because it's with the opposite sex, although, many times it has been.

Brandon was getting ready to get in the shower when his phone rang. I wonder which one of my women this is now. They've all been calling me today. . He chuckled and walked butt naked into the kitchen, where his phone was, on the island. The phone read Chavon. Damn, I'd like to tell her thank you for the other night. He picked up.

"Hey, beautiful, what's up? I want to thank you for the other night. You really was solid from beginning to end. You could have left. That was big of you."

"Yeah, well, I'm a big girl who's big on loyalty. I'm glad

you're okay. I wanted to come to your arraignment, but I didn't know if it was okay. Did you plead not guilty?"

"Of course I did. My lawyer got me. I should be good. I have a good feeling that I'll get off. I mean, I will get off."

"Yeah, if it ain't yours, the truth will come out. So what are you doing tonight? You feel like having a private party?"

"No, I'm really in kind of a foul mood, and I don't want to take it out on you."

"Well, I'd hope you wouldn't since you know it wasn't my fault."

"I know. I just need a few days to get myself back to normal; plus, my kids are coming for the weekend."

"Oh, well then, okay. I hope to hear from you soon. Take care of yourself, and if you change your mind, you know how to reach me."

Brandon agreed but knew he probably wouldn't be reaching out to her anytime soon.

Brandon swung open the door after hearing the buzzer. They were standing there just bright-eyed and ready to come in and explore. The jury was out on if he was going to be happy spending time with Ciara. Ciara walked in with an orange fatigue sweatsuit, blond hair cut short and curly. Her lips were glossed up and shining, and she strutted in like she had arrived at her surprise party that she had already found out about. He loved that she didn't have extra-long, fake, spider-looking lashes on her eyes. She looked naturally beautiful because she naturally was. She had her phase of wigs and weaves, but she didn't realize how much better she looked without all of that extra stuff.

"Hey, y'all are just who I needed and wanted to see. I missed y'all." Brandon grabbed his son and began to fake box with him and softly punch him. Major laughed and pretended to fight his father back, but then just grabbed him and held on tightly. Major started sniffling, not wanting his father to know that he was crying. Brandon pulled him back, still holding his arms, and assured him, "Listen man, I'm gonna talk to the family once you get settled, but I'm telling you I'm gonna be okay. You don't have to worry about me. Go get comfortable and come back."

He grabbed his daughter, Malika, and hugged her tightly. "Go with your brother." Malika took her bag to her room.

Ciara sat at the island and just looked at Brandon. He looked back. "I spoke to your mother; she filled me in. I'm sorry to hear what you're going through." Ciara seemed sincere, but Brandon knew how she could be nice-nasty. He was cautious before falling for the okey-doke.

"Are you sure about that, or are you happy on the low? You sure you didn't put no roots or voodoo on me?" Brandon laughed.

"First of all, I'm glad that you are joking with me, but I know damn well deep down, you mean that, and you ain't right for that." Brandon looked at her in a way that said, oh, here we go. You ain't been here five minutes, and you're ready to tell me off.

"Is this going to be a long weekend or a short one?" Brandon laughed.

"I'm not trying to argue. I'm here because the kids said they wanted me to stay, and they wanted me to ask you..." Brandon cut her off.

"Oh, so you're saying that you didn't want to come yourself?"

"There you go, wanting some accolades." They both laughed. "You know what I want, Brandon?"

"There you go, making it about you." They laughed again. "What do you want, Ciara?"

"I just want a nice hug. That's all."

Brandon grabbed Ciara and they embraced. He held her and smelled her, and she smelled him. They were squeezing each other tightly, and then he pushed out of his mind the thought to squeeze her ass. He laughed to himself and let her go.

"How was that?"

"That felt good. I still felt a spark. Did you?" Ciara was never scared to speak her mind, and it drove Brandon crazy sometimes.

"We'll always be connected. I'm glad I didn't feel any bad energy. You know you scare me sometimes. But look, keepin' it a G, I am glad that you're here, and I hope that we're gonna have a peaceful and meaningful time."

"We will. I brought groceries. I'm going to make you dinner, and we can play games. Let's just enjoy each other's company." They gave each other dap. The kids came out, and they all sat in the living room.

"Now, ask what you want."

"First, let us pray. Father, we love and honor You. We are nothing without You. You know that we know that Your will is the best will for our lives. Please know that we love Daddy. We love Brandon. We need him. Cancel any plans that the enemy has to destroy him, because, without him, our head is missing. Cover this family, Lord, and prosper us. Keep us safe and please let this just be another test that we can use as a testimony of Your grace and mercy later. Amen."

Of course, Ciara had to interrupt with her bossy self, Brandon thought. I do love her faithfulness to God; it's very attractive and makes me think of my mom. They say we look for our moms in our women. I just wish she wasn't as sassy as she is. Although it is sometimes sexy, I must admit.

Malika interrupted his thoughts. "Daddy, are you going to prison? We need you out here, Daddy. I know I don't like you being overprotective and strict, but I cannot grow up without you," Malika whined.

"Well, you wouldn't either way. Once this is done, I'll be able to talk more. Just know that people will hate you for nothing at all. They'll hate you because they don't understand you. They'll hate you if they feel inadequate themselves, and they'll hate you when they see your greatness. And that is the lesson that, once you understand, you'll learn to navigate around that hate no matter who it comes from. Nothing matters but your integrity, your character, and your convictions. Do not become what someone else says you are just because they say it. Be the opposite of what they expect, but never feel that you have anything to prove. Nothing matters except God and love. Everything after that should come from hope and determination. Be determined to be great and greater each day. Now, let's order pizza and watch movies!"

* * *

The family had a nice night, and all fell asleep on the couches in the living room. Brandon woke up extra early Saturday morning to cook breakfast for them, like he used to do when they all lived together. He was planning his time very carefully, knowing that he had to meet Grace on the playground at 3 p.m. They ate breakfast and played a backgammon tournament.

"Who wants to go outside to the park downstairs?" Major raised his hand. "Oh, Malika, you too grown for the park?"

"Hell no." They all stopped and looked at her. Malika started laughing. "Got ya. You know I would never say that to my parents."

"Yeah, well, you ain't even gonna joke and say it. Come on." Brandon figured he would have to tell Ciara what was going on with Grace because he had to talk to her, and Ciara would have to understand. He wasn't going to deal with female cattiness while trying to take care of this situation.

"Y'all go ahead; I'm gonna start cooking." Brandon knew there was a God. Thank you, Lord, he thought. She's not coming with us. Yes!

When they approached the playground, Malika and Major quickly noticed Peter and Rebekah. They ran over, and Brandon walked directly up to Grace.

"Is the coast clear?" he asked.

"Probably not, but you made a great plan. We're good now." Grace looked Brandon up and down. He noticed but wasn't going to feed into it.

"So what happened? Did you speak to the girl?"

"Yes. I talked her into taking five thousand to call the precinct. She emailed the pictures and told them that he should be given a drug test, and I sent her a picture of the safe. They asked her to bring in some evidence from the safe if she can. She's meeting me tomorrow, and after she drops off the evidence, she'll get another five thousand. And then, if she has to testify about the other night and how he forced himself on her, she will. She said they were at Jerry's."

"I knew it. I told you." Brandon didn't ask her anything about the money. She obviously felt the money was worth getting rid of Mark for her own sake.

"Wow. Well, if I get lucky enough to get the case dropped, I may be able to contribute something. In all honesty, him using drugs isn't going to be as damning or detrimental to him as whatever is in that safe is. He can get put on a leave and sent to rehab, and that won't affect my case. His illegal activity is the only thing that can save me and hopefully save me from having to fight this bullshit case at all."

"When can we have a drink and go somewhere far from here?" Grace was getting bolder and that made him a bit uncomfortable. He didn't want her to equate her help with his obligation to act on it. He half-jokingly considered suing her for sexual harassment when this was over with.

"Right now, this is all I can deal with, honestly."

They were both startled when Gabriella walked up to them.

"Hey, how are you two? Hey, Brandon, the last time I saw the two of you, it was me and Brandon together. Haven't heard from you." Gabriella started throwing hints and eyes at him just like Grace had.

"We're out here being held hostage by our kids, of course," Grace said to throw cover over their meeting.

"Brandon, Chavon told me what happened. That's unfortunate." Gabriella was continuing to drop hints that she knew what was going on. He could sense that she was a bit disturbed about Chavon. "It was surprising that you two hung out after we did." That was what her mouth said, but he deciphered that to mean, "How can you fuck my friend after me?"

"Yeah, she gave me a call. She's cool, like you. I see why the two of you are friends." Brandon didn't owe anyone any explanations. He wasn't committed to either one of them—or anyone, for that matter.

"Oh, well, have a good day." Gabriella walked away as if Brandon was supposed to convince her not to leave, like she didn't really want to say goodbye, but had nothing else to really say. He was glad that was brief because there really wasn't anything to say.

"Seems like you have an admirer," Grace teased sarcastically.

Now, here she goes being jealous. What is wrong with women, always trying to be possessed by someone?

"Hey, I guess I'm a likeable guy. What is it that seems to have you so much wanting to help me or being drawn to me?" Grace looked at this black man with dreads, perfect skin and hairline, sexy beard and mustache trimmed just right, and followed down to his broad shoulders and chiseled chest that could be seen through his shirt, his muscular arms...

"Excuse me, Miss, I feel like you're undressing me with your eyes. Is that all it is? That I'm something different that you're intrigued by or because I'm taboo for a white Jewish woman to even think about at all? Or am I a pawn just to get back at your husband for all of his mistreatment? Really, what is it?" Brandon was joking and serious at the same time. He often felt that women just saw him as something they could use, get pleasure from, without compassion or understanding of who he was as a black man, not just a man. A black man is always going to be black first in everyone's eyes. His pride comes from embracing that fact and walking in it.

"I must admit, I was undressing you." Grace paused. "I know you see me as a typical white girl who's spoiled, sheltered, and oblivious to you and your struggle. I know you may think that I think that you're beneath me, and I must admit, I have thought that at a time in my life. I had to really ask myself why I was thinking about you so much, and I think, for some reason—and especially after the day you helped Rebekah, I saw you in a different light. I may have been racist and didn't realize it... if I could allow or accept the racism in Mark. I don't know, I have been questioning myself a lot about who I am and what my priorities are, and I think just wanting to be comfortable and taken care of made me selfish and inconsiderate. I shouldn't have given up my career to be a housewife, and I gave Mark my power, my identity."

Brandon immediately thought of Ciara and how, no matter what, she always took care of herself and the kids, with or without him. That was the strength and resiliency that most black women carried and were raised on. The struggle has been our strength in many ways; not that all our struggles have been warranted or deserved. He smiled. That's why I have to be with a sister. She knows what I'm made of, because we're made of the same essence.

"I'm glad that, although this is a hard situation for you, it seems to be growing you. My dad always told me that the prize comes after the sacrifice. We have to shed our skin sometimes to make way for a new being. We're always evolving as people... or we're supposed to be. I know that life is short, and I'm not going to be miserable for anybody."

"Yeah. I think it was also the day I saw how you were teaching your children in the elevator. Mark doesn't even do that. Here I was thinking, wow, this black guy is teaching his children. Then I wondered why I was surprised about that, and that's how I began to realize that I was biased, if not somewhat racist, and I don't want to really think that I am—no, was racist. I didn't hate black people like wanting them—or you—to be dead, but... I guess I just never really saw you as the same. I don't know, I guess I was confused about how you're different, not how we're the same. I feel bad. And I feel bad about what my husband is trying to do to you and my children. I don't want to make my children think this is okay or have them be that way. I've never spoken badly about black people, and I never stopped my kids from playing with black children, but bringing them home never happened. So, I had to realize that as well. I've never spoken against injustice, and now my husband's carrying out an unjust act, and I cannot stand by because I now know this is probably not the first time, and if I don't do something, it won't be the last. And, on top of it, I want out. I can't bear to love someone like him any longer. His being a monster will make me one too."

Brandon was impressed with what Grace was saying but had the sudden urge to go back upstairs and be near Ciara. He and Grace agreed to meet up on Monday to discuss any further developments. Brandon had a week off to get himself together and prepare for this fight.

Melinda walked up with her grandkids, who went to play with Brandon's and Grace's kids.

"Hey, guy, I need to talk to you for a minute." Melinda walked away from Grace after saying hello to her. Brandon followed.

"Listen, do you trust Grace?"

Brandon was stunned at the question. "Yeah, I actually do," Brandon confessed.

"Okay, just making sure because Jerry called me over to help clean up some vomit and shit that Mark had done after they had two girls there. He started saying how he's tired of Mark trying to treat him like his pauper and shit like that. I didn't want to ask too many questions and pry, but I'm gonna get it out of him if he had anything to do with planting that gun. I just wanted to tell you that."

They walked back over by Grace, and Melinda said, "Grace, girl, be careful talking to this here fine specimen of a black man. Just you talking to him can get him lynched." Melinda walked away, leaving the sting of her comment ringing in Grace's ears.

The kids stalled them out for another half hour, asking if they could have "a few more minutes" five times. They continued to have deep conversations, and Brandon gained more understanding of Grace, which he was glad, seeing as she was the one helping to save his life.

They all rode the elevator back up, and as they approached Brandon's apartment door, Ciara swung it open. Grace was walking past, and Brandon could see the shock and disappointment in her face.

"Can we go over their house?" Rebekah asked.

Grace said, "Not this time," and kept walking. The kids said their goodbyes, and Brandon walked into his home.

He took a deep breath. "Um, what's that crazy-delicious meal I smell?" He walked up to the pot to try to uncover it, and Ciara hit his hand.

"You know the drill. Get out my kitchen—I mean, your kitchen—while I am cooking. And y'all need to go wash up."

"Can we all go roller-skating tonight, like old times?" Malika asked. Brandon agreed that they could all go, and the kids cheered.

Ciara was enjoying playing house at Brandon's. She just hoped it would end well. With them, things could explode in seconds, and a war could start in an instant. She was trying to have fun and not think too much about what was going on and what it meant. She told herself not to expect any major change, but to just be content that he wanted her to just be there for him through this hard moment in his life. She didn't want anyone else to be able to be there for him more than she was.

They enjoyed going to Branchbrook Roller Rink in Newark, and it was just like old times. Brandon played around with Ciara, and they skated and held hands a few times. Ciara enjoyed it, but she didn't want to get the kids' hopes up too high.

When they got back to the condo, they watched movies, and the kids fell asleep.

"Go to your rooms," Brandon told them after they conked out on the couch around 1 a.m. No one budged, so grabbing them and steering them to their beds was a must because he was striving to have some alone time with Ciara, who picked up on it when he came back and nearly sat on her lap. She adjusted herself to put a bit of space between them.

"Excuse you," she joked while scooting over.

"I don't want to be excused." Brandon closed the gap.

"You are too big to sit on my lap." Ciara was hoping that Brandon wasn't going to be a typical male and try to get nasty. Her suspicions proved her intuition was on point.

"Ok, no problem. So can I put my face in yours?" Brandon slid to the side and laid his head in Ciara's fully clothed crotch.

Pushing him away and standing up, Ciara had to count to ten in her head instead of blowing her top and screaming, waking everyone up.

"What's wrong?" Brandon stood and moved closer to attempt to kiss Ciara on her lips, but she turned her head just in time for her to catch her cheek.

"Oh, it's like that? I can't even get a kiss?" He walked over to the huge window and looked at New York, agitated.

"Brandon, first of all, I may have given you a kiss, but you started with can you eat my pussy."

"I thought you may have missed me doing that." He did not look at her.

"I miss way more than that, and I am not one of these chicks out here that are just going to let you fuck because we have kids. You don't obviously want what I want, so I don't want anything at all. You forgot that I am an all or nothing type of girl, huh?"

"No, I just want to be the exception to the rule." Brandon walked past her and into the kitchen to pour himself something to drink.

"For what? So I can have my feelings all messed up? I am trying to move on with my life like you have."

"We obviously really haven't, or you wouldn't be here, but okay. I apologize. I just got caught up in the moment. Goodnight." Brandon left Ciara standing in the middle of the living room in disbelief.

"This guy never ceases to amaze me. When will he grow up?"

Ciara put her blankets out on the couch and fell asleep. The next morning, she gathered her belongings and her children, and they left.

Tuesday morning, Mark walked into the precinct and was called into the Lieutenant's office.

"Hey, Captain. Lieutenant, what's up?" Mark said to both of the gentlemen in the room and sat down, eating an apple, oblivious to what was about to transpire.

"Can you throw that apple in the trash? This is serious," Mark's supervisor warned. Mark did as he was commanded, throwing the apple in the garbage can as if shooting a basketball into a hoop.

"Mark, take out your badge and gun and place it on my desk."

Mark sat up and looked puzzled. "What's going on here, sir?"

"As I said, please place your badge and gun on the table and I'll explain."

Mark huffed and sat still for a few seconds. He shifted in his seat, and as he was about to be instructed for the third time, he reached into his back pocket and pulled out his badge. He went to his holster and took his gun out and slammed it on the desk.

"You have the right to remain silent. Anything and everything that you say can be used against you in a court of law..."

Mark was handcuffed and processed. He was informed that he was being arrested for bribery, stealing evidence, conspiracy to commit murder, illicit drug use, possession of controlled dangerous substance, among other misdemeanors. He was taken to the county jail to await arraignment.

Mark called Grace. "Grace, I'm going to need you to bail me out as soon as I'm granted bail. I'll call you. Don't come to the arraignment."

"What's going on? What are you talking about? You're under arrest? Oh my God, are you serious? Why?" Grace put on an award-winning performance, all while smiling from ear to ear on the other end of the telephone.

"I gotta go, honey. I love you. I'll call you as soon as I can. Call my lawyer and send him down here."

Grace agreed through her sobs and sorrow, which were really sobs of joy. She hung up the phone and started clapping and jumping up and down. The kids were at school, and she couldn't wait to tell Brandon the good news. They hadn't met the day before as planned because his family stayed until Monday night instead of Sunday. Grace dialed Brandon's phone, and he picked up.

"He's behind bars! He's being charged with conspiracy and a whole list of things. Thank you. Thank you for giving me the motivation and the courage to fight for my own life. And to be free. I'm getting stronger every day, knowing that I don't have to spend the rest of my life with that animal. When I saw those pictures of him, I didn't even recognize him. It wasn't the man I fell in love with. And he isn't even a good example for our kids anymore. His greed to succeed by any means necessary took over his good sense and character."

"Well, I'm glad that you're searching for your true happiness. Just be sure. Maybe your marriage can be saved." Brandon didn't want to be the cause of a marriage breaking up.

"Well, maybe your family can be put back together. That was the mother of your children on Sunday, right?"

Brandon looked at the phone in disbelief. "Yes, but that's off topic," he joked, trying to lighten the conversation and change the subject.

"It's early; let's have breakfast. I'll make you breakfast. Just come by so we can talk in person." Brandon's mouth dropped. He had to think fast. Okay, I can actually go in this guy's house. I know he isn't gonna show up, and I can see if there's anything else that I can use that might help my case. I need to go. But, damn, I'm not trying to be seen coming out of that door. She should know how the cameras work.

"Are there cameras that show our doors in the hallway?"

Grace laughed. "No, there are no cameras in the hallways, just by the stairwells and elevators. They don't want to invade the residents' privacy, and anyone committing a crime will be seen leaving one way or another."

"Oh, okay. But you know this is serious. It's not funny. He would have me killed if he found out that I was in his house." Brandon again wondered if he should even chance it.

"I know. I mean, he'll never find out. I'm not trying to bring any harm to you or your life. I am just trying to show my appreciation. I just need a friend right now who understands what I'm going through. My situation is going to be a hard enough transition for me and my children, but I know that I'm going to have to deal with his family and my friends, who will not be understanding or supportive. So are you coming? And do you like French toast?"

"Yeah, that's fine. I'll be over in a few minutes." Brandon didn't change his Nike shorts or T-shirt. He wasn't going to get dressed up to go down the hall.

He rang the doorbell, and Grace came to the door with yellow terry cloth shorts and a white cotton camisole. She had on Nike slides, and Brandon was surprised that her toes were painted black.

"Come in; it's nice to see you." She reached out for Brandon to hug her, and he gave her a quick tap, nowhere near an embrace. Grace led the way into the kitchen, which had a different set up than his. It was to the left of the living room instead of in front of it, but they were on opposite sides of the hall. Grace's apartment was in the middle of the complex, so she didn't have the big window. Her apartment appeared to be wider, where his was longer. Hers and Gabriella's apartments had terraces off the living room. His terrace was off his bedroom.

"Sit. You came just as I finished making your plate. It's still hot. Would you prefer orange juice, pineapple juice, or apple juice?" As she turned around and he sat at the table, he noticed how short her shorts were. He wondered if she always walked around the house like that or if that was for him.

"I'll have pineapple juice and thank you." Brandon poured syrup on his French toast and held his hands palm up and said, "Thank you, Father. Bless my food and the preparer of it. Amen."

"I always wondered what it was like to be black. I hope that is not offensive." Grace sat down at the table and watched Brandon as he ate.

"Why would I be offended by that? Black people are very soulful, and that's attractive. We attract a lot of love and just as much hate." He surprisingly liked her French toast; he didn't eat everyone's food.

"I don't know, it probably sounded weird, and I don't know. I always wondered how I would feel. I mean, to be honest—and I may have told you this—but white people just don't understand black people."

"I get it; y'all don't." Brandon laughed. "I mean, I just figure that some white people are intimidated by our strength and tenacity, and they're offended by our survival skills. We're a threat for more reasons than us wanting to rob somebody, but it's better for the adversary to put it all on us wanting to rob somebody than us being great."

"I understand. Do you want more? You must have been famished."

Brandon laughed to himself, thinking, See, that's why I have to have a black woman. I was just hungry, not famished.

"No, that was good. I don't want to be stuffed. I'm going to the gym."

"Oh, you should train me. I've been getting back into going. I'll be right back."

Grace came back in the living room and walked over to Brandon and lifted his hand in hers and pulled him to follow her. He hesitated and then got up and followed. He knew where he was going. He thought, fuck it; Mark was trying to fuck me, and now so is his wife. He smiled from ear to ear. Then a horrifying thought came into his head. What if he's using his wife to frame me, or what if he isn't locked up and told her to pretend I came in to rape her? Wait, he isn't going to let me get this close to his wife, and she did help with telling me what happened to him. I have to be sure. As they entered the bedroom, he paused at the door.

"You never told me what happened with the girl and how your husband got arrested." Brandon looked at her to see what kind of vibe he would get.

"Can I tell you after?" Grace asked, sitting on the bed.

"Nay." Brandon stood his ground.

"Okay, so I met with her and gave her a sample of everything—the drugs, shell casings, some of the money too. And I pocketed some for myself. I left everything in the safe because I figured they would get a warrant. When he left for work Monday, the girl took everything to the precinct. By two o'clock, my house was being raided with a warrant, and he had no idea.

I guess they had run all the tests by this morning because he called me and told me he was being charged. They tied the casings to two murders. One of two twin brothers and another man. I got this information from his partner. His partner was shocked."

Brandon shook his head and smiled. This should definitely help. He hoped the casings were connected to the gun that was found in his apartment. "Wow, he done fucked up, didn't he?"

"Looks like it." Grace shrugged. "Now, can you come and sit down?" Brandon was ready for his "Becky" moment. He knew exactly what was about to go down.

Brandon sat on the edge of the bed, and Grace went straight for the prize. She had Brandon in her mouth in less than two seconds. He just watched and marveled. As he got ready to cum in Graces' mouth, he looked at a picture of her and Mark on the dresser. He wanted to stick his tongue out, but he didn't want her to look up and think he was ridiculing her. He had to decide if he was going to deposit in her mouth and end the scenario or go all the way. Fuck it.

When he ejaculated, Grace swallowed and hopped up and ripped her clothes off while he sat up, asking himself if this was really happening. Let me get this shit over with. I cannot believe I'm really doing this shit. What the fuck?

Grace leaned back and waited for Brandon to get on top of her. He did. She gazed up at Brandon while he put his back and front all into her gate. He was exploring her insides. She felt good to him, but he wasn't thinking about getting comfortable there. That was the apple in the Garden of Eden. He knew that he was only going to visit this place one time, so he didn't rush, but he also didn't want to make Grace addicted. He was already flirting with disaster; he didn't need to create a fatal attraction.

Brandon's phone rang and startled both of them. He reached over to grab his phone and didn't realize that he accepted a video call. When he picked it up and touched the accept button unknowingly, the video that he saw when he looked at the phone wasn't half as bad as what Ciara saw on the opposite end of her phone. Ciara and Grace both gasped at the same time.

Brandon quickly hung up and buried his head in the bed. Grace sat up but remained quiet and quite nervous, wondering if Brandon was going to leave, hate her, and never give her any more of that good dick she just got. She was hoping that he was going to resume, but the odds were probably against it.

"You okay?" she cautiously asked.

"I don't know. I'm trying to figure it out. Just give me a minute." He turned on his back. "Are you okay?"

"I was great; now I'm just okay, I guess. You want to know what would make me great again?" She figured she'd take a shot at it.

"What's that?" Brandon really didn't care, but he was there. He was trying to work out his exit plan.

"If you just finish what you started. I know you probably have to go, but I waited a while for this. I thought about it a lot."

Brandon's eyebrows raised. "Well, was it what you thought it would be?"

"Nope." She shook her head, and Brandon raised his eyebrows again.

"It was better, but let me make another informed decision, just to be sure." Grace got on top of Brandon. She sat on him and gyrated until he got erect. He helped himself back into her for round two.

Brandon and Grace went two more rounds, and he didn't hesitate to get dressed and leave. He was no longer worried about anyone seeing him come out of Mark's apartment. He was more worried about Ciara. Brandon told Grace that he would call her the next day. He tried not to feel guilty about Ciara seeing him in the bed with Grace, but all he could think about was what he was going to say. He tried to decide on the best story but knew that no story would work except the truth. He started calling her number on his way down the hall to his door. Ciara answered on the first ring but didn't say a word.

"Hello, Ciara. Ciara, say something," Brandon said. He let himself in the apartment and paced in front of the living room window, looking at New York and wondering how he had gotten to such a low place in his life after experiencing one of the biggest accomplishments in his life.

"You say something. I just want to see how creative you're gonna be. This should be good." Ciara sat on her kitchen stool, looking out of the window at her kids playing basketball. They were living in a two-family house. After Brandon left the family, Ciara, too, felt the need to move. She had too many memories of them, and it was too painful for her to stay there.

"Listen, I'm in a fucked-up situation. I am going to do whatever I can to beat this muthafucka at his own game."

"Oh, okay. I understand now. So you trust the wife of the man who's trying to destroy your life. You'll even risk your life to save it too, right? I mean, I'm sure that fucking her will definitely guarantee that you'll come out of this good. And if not, at least you got some white pussy. And listen, don't worry; I'm not that much into you anymore." Brandon looked at the phone and thought to himself, Yeah, right, but I know why you have to pretend that that is true.

"Basically, I took audio so that she can't say I raped her. And I needed her to trust me enough to tell me everything. He's in jail and is facing a whole bunch of charges."

"So what was the point? She only decided to help you if she got to get some of that big, black dick?"

Brandon grinned from ear to ear. "The point was, it won't happen again if you don't want it to." Brandon didn't know where that comment came from, but it came so naturally out of his mouth.

"Brandon, I'm really not in the mood for games. I just think you're doing dumb shit. I get that you're in a crazy ordeal right now, but you trippin'." Ciara let a tear roll down her face.

"It might seem like that, but I got this. You trust me?"

"I don't. And I don't have to. And I'm glad that I don't."

"Ciara, what do you want me to do?" Brandon was so confused, but then he wasn't. He knew what he needed to be doing, and he felt that God was trying to show him something and he needed to man up to receive it.

"I'm not gonna tell you what to do. You ain't beat for me, so I ain't beat for you. You want to keep playing me like I'm an option for you, and when you finally wake up, I'm gonna be gone. And don't ask me now, because you're fucked up, about what I want. You got what you wanted, right?" Ciara was so disgusted with Brandon's antics that she was ready to leave him alone. Enough was enough.

"Ciara, maybe I didn't think things through, but our relationship wasn't getting better. I forced my feelings to become dormant. When you came for the weekend, I just wanted to see how I would feel, and I can't lie: it felt good. I don't want to use you because I'm in the middle of an ordeal. I want to see what we can do." Brandon felt that Ciara was at the end of her rope with him.

"Why the change of heart then? And listen, I am not fully convinced that this is a genuine feeling either. You're still the same inconsistent, irrational, unstable—"

"Okay, so we're back at the putting-me-down stage? This is what I mean." Brandon's blood started to boil, and he was losing his cool. He did not have the patience for the nonsense at the moment

"You're right. You don't need that right now. I'm gonna let you go now. Have a good day." Ciara hung up, and Brandon's mouth dropped.

Before he could digest what happened, his phone rang again. It was Grace.

"Hey, I forgot to tell you that I'm going to see Mark tomorrow." There was dead air.

"Okay." Bitch, so what? You just ruined the peace I had with Ciara.

"So I will call you tomorrow to tell you what happened?"

"Okay." Brandon shook his head. They hung up, and he sighed. Please don't let this chick start stalking me, he prayed.

Brandon lay down on his back and looked up at the ceiling. "What do I want to do? What am I gonna do? What can I do? What will I do? How can I do it?" The questions kept coming and he didn't even have time to answer before another one popped up. He picked up his phone and looked in his contacts under Cougar, and Cougar Shantel Fume popped up. He made the call.

"Hello?" the lady from the lounge answered with uncertainty.

"Hey, Shantel, it's Brandon. I met you at Fume.

"Oh, is this cutie with the dreads? I've been waiting to hear from you. Actually, what are you doing tonight? My girlfriend's daughter is having a birthday party tonight at Trust Lounge in Harlem, and I don't want to be the third wheel with her and her husband. Would you like to accompany me?"

Brandon wanted to laugh at her vernacular trying to set up a date like it was a corporate meeting.

"Sure, I will join you."

"Okay, I can pick you up. I live in Bloomfield, right next to Montclair. Is nine okay?"

"Yes, that's fine."

"Okay. See you tonight. And it's not dressy. Come with your face that's all you need." They laughed and hung up, and she called right back.

"Hello." Brandon was entertained by her big energy.

"I'm sorry, honey. I didn't even ask you what you were calling about." Shantel was too much, and it was apparent that age was not a hindrance to her at all.

"It's okay. I kind of wanted to get your advice about something, but we can talk later." Brandon was so confused about what was going on he was calling Shantel because he wanted some advice.

Shantel picked Brandon up at 9 on the dot, in a crispy

white and bright Range Rover. He was waiting outside in a blazer and slacks. He wanted to look mature and not street. They made small talk on the way, and he found out that she had two daughters not that far from his age. He didn't really care because he was not looking for anything serious with her. When they got inside the lounge, it was not too crowded. There was a nice crowd. After meeting Shantel's friend, her daughter, and a few other people, they went to a table that was not in the center of the party. They ordered light appetizers, and Brandon found the right moment to bring up the conversation he wanted to have with her.

"Can I ask you something?"

"Of course." Shantel sipped on her drink.

"How come women are so hard to please?"

"Wow. That's a loaded question, and I don't necessarily believe that to be true. Some women and men are never satisfied, and there is nothing you can do about that, but if you are referring to a woman that has given up on you, then pleasing is not what you should be trying to do. Have you ever heard the saying 'The best apology is changed behavior'? I know you have. Well what is even better than changed behavior is having the right behavior from the start.

"When you do things the way you should, a woman, a real woman will appreciate that and act like she is supposed to. Men are always acting like women just want to complain over nothing and for no reason, but that really makes no sense." Shantel was distracted by a woman who seemed to be staring at them from the bar.

"I think you have an admirer or a stalker. By her look, I cannot tell which one."

Brandon turned around and saw Ciara looking at him. He also witnessed a man handing her a drink and Ciara walking to a table to sit with him. His heart sank. He began to stutter as time seemed to stop.

"That is my ex-fiancée and the mother of my two kids." Brandon and Ciara's eyes locked again, and his head sank.

"Wow. You seem to be suddenly upset. Did the two of you just break up? Is that her new beau?" Brandon wanted to ignore the pounding of his heartbeat and was glad that Shantel couldn't see his heart beating outside of his chest. He couldn't even speak, so he shrugged his shoulders.

"Do you want to leave?" Brandon wanted to leave, but he more so wanted to stay to see the interaction that Ciara was having with the unidentified man, to see if they were platonic or involved. To his horror and dismay, before he could answer, they quickly finished their drinks and left without any dialogue between him and her. Brandon felt like a knife was thrust into his heart and he could hardly breathe. To save face, he attempted to act normal and unbothered. He couldn't even finish his food and was pretty quiet the rest of the night and in agony. His clenched fists and short breathing let him know just how bothered he was.

After a few minutes, Shantel said, "I'm ready because clearly your head is messed up right now."

Brandon didn't care if Shantel had felt his disturbed vibe. All he could think about was if Ciara was getting fucked tonight and if she was going to have a big black dick in her mouth. He almost gagged at the thought of it.

The quiet ride home was deafening, and Brandon kissed Shantel on the cheek as he exited her truck.

"Get back with her; you care." Shantel pulled off after he closed the door.

Brandon felt dejection as he moped in the house, headed

all the way down, and went straight to bed after walking out of his clothes and leaving them on the floor.

Ciara breathed heavily while her date licked her clit as she held her legs wide open and had her head back, enjoying the moment.

"Damn, Cee Cee, you taste so good. You ready for me to fuck this juicy pussy?" The man she had accompanied to his cousin's party licked his lips with her cum on them.

"Yeah, I want that dick right now," Ciara moaned.

Brandon's body jumped, and his eyes opened, helping him to realize that he was dreaming and that it was morning by the sound of his lawyer's voice. "Hey, Brandon, how's it going? I have some good news."

"Yeah? What is it?"

"The officer who accused you of having the gun has been found to have the shell casings to that very gun, and the gun is attached to some homicides."

"You're kidding me!" Brandon was glad that he didn't have to explain to Reigel that he knew and how he knew. He was trying to come up with a way to tell him that didn't include Grace, and, again, God did the work for him.

"How do you know that?"

"Listen, I have friends in good places. Let's just say that your case may turn out to be a piece of cake," Reigel suggested, and Brandon wasn't convinced or satisfied with that answer.

"Why wouldn't it be thrown out? Won't you be making a motion to dismiss?"

Reigel laughed. "Hey, you know your stuff."

"It seems self-explanatory. He's connected to the gun. It ends up in my apartment. It's pretty cut-and-dry to me." Brandon's blood was about to start boiling. He didn't like when people took other people's misfortunes lightly. This asshole was actually chuckling like this shit is funny. This is my fucking life.

"Yes, but in law, it's hardly cut-and-dry, and I'm not saying that it isn't possible, but there are steps and procedures. I'll put in a motion to dismiss, but I have to wait until he's arraigned in court. He'll be arraigned at nine a.m. tomorrow morning." Brandon wondered why Grace hadn't said she was going to the arraignment. Did she not want him to show up? Was she starting to protect Mark for some reason?

"I will be there." Brandon's mind was working in overdrive.

"Good idea," Reigel retorted, and they agreed to see each other first thing in the morning.

"I wish I could turn my brain off." Brandon was drained. He took a shower and decided to go to bed early. When he got out of the shower and in the bed, he saw that Gabriella had texted him.

"Hope you're okay. I see things have been crazy for you. I was seeing if you wanted to stop by for a little while. I'll be up for another hour or so. Hope to hear from you." She ended her message with a wink emoji.

Brandon smiled. He liked the attention. He loved women. He loved them more it seemed when they weren't attached to him. Ciara was only his third time being in love. His first love was his high school sweetheart, and the girl who cheated on him with the local drug dealer was his second. She ruined his trust in women, and he believed she's the reason Ciara got so much grief from him.

He never got emotionally attached to every other situationship that he was in. Women were a handful, and ironically, a handful of them were easier to deal with than one. At the same time, Brandon knew that, combined, a handful wouldn't do and amount to what one who really loved you would.

"Why is this manwoman, Venus-Mars thing so damned complicated? I can't even figure it out."

Unfortunately. Brandon had another emotional dream. His mind took him, in slumber, to the day that he told his children that he was

moving out. The scene was clear as day and felt as real as ever. Malika was crying hysterically as he explained to her and Major the reason for the destruction of their family.

"This is not fair! You don't love us!" Malika ran into her bedroom. Ciara went to get her and brought her back to the family discussion."

"Malika, I will always be here. I will never leave you. Me and Mommy just don't get along anymore." He wiped her tears and looked over at Major whose anger was showing in his crossed arms and vexed face that was staring at the wall.

"Then get along! If you're not getting along then start!"

"It's not that easy," Ciara responded.

"So breaking up your family is easier?"

Brandon woke up in a frustrated mood and looked forward to seeing the tables turn on Mark's piece-of-shit ass.

He took out one of his favorite suits. He was dressed as if he were the prosecutor and wished that he could snap a shot of Mark coming in front of the judge in an orange jumpsuit, like the criminal that he is.

He got in his car, put on his shades, and drove to the courthouse, listening to Fabolous' The Soul Tape 3. Brandon was a smooth, calculating, meticulous go-getter. He was a good person. What he didn't realize was that he was a runner, a track star. When it came time for him to deal with certain things head on, he would flee from the thought and the appropriate action, which made him look like a fraud. Mechanical things like work, car maintenance, and financial responsibility were his strong points. Emotional responsibility and maturity, accountability for his actions, and acceptance of his shortcomings were issues that he did not address well, if at all.

Ciara had told him countless times that he was a narcissist. He never received it. He felt that he was the perfect catch because he looked good on paper. What he was about to realize was that he had a lot of soul searching to do if he was going to be able to move forward in life beyond his safe place. Although Brandon's job was a good and secure one, his dream was to be an attorney. He always wanted to be a lawyer, but never felt he had the stamina to complete that mission. Being a talker was easy, and his position as an advertising executive came naturally. Being an attorney would mean that he would have to look outside of himself and be able to empathize with others if he was going to be good at it.

Reigel was waiting when Brandon walked into the courthouse. They went and sat as close to the defendant's table as they could.

The judge, who was black, to Brandon's pleasure, came in, and they got started after everyone rose. Brandon was thrilled that the jurisdiction was Montclair and not Newark because he knew that Mark didn't have as much pull there. The drugs and evidence were found in his home, so, once arrested by his superiors, Montclair officers came to transport him to the Essex County Jail.

There were five or six other arraignments before Mark's, and before Mark's, a few more officers than usual piled in the room. The blue code always remained in effect. No matter what police officers did wrong, there were always those who would support and overlook their behavior.

The doors opened and all eyes looked in awe as Mark came out in handcuffs, with his head down and ego bruised. Brandon's eyes were bright and his smile wide. The adversaries locked eyes when Mark lifted his head. Mark immediately put on a facade of wellness and arrogance, winking at Brandon. Brandon laughed. A confident Brandon winked back. Reigel's sharp glance at Brandon let him know that he should remain quiet and calm.

Grace rushed in and did not see Brandon in the front.

"Officer Stephens, I have read the charges against you, and they are rather serious. I'm sure that you have an explanation. I'm hoping you do. After I read them to you, you can enter a plea of guilty, not guilty, or no contest, at which time I'll set a date if you're indicted."

Mark's attorney spoke up. "Your Honor, my client has requested not to have his charges read."

"Well, your client has made hundreds of arrests in his career as a police officer, and although he's a public servant, that doesn't shield him from the same justice that he's exacted on others. So the charges are as follows: two counts of conspiracy to commit murder, two counts of possession of illegal ammunition, three counts of possession of controlled dangerous substances, two counts of tampering with evidence; seven counts of an officer of the law engaging in unlawful practices..."

A pin could have dropped, and it would've been heard. The silence was deafening, and the tension was thick. The stiffness of the officers who came to support gave way to red-faced embarrassment.

As the judge continued to read Mark's charges, Brandon

began to get riled up. Under his breath, he said, "I can't wait to have my day in court." The sound of two hands clapping broke out when Brandon applauded the charges. Reigel shook his head and motioned for Brandon to stop.

Brandon looked down and saw Reigel waving his hand from side to side. No one could see it, and it was quick. The bailiff called out for quiet in the courtroom.

Mark had beads of sweat running down his face. He looked like he had seen a ghost. He looked at no one—not his attorney, his wife, his adversary, or his supporters.

"I plead no contest, Your Honor." Reigel shook his head again. Brandon didn't know if that was bad or good.

Brandon's eyes squinted as he kept trying to read lips when Mark would ask his lawyer questions based on what the judge was asking him.

"Mr. Stephens, did anyone harass or coerce you into doing so?"

Mark, still looking down, answered no by shaking his head.

"Please answer the question, sir."

"No."

"Your Honor, my client, Mark Stephens, is requesting to have a hearing before sentencing, where Mr. Stephens would like to make a statement to the court."

Judge James Young looked at Mark's lawyer and said that he'd consider, but it wouldn't be likely. "As we hold citizens to the law, we must hold police officers to it, and even more so because they took an oath to uphold it. They swore they would. Officers ought to be held to a higher standard, not allowed to do their own will."

As people filed out of the courtroom, Grace approached

the defendant's table, and Brandon stood staring as Mark was permitted to lean over the wood barrier and give her a kiss and whisper in her ear. As he leaned over to Grace, Mark's eyes were set on Brandon's, who were just as set on his. Brandon winked, and Mark's face appeared to turn to stone like Fantastic Four's Thing. He thought about mouthing, I fucked your wife yesterday, but decided against it. He looked at Mark and smirked. The crowd piled out of the courtroom.

Reigel seemed agitated as they stopped in the vestibule. "So is this good news?" Brandon probed.

"Listen, Mr. Phillips..."

"You mean Brandon?" Brandon asked, oblivious to the fact that he was almost unruly at the arraignment.

"I'm speaking as your attorney. I'm going to need you to contain yourself during hearings. Now, what this means is that there will be no trial. He'll get a sentence, and I'm about to go back and put in a request for dismissal of your case due to the circumstances."

"So isn't that good news?" Brandon asked worriedly.

"It means that we don't have to worry about a long, drawn-out trial or him being found not guilty. He knows he has no chance with the evidence and where it was found."

"So will I still have a fifty-thousand-dollar bill?" Brandon held his breath.

"No, unfortunately for me, you won't. The fee will depend on how many motions we have to file, court appearances we'll have to make, and any circumstances that pop up. Hopefully, this will be quick. I'll call you in a few days." Reigel walked away from Brandon and back into the building.

Brandon felt a tap on his shoulder as he was walking away. He turned around to see Grace and was both unhappy and curious.

"So why did he plead no contest, and are you sure we should be talking right here?" Brandon looked around. He was glad his mother wasn't there, because she may have had to take a vacation from her Jesus to curse Grace out. He didn't tell his mom about the arraignment because he didn't want to get her hopes up and nothing good would come of it. Now he wished he had told her so he could celebrate with her. He felt damn good. The ordeal wasn't over, but it sure was looking hopeful.

"I don't care." Grace didn't seem the least bit concerned. She gazed in his eyes and looked like she was about to lean in and kiss him. Brandon took a step back.

"Well, I do. Let's talk later." Brandon turned and walked away. He wanted to start jogging so that she could not find another excuse to approach him. Getting to his car and taking a deep breath was a sigh of relief. Then his phone rang, and he paused, feeling like he was in a horror flick seeing Grace's name.

"Grace, this is rather stressful for me, and I'm not trying to take my frustrations out on you, but I don't want to begin to feel like my life is recreation for you."

"Brandon, please don't say that. I put my marriage on the line for you..."

"And I didn't ask you to. I told you that I appreciated it, but I asked you if you were sure, and now you're already throwing it in my face?"

"No, I was calling to apologize. You have every right to feel how you feel. I'm just so glad that Mark's going away for a while."

"How do you know that?"

"It seems pretty obvious. He pleaded no contest, and the judge didn't seem too thrilled with him."

"What did he say in your ear?" Brandon was ready to put the pressure on Grace.

"Oh my goodness, my daughter's calling me. I'll have to call you back." Grace hung up the phone, and Brandon had a funny feeling.

Brandon called Melinda when he got in his car. "Hey, man, what's going on with you? How do you keep getting yourself into so much shit?"

"I'm not getting myself into anything. It's these damned racist people. Why did you say that, though? Do you know something I don't?"

"I know that the rumor is that you're messing around with Grace, and don't think that because he's locked up, he doesn't have cronies to do his grimy work. He may be down, but don't count him out yet."

Brandon shook his head and thought, how fucking stupid can I be? What the fuck am I doing? "I'm not messing around with her, Melinda. I—"

"Did you fuck her?" Brandon's hesitation gave away the answer.

"Oh my God, you black men ain't shit. Every freakin' chance you get to stick yo' dick in some white meat, you screw your head off for it. That meat cannot be that good. Everybody know white meat is dry."

Brandon busted out laughing. He didn't even know what to say. "Melinda, you are so crazy. I don't know what you're talking about."

"Yeah right, mothafucka. You know exactly what the fuck I'm talking about. But, anyway, you better know what you're doing."

"Melinda, I need your help," he confessed.

"Anything, man, anything... except helping you get some more of that white pussy. You should have enough of that for right now. You got a cracker trying to stick his meat in you too. Leave them evil folks alone."

"Seriously, Melinda, please stop. I need you to find out from Jerry if he had anything to do with me getting set up. I need you to see if he'll talk to me. I can't just run up on him and then get a harassment charge on top of everything else. Can you do it?"

"Definitely. One thing I won't do is throw a black man under a bus or allow him to be thrown, if I can help it. That is unless he crossed me first, but that's for another conversation after you get your shit out the way. I'll go see him tonight."

"Thank you. You don't know what I'm going through." Brandon took a deep breath.

"I can imagine. Listen, sometimes God has to shake us up because we're living like we can do whatever to whomever whenever, and it ain't like that. Just think. When the devil sees that you aren't being strong in your position, he will come in and attack."

"I already know. My thing is that I can't let nothing stop me. I don't care what he tries."

"You can stop your own progress with poor choices. A man is supposed to lead and not get his family involved in danger. You have to ask yourself when you dropped the ball. You have a beautiful family."

Brandon instantly realized that Melinda was trying to talk to him about Ciara. Oh boy! he thought.

"Melinda, I appreciate where you're coming from, but not right now, please, respectfully," Brandon said gently, not wanting to get on her bad side. He needed her.

"I hear you, sweetie, and I get it. But I'll reserve my right to get in yo' ass in the very near future and that's a promise. My brothers be so disappointing. Oh, I said I was going to stop. Okay, I'll call you later with any news." Melinda hung up.

As soon as Brandon got in his house, Gabriella called him. He saw her name on his screen and picked it up.

"Hey, beautiful."

Brandon gently knocked on Gabriella's door. He felt like he was sneaking, and he didn't know why. Grace was a married woman, and Ciara was uncharted territory. He didn't know if he wanted to chart her territory again or if she even wanted him to. Of course, Ciara wanted her family, but he wasn't going to be with her just because of their kids. He wondered if they were going to be able to put the past behind them and be able to love each other deeply and passionately again.

Chavon came to the door in lingerie that abruptly wiped Ciara from his mind. His mouth dropped as Gabriella came up behind her with the same sex-slave getup on. His tool became rock hard and led him right through the door without asking any questions.

Gabriella grabbed one of his hands, and Chavon grabbed the other, leading him to the couch. They pushed him down and Gabriella got on her knees and unzipped his zipper as Chavon stood on the couch and put her package close to his lips. She bent her knees and looked down to see what was about to go down. Brandon went on auto pilot, not thinking twice about licking Chavon's clit as she sat spread-eagle. He grabbed her ass, wrapped his arms around her thighs, and shoved her into his mouth.

Gabriella was working on his jackhammer, slurping, slobbering, and bobbing her head like a bobblehead. Brandon felt like a king with his concubines. He took his face out of Chavon's crotch to take a peek at Gabriella, who had his dick in her mouth. She looked up in his eyes, and he winked at her. He put his head back on the couch.

"Chavon, go eat Gabriella's pussy while I watch."

Chavon stepped backward off the couch and kneeled behind Gabriella and planted her face in her backside. Gabriella jumped and giggled, then relaxed into Chavon's mouth. Gabriella began to moan, which turned Brandon up a notch to start gyrating and thrusting himself into her deeper and harder.

"Oh, y'all set me up, huh? Y'all come and get this cum in both of y'all mouths at the same time. Chavon, come up next to her."

The two women sat hip to hip as Brandon grabbed his dick and held it while he squirted into their mouths, and they lapped it up, kissing each other's tongues and sharing his juice. He wished he could take out his phone and take a picture. Why not? he thought and whipped his phone out and started snapping pictures.

"Let me see y'all give me a nasty photoshoot. Give me, like, ten freaky photos to look at later."

Brandon started snapping shots as the girls gave him exactly what he asked for. He was loving every minute of it until the doorbell rang. Brandon and Chavon froze as Gabriella jumped up and went to peep out of the peephole. They didn't expect Gabriella to swing the door open, but she did, knowing that Grace was on the other side. As soon as Grace saw Brandon sitting there with his dick outside of his pants, she froze.

Gabriella seemed to be amused.

"Oh, I'm sorry, Grace. I mean, I'm sorry Brandon and Chavon." She closed the door to cover them and herself.

"Yes, Grace?" she asked, peeking out of the side of the door.

"Gabriella, you told me to come and get the book that I wanted to borrow."

"Um, okay hold on." Gabriella closed the door in Grace's face and ran to her bookshelf to grab The Secret and quickly tossed it into Grace's hands and brushed her off.

"Okay, call me, Grace. See you later." She slammed the door.

"Yo, why would you open the door like that knowing we in here butt naked? That wasn't funny. What the fuck was you trying to prove? You wanted her to see me here?"

Brandon got up and zipped up his pants and sat back down.

"Calm down, Casanova. Why do you care if she saw you here? She's married."

"I care not to have people in my business. Yeah, she's married, and her husband set me up. You think I want her to have any ammunition to use against me? This isn't a game. You on some drama shit. I don't do drama." Both women were sitting quietly as Brandon scolded Gabriella.

"My goodness, I'm sorry. I didn't mean to get you upset," Gabriella humbly admitted.

"Well, think then. I just lost my mood."

"Well, can you get it back? Because I'm horny." Chavon was frank about it.

"First of all, how did this happen?" Brandon asked, referring to the two of them jumping his body.

"We got tired of fighting over you and you not giving either of us the time of day, so we figured we'd just share." They both started laughing.

"Yeah, but do I have any say in the matter? Why do y'all women always feel it's okay to make a man's decision for him?"

"You seemed to enjoy it," Gabriella joked.

"Of course, but I never told either one of you that I was interested in having anything with either one of you, or at all for that matter. I never led either of you on either."

"No, but you were with both of us, and you knew we were friends," Chavon said.

"And, obviously, both of you knew it, but I didn't know what either of you had spoken about regarding me, and I wasn't going to quiz you. I'm a free man. I see that you planned this well, though. Thank you," Brandon chuckled.

"Well, it ain't over." Chavon straddled Brandon and started kissing him while taking his T-shirt off. The two women took turns riding him on the couch and then made the move into the bedroom to engage in more creative positions.

He was ready for all of the action they were giving him, and it helped to take his mind off his case. He deserved this stress relief. Shit, this is how a G handles life's bullshit, by playing in some shit. He laughed but wouldn't say why when they asked and just replied, "Just a G thinking to himself."

Brandon was getting aroused and didn't fight it. He figured this would be the last time this would happen because he was done with these two. The finale was great. Brandon spent another five hours with the girls, drinking and sexing off and on in between eating and was worn out when he got home at 2 a.m.

He woke up the next morning and looked at the clock, which read 11:30. He had come home and continued to drink himself into a stupor. He didn't remember anything that happened after leaving Gabriella's, but he woke up butt-naked in his bed.

"Damn, did they come here too?" He laughed.

He reached over and grabbed his phone and saw that Grace had sent him five text messages that he didn't open. Ciara had called twice, his mother three times, and Melinda once. He listened to his voice messages, and Melinda said, "Listen, Jerry said he'll talk to you tonight. We're gonna meet in my apartment at nine o'clock. Come by eight thirty so we can talk before he gets here."

Brandon smiled, looked up to the sky, and put his hands together. "Thank you, Lord," he said.

Ciara's message was disturbing. "Your daughter is in Hackensack Hospital. Why is your phone off when you have kids?" His mother had also left frantic messages for him to call her, the difference being that she didn't say his daughter was in the hospital on the message, but just for him to call her, knowing that it would get him worried.

"Ma, what is wrong? What happened to Malika?" He was getting dressed, his mother on speakerphone.

"She was in a car accident with her friend and her friend's mom. God is so good. Do you hear me, son? A drunk driver. I'm at the hospital. Just come, son. Where were you all day, and how do you not make sure that your phone stays on when you have kids?"

"Is she okay? Is she hurt badly? Is she conscious, Ma?"

"Brandon, she's in an induced coma. She's going to survive, but it's very critical right now. She broke a rib, and the pain is going to be too unbearable for her, and she has some internal bleeding, so they had to let her rest. Now come on, son."

Brandon hung up the phone, grabbed his keys, and ran

out of the door. As luck and the devil would have it, Grace was waiting at the elevator. Damn! What the fuck is going on right now? Is the devil trying to attack me? Why would she have to be here right now? Maybe this bitch been here for hours waiting for me to get off or on the elevator. Shut up, Brandon, don't be an arrogant asshole. He shook his head to clear his thoughts.

"Hey, Grace, how are you doing?" Brandon didn't give her any energy or feeling that they had just had sex days before and then she saw him having sex with two other girls. He acted as if she were a neighbor that he knew casually, which was the truth,

"Hi, Brandon, did you get my texts?" She looked at him as he looked at the elevator control to see how close the elevator was.

"I saw that you sent them. I just have to get to the hospital. My daughter was in a car accident. I'll read them as soon as I can." Brandon was thankful that the elevator showed up. They entered.

"Oh no, I'm sorry to hear that. Call me when you get back." Grace was holding Gabriella's book in her hand. "That was a surprise yesterday," she continued.

"It sure was." Brandon was elated that the elevator stopped and received more passengers.

As more people entered, Brandon shifted to the other side to allow the newcomers to stand between him and Grace. He was the first person off the elevator at his parking level. Brandon didn't know whether Grace got off on their parking floor or not, because he sprinted to the car in less than two minutes and was already on 95 North within ten minutes and at the hospital in twenty.

The people in the hall moved out of the way as Brandon

ran into Malika's room, instantly teary-eyed when he saw her. He couldn't help but to break down seeing his daughter hooked up to a machine through a window.

"Lord, here I go again needing you. Lord, heal my daughter. That's my baby right there; that's my baby right there." He felt his mother's comforting embrace, and her arms wrap tightly around him, making him feel like he was six years old again. He squeezed her back and let out all that he could so he could gain some composure.

Brandon was not a man who felt embarrassed about shedding a tear because he was secure in his manhood, but crying wasn't something that he did often. He had never seen his father cry and always knew why. Men had always been taught that men don't cry. He also knew that crying stopped him from losing his mind, and he was glad that his mother had instilled in him that it was okay.

Brandon was a real man with a bit too much of an ego, but that's for another part of his story. At this moment, he was a real man who was unable to help his daughter. All he could do was pray for her.

Major came up and hugged his dad, and Brandon embraced his son. He looked over as Ciara was sobbing quietly in her chair. He squeezed his son and put him in his mother's arms and went over to Ciara.

Brandon leaned down, took both of her hands in his, and picked her up and embraced her like they had never separated. Like they were in love and like they were a team. "You know God has her, right?" Ciara asked him through muffled tears as her head was buried in his chest.

"I know, so we can't keep crying. Let it out and then we gon' be strong for her and Major, okay?" He brought her chin up to look her in the eyes, and he kissed her on the lips. The moment was really real, and he was glad that they could come together in love for their daughter no matter what was going on between them. They had come a long way because this time a year ago, they were warring every day. They couldn't stand each other or be in the same room together for more than two minutes. He pulled up a chair next to hers.

"Did you eat anything? And what the hell happened?"

"They were going to a birthday party at Sky Zone and a drunk driver hit them. You should see the car. I went to the scene first. Look." Ciara showed him a picture of the mangled car that Malika was riding in.

Brandon was so shook, anxious, and always thankful for his blessings. He and Ciara talked and laughed as they recalled things Malika had done as a sassy little girl. When Brandon brought up a time when Ciara's aunt had thought she lost Malika at the zoo, he reminded Ciara that she was supposed to call her Aunt Gem.

"Oh shit, wait. Let me use your phone to call Aunt Gem. My phone is dead, and I have to see if she was able to get a flight. She wants to come stay at the hospital so I can keep working so that I'll be able to take time off if I need to when Malika comes home. Go to the nurses' station and see if the doctor is still here. He was just in here a half hour ago. He can tell you everything he told us. It could have been much worse, and he said she's very lucky; I said she's blessed."

Brandon passed Ciara his phone without thinking. He went out and requested the doctor come and speak with him. He waited for the doctor, who started talking to him, and he mentioned that Brandon should ask to see the wreckage because the pictures would show him just how lucky his daughter was considering the carnage of the car itself. He said, with technology, a doctor can be sent pictures of the crash to give the physicians an idea of what the patient's trauma was and the possible injuries that the person could be dealing with.

"Pictures?" Brandon's heart dropped when he realized that he had just taken naked pics of Gabriella and Chavon. He wanted to run back to the room and grab his phone, but, instead, he continued to listen intently at the doctor, all the while scared of what Ciara may find on his phone, not to mention that he didn't even know what Grace's text messages were about. He took a deep breath and tried to remain focused on his daughter's condition.

"Doc, I thank you. Do you know how long she might be in here, and will she have to go to a rehab before going home?"

"No, she's young. She'll probably be in here for a week, no longer than two, depending. It's a bit early to tell, but she's stable, and she will bounce back as long as everything in these next few days continues to go well. She's a strong young lady, and she has family support, and a praying family always has power. Believe me, I see all types of families and those with faith usually prevail more often than those without. I cannot lie to you," the young white, hip doctor confessed and gave Brandon the ease that he needed to trust in what the doctor was saying, which made Brandon comfortable and optimistic.

"Thank you, Doc, and I know that to be correct too." They shook hands, and Brandon returned to the room connected to his daughters, only divided by a glass.

He was glad that the doctor said they would be able to go in and touch her and be in the room with her the next day. He had three more days off work and would spend the night with her. He had to go back home to meet up with Jerry and Melinda.

His mother was the only one in the room. "Where are Ciara and Major?" He looked and saw his phone face down on the table, and his gut told him the answer wasn't going to be good. He walked over to the chair where Ciara was sitting and sat down and slowly picked up his phone.

"They went home. Boy, I don't know what the hell is wrong with you. You're just never satisfied. I don't even feel like talking to you right now. I'm concerned about my granddaughter. You're grown. I tried to instill the right things in you, and you're still acting like a damn fool. I said I don't feel like talking, so I'll stay tonight. Get out my face. I'm disgusted with you. And Ciara said that she and you will alternate visits. She don't wanna see you either. I'm staying tonight. She said you can stay tomorrow and then the next day, since you just came because you were busy having a threesome while your daughter was almost dying in a car crash. Good night."

Brandon stood up and stared at his mother's back as she stared through the window at her granddaughter and began to pray out loud as usual. He felt like a demon who was banished from the throne of grace and humiliated for his behavior. He didn't dare say a word to his mother for fear of being chewed out. He looked at his daughter and blew her a kiss and walked out the room. He drove home in complete silence.

As he walked from the parking level to the elevator, he told himself that if he saw Gabriella or Grace, they might need to turn and walk the other way because irate was an understatement for what he was feeling at that moment. He still hadn't read the messages from Grace and knew that they were just the icing on the cake from Ciara seeing those pictures.

He shook his head and walked in his door and sat down on the couch. He put his phone on the end table and walked over to his gigantic window and looked at the skyline. It was

4:30, and he had four hours before the next ordeal would take place. Brandon's mind was exhausted. He stared out the window and thought about all the stories in the "Naked City" and felt that his story was just as insane.

PRESTO-CHANGE

Brandon woke up at 7:40 p.m. and jumped in the shower. He threw on a sweat suit and took a minute to finally read what Grace had texted him, but her messages were gone. Ciara had obviously read and deleted them, so he didn't even know what they said.

He texted her, "Call me at eleven o'clock tonight."

Brandon went to Melinda's house at 8:15. She had a mouthful for him. She almost grabbed him by his collar and threw him on the couch.

"Do you have a game plan?"

"Yeah, I have some ideas, but I want to hear what Jerry will say first and what he told you. Where is he?"

"He's an easy target. He's nervous. He's scared of Mark, but he wants Mark off his back. He's on his way. It's in his best interest to side with you because if he sends Mark away, he'll be free. The only thing is not knowing if Mark has people out here who'll still be loyal to him and tie up loose ends, and that's why you need to stop fucking his wife. You don't know if he got that bitch's phone tapped or cameras in their place without her knowledge. You know a lot of cops are power trippers who have to control everything. The last thing you need is for him to find out that his biggest fears are really happening.

"He's just paranoid because he got a big black man in reach of his wife for her to obsess and lust over, so he wanted you off that floor. She probably screamed your name out in her dreams; you never know. You know you a sexy, black mufucka. Come on, don't play modest with me, looking all innocent right now, like, 'Who, me?' Knock it off, buddy." Brandon and Melinda busted out laughing.

"So here's what you're gonna do. You're gonna feed him what I just told you without acting like I told you shit. You dig? He's not that bright. Believe me, you can run circles around him mentally."

Brandon gave another surprised look and joked, "Who, me? Nah." He shook his head, and they cracked up again. "I got this."

The doorbell rang, and Melinda led Jerry into the dining room, where he joined Brandon at the table. They didn't shake hands or speak, just nodded at each other.

"Listen, guy—Jerry—I'd like you to speak first."

"I'll tell you what I know for fifty thousand." Jerry twitched in his seat, and Brandon leaned back slowly, then leaned forward, putting his chair back down on all fours. He smirked and looked Jerry directly in his eyes.

"That's the best you got, to try to charge me for information that I already know? Look at it this way: You work here. You've had numerous dealings with this cop, and you know a lot about him. You're scared of him because of the way he operates. I already know he's had you wrapped around his finger. If you let him get out, you'll forever be his slave. If you help me, you'll set yourself free. So how about this? We make it to where you're not a cooperative witness, but a hostile one. We make it to where you're in trouble and you have to testify. That way he'll think you were forced to tell on him, not that you willfully gave him up. You'll be arrested for planting the gun in my apartment, but all along, you'll be cooperating with the police as a confidential informant."

"Mark will probably have me killed, the way he's probably gonna try to have you killed over his wife." Brandon looked at Jerry and turned his head away.

"You're telling him my every move, man, and you want to charge me because you're his flunky? What makes him think I'm fucking his wife? Did you tell him that to make yourself look good? Because there's no reason for this man to think that right now unless you told him. She surely wouldn't tell him." Brandon caught himself and so did Melinda.

"Well, Brandon, you don't even know her like that, right? At all, right? I mean, how would you know what she would or wouldn't do? You only used to see her when you guys' kids were playing together in the park. Don't put nothin' past no woman. She may want to make him jealous. I'm sure he's cheating on her," Melinda scolded.

"He sure is. I have pictures that these prostitutes took for me after pretending that they were robbing us. I set that whole thing up just in case I needed some ammo against him, because I just couldn't trust him anymore." Jerry's face turned red when he realized what he had just confessed. Melinda smirked at Brandon, as if to say, "I told you he's a dummy."

"See? That's what I'm talking about. And I can't pay you because that's bribery. But I can pay you after. I won't even have to pay my lawyer so much without a trial, and I can sue the police department too, because I know that redneck got bad shit on his record."

"I have a lot on him. I just didn't know how to go about getting that prick off my neck."

"Yup, he's just as bad as the piece-of-shit cop Derek Chauvin, who stood on George Floyd's neck. He is going to get off mine. Listen, what he did to me is wrong, and I know that you had something to do with it. So do you want to take the chance of going down with him or what?"

"I guess I have to get a lawyer and see what's best for me." Jerry was flip-flopping, which meant that he was nervous. Brandon knew that he had him.

"Listen, Jerry, I'm gonna talk to my lawyer tomorrow. Don't just help me; help yourself. I'm gonna win this fight, I'm telling you. He messed himself up. Don't be loyal to someone who used you like his flunky. I ain't threatening you. You have to make your own mind up, but it's not looking good for ya boy right now.

Believe me when I tell you, he's done either way. Give me your number and I'll call you tomorrow after my lawyer speaks with me. I gotta run. Thanks for agreeing to come and talk to me. Thanks for slipping up and telling the truth. Melinda, thanks for having us be able to meet up here. I can't trust anyone and you, Jerry, definitely can't trust Mark. Good night."

Brandon saw his way out and gave himself a high five on the way to the elevator. "Shit, I would have made a great lawyer and a better detective. Now, I'm about to have a lawsuit and let this prick suffer for trying to go after me from day one. I love how them tables turn." Brandon knew that Melinda would seal the deal by encouraging Jerry to do what was right. He knew not to badger the guy or try to scare him. He definitely played good cop, and he was sure Melinda was probably in there now, playing bad cop and scaring the shit out of him. Thank God I met her. I would be up shit's creek right now.

One thing that began to weigh on Brandon was the possibility that he may not be safe in that building until things were finalized. He wished that he could go stay with Ciara and the kids, but after what just happened, he didn't know if she would speak to him again or at least in the next few years. That reminded him that he needed to find out what Grace had texted him. His watch showed 9:30. He didn't want to wait another hour and a half in suspense. He texted her to call him, and no sooner than he sent the text, his phone was ringing with her name on the screen.

"Hey, Grace, how are you feeling?" It took everything out of him to be nice to her. He was just over it already. All of this had happened because her husband couldn't share a floor with a successful black man who was minding his business and realizing one of his dreams of moving into a high-rise building overlooking Manhattan.

"I'm sorry. I'm really, really sorry." Grace was crying. Brandon was like a stone wall.

"Come by." Brandon hung up the phone and took his sweatpants off and put his basketball shorts on and poured two glasses of wine. He had no guilt. He was on a mission of warfare. He was out for revenge, even though he wasn't supposed to be. He knew that God would handle everything for him, but he had the immature thought that he would fuck Mark's wife for all the strife that he had put Brandon through, and Grace knew what she was getting into and had used Brandon to her benefit too. His life was in danger because of her.

Grace came through the door, drunk and stumbling. She started kissing Brandon, and he kissed her back. The kissing was passionate and lustful. He started grabbing on her ass, and she pushed him against the window and turned him around so that he could see the lights of the city while she electrified his penis with her saliva and throat. Brandon wasn't going to be polite. He was going to make sure she never ever forgot about his dick. He was going to dickmatize her to loyalty and make sure that she never wanted to cross him, hoping that one day she just might get this dick again.

Brandon was thrusting as Grace rode his penis in her mouth like it was a rodeo. She was trying not to let it fall out as much as he was moving and putting his back into it and hitting the back of her throat. She licked his balls to his tip and straddled his penis like her tongue was a Slinky.

He came in her mouth and sat down and let her have it.

"What should you be sorry for?"

"I know you think this is all my fault."

"I just want to know what made your husband target me. Why me?"

"His power went to his head, and he's a racist."

"So what did your texts say?"

"I sent you some nude pictures, and I said that I want to fuck you again... and I said that I was falling in love with you."

Ciara's tear-streaked face popped up in Brandon's mind. He sighed and looked at Grace. "Listen, I cannot continue this any longer. Whatever happens from this point on, we just have to handle it as it comes. I have to tend to my family. I need to make things right with my family and my woman. I'm not a man if I can't cover my family, love my family, honor my woman, and be an example to the children that I helped bring into this world. And some of this I knew, but your deadbeat husband reminded me. Do you understand?"

"Can you make love to me one more time?"

"I can fuck you one more time. I never made love to you. Do you understand that as well? I don't need any more problems."

"I understand." Grace took her clothes off, and Brandon fucked her like she was a whore—in the kitchen, on the counter, and on the living room floor—and sent her home.

* * *

Brandon woke up in the morning and called Riegel. He shared with Riegel what Jerry had told him. Reigel was excited to hear the newest developments, but probably wished that the case would have gone to trial so he could collect the $75,000 fee. Riegel shared that the judge had granted Mark the pretrial hearing he requested in two weeks, and, in the meantime, he would find out the best way to approach the information that Jerry confessed. The motion to dismiss the case would be heard at Mark's hearing, which was awesome. He told Brandon that this was almost a slam dunk, but there were still steps that had to be taken. Brandon felt good about their call and got ready to go to the hospital.

When he walked into his daughter's room, Ciara was there with his mom, Major, and her Aunt Gem. He wasn't expecting to see her there after what had transpired the day before. Malika was awake and seemingly alert, her eyes brightening when he walked in.

Brandon walked up to Malika's bed and kissed her on the cheek. "I love you, little mama. I'm so glad you're gonna be okay. Can she talk?" He looked around for anyone to answer, and no one seemed to be paying him any mind, which told him that everyone knew what was going on, including Major and Aunt Gem. He felt like a loser, an outsider, and all because of some whores.

"Yes, Daddy, I can talk. Not a lot, though. My rib hurts."

"Okay, baby. Don't talk; just relax. I'm staying here with you tonight. I'll be back. Mom, let me know when Ciara leaves and I'll come back." Brandon wasn't going to sit there and be demonized. He had enough pressure on him. He was womaned out and didn't want to even talk to his mom. It was all women. They always had to mess everything up with their emotions. Brandon walked down the hallway and didn't realize that Ciara was behind him until he stopped for the elevator, and she walked up. He wasn't going to say anything to her because he didn't want an audience if he said the wrong thing. They both stepped into the elevator, and she let him have it.

"So you gonna run to the blonde, the sister, the cop's wife or the old chick you were whining and dining? You have a whole variety of chicks. Good for you."

"I ain't got shit, and I'm not in the mood, Ciara. What you saw you shouldn't have seen. You shouldn't have gone looking in my phone."

"Maybe not, but I don't like a fake, and you're a fraud. You came in there yesterday like you're the father of the year, and you're just a fucking whore. A man with no purpose. A man with no discretion. You made it, right? You moved on up to a deluxe apartment in the sky to do you at the expense of your so-called family, and you really think what you're doing is right in the eyes of God?"

"I'm doing whatever a single man can do, that's all."

"As I said, at the expense of your children and the queen who gave you them. I could see if you had a girlfriend... one. One female who you connected with, who you fell in love with. No, I can't even see that, but you out here just slinging dick anywhere? That's not what a Kingdom man does."

"Ciara, you know so much, don't you? So much that you didn't even treat me like a man, but just your toy when you had me. You thought you could give me attitude like most black women do, you could tell me what to do like you were my mom, and not respect what I had done as a father for my children or a man to you. I took you from a dysfunctional family to love you, and you didn't even know how to receive the love because you couldn't trust that anyone could love you. You pushed me away too, with your insecurities and trauma that you never dealt with sufficiently. Yeah, you'll go to church, and yeah, you take good care of the kids, but what are you doing for yourself to let go of your hurts that make you a bitter, uptight woman?"

"What! You're a narcissist. Every time something happens, it's never your fault. You're always the best thing, and if you aren't appeased and your ego isn't stroked, you're out. Just like now. You're the one having time to fuck a whole bunch of women, but when we need you, we can't get to you. Your only priority is you."

They stepped off the elevator, and Ciara followed Brandon outside. "Ciara, where are you going? I'm leaving so you won't have to be disgusted with me, so I don't have to ruin your day. I'm leaving so that you can visit with Malika in peace and then when you leave, I can do the same. I'm not in the mood for you to belittle me right now. I'm going through enough."

"Exactly my point. You're only concerned about you."

"Ciara, what do you want me to do? I've asked you this before. We can't be together if we can't get along."

"Are you making any effort?"

"No, because everything is a battle with you. I do want my family. I learned my lesson. This move didn't turn out at all how I expected it to. My dream came true and turned into a nightmare, and I have nothing. So you should be elated. I failed. Okay?"

"I didn't want you to fail, but I wanted you to care. I

wanted you to try harder, fight for us. I wanted you to see that even in that beautiful building and condo, a house is not a home without love in it. You can put beautiful all-white furniture in a beautiful place, but it will still feel empty when the right souls aren't there."

"I get it, Ciara, I get it. Be amused, like I said." Without realizing it, they ended up walking into the hospital's garden. The serene setting calmed them both down.

Brandon walked over to a bench and sat. Ciara sat next to him, and they didn't say a word for a few minutes. He looked over at Ciara and put his arm around her, and she leaned into him, under his wing.

"Brandon, we had some great times. I think about all of the things we did before the kids. The concerts. The trips. We had some rough times too but there is no relationship that doesn't. Even after the kids, we had a dope family."

"I know Ciara. I don't even know how we ended up here."

They sat. Neither of them wanted to ruin the moment, ignore the undeniable love that was still there, or question what was going on. They just felt good in each other's arms. Brandon wasn't confused about his feelings for Ciara; he was just at a loss of what to do or how to fix things with her or if they were even fixable.

They sat and then Brandon's mother called them back to the room to speak with the doctor who came in. They held hands the whole way back to Malika's room.

Brandon spent the next two weeks back at work, preparing for his hearing for his case's dismissal, and around his family. Grace continued to try to run into him and text him here and there, but he ignored her. He felt that he needed time away from all women to get his thoughts together. He set up a counseling session with a teammate friend from college who was a therapist. The white male welcomed Brandon into his office with their basketball-team handshake. They embraced and sat down.

"Brandon, it's good to see you, man. I was surprised to hear from you."

"Yeah, we haven't had a meetup in a while. I'm ready to tear you down on the court whenever you're ready. What do you think about this Kyle Rittenhouse mess? You know that white boy is gonna get off scot-free, but if it was me or someone who looks like me, we would be in prison for life. I just saw on the news how he walked freely past the police with an AK-47. Man, you Caucasians have it made in America."

"Yeah, I can't lie; it's really unfair, and you know I don't agree with that injustice. He's definitely gonna get off and have other boys thinking they can get away with murder too. But, man, that's bad news. Let's talk about something good. I'm ready to demolish you on the court. But, anyway, what's going on with you? You always joked that therapists were crooks capitalizing on other people's sorrow," Jason Weaver teased.

"Yeah, well, my sorrow is so deep right now that I'll take the chance. I trust you, guy; I wouldn't talk to anyone else. Well, except the times my ex forced me into it. But it didn't work."

"Well, did you give it an honest chance or go in there thinking that? Because nothing will work that you don't believe in."

"Oh, you smooth operator. You're getting to work right away. No fair. You just said something deep and meaningful that fast? Okay, I'm sold. Sign me up for every day." Brandon and Jason laughed.

"Man, it's really not as complicated as people make it. A lot of what people's problems are is fear. Fear of failure. Fear of the unknown. Fear of being wrong. Fear of being found out. Are you hiding anything about yourself?" Jason got serious.

"Shit, I don't know. I know I ain't crazy. I don't think I'm a bad person..." Brandon leaned back and thought for a moment. "I thought I was doing everything right—not perfect, but I didn't think I was doing anything wrong. I finally moved into my dream apartment, and everything just fell apart. From the first day, a racist detective had it out for me; pulled a gun on me. Our kids become friends, his wife starts to lust after me, and he sets me up with a gun in my place. Then the wife helps out and gives evidence that he was robbing drug dealers and even killed three of them and set up others." Brandon was taken aback just hearing himself talk about it.

"Whoa, that's a lot, dude. It sounds like a book or a movie."

"I wish. It's my life, though, and I just got blindsided. And then..."

"Uh-oh, there's more?"

"Yeah. I kind of fell victim and started sleeping with the wife."

"What wife? The cop's wife? No way! You got on a bulletproof vest?" Brandon's mouth dropped. "I'm sorry, that wasn't funny. Let me stay in therapist mode and out of friend-bustin'-your-chops mode."

"Please do. I can't even believe it myself. So what do I do?" Brandon asked.

"What's the current state of your case? What do you think you should do, or what do you want to do? Seriously, do you feel like you're in danger?"

"Shit, I'm a black man in America. I'm always in danger, but I'm not as worried as I was a few weeks ago. I'm not having any dealings with the wife or her friend who lives in the building that I was fucking with her other friend." Jason's eyebrows raised, and Brandon put his head down in shame. "Man, what's so wrong with having a lot of chicks?"

"It's not that there's something wrong with it, but what does it create? What comes from it? Has it made your life better? Has it fulfilled your needs or created more drama for your life? It sounds like it's brought a lot of drama."

"Man, it sure ain't like it used to be back in the day. Casual sex was the bomb. No strings, no guilt. Damn. I feel like a horrible person. My ex found out. She thinks I'm a piece of shit."

"Okay, so do you want to be with her again?"

"Yes. I wasn't sure, but my life is so empty without them."

"Okay, without them or her? You cannot go back to her if it isn't for her. You can raise your kids and coparent in a healthy way if it's not about her. You won't be happy for your kids. Yes, your kids deserve to be happy, but the parents must be happy for the kids to inherit happiness and know that happiness starts from within and not from someone else giving it to you. So be sure. Don't dig another hole for yourself."

"Listen... I want her, and I love her. I just don't wanna be miserable. I'm not gonna get married to get divorced. I've been fighting it. But I don't want any of these lame chicks out here. They're only good for one thing, and after that, I have no use for them. I have a daughter. I don't want to treat women that way. I want to honor Ciara. She deserves to be my queen. She's been there every step of the way. I could never handle it if she found someone else."

"So then, get married and don't get divorced. If you want the marriage to work, make it work. Nobody can do it but you. That is what I mean by fear. Have the power. Use your power to get what you want in life. Go after the good things, the way you can easily, without fear, go about the bad stuff. You accomplished your goal in moving where you wanted to move. I'm sure it wasn't easy, and it was probably worth it. You learned a lot of lessons, right? What can you say you learned from getting what you always wanted?"

Brandon thought hard. "I learned that everything you think you want may not be what you thought it was when you get it. And what you think you don't want may be just because you don't want what doesn't come easy."

"And what doesn't come easy is usually what's best for you or will bring you the greatest reward when you conquer your fears about it."

* * *

Brandon had on a brand-new suit, and Ciara had on a matching Tahari suit dress. They walked into the courtroom hand in hand, his mom and her aunt with them.

They stopped before entering the courtroom and held hands while Ciara prayed. "Lord, You have brought me and this man, whom I love with all of my heart, back together. We have had many trials, and You've been there through them all. We need You now again. We know that You'll exonerate Brandon. We just ask that this ordeal be over today. We ask that this demon, Mark Stephens, gets his just reward for trying to ruin other people's lives. Just cover Brandon, Lord, and give him the victory. We love You, Lord." Brandon kissed Ciara and his mom and hugged her aunt, then walked into the courtroom.

The ladies sat behind Brandon and Riegel. Brandon was surprised that Grace wasn't there.

Judge Young came out, everyone rose and sat, and the proceedings began. "We are here to have a presentencing hearing for ex-officer Mark Stephens, who has pleaded no contest to the charges against him. I read his charges at his arraignment, and he has asked to speak to the Court. Mr. Stephens, you may speak."

Brandon looked behind him and saw a few different black men who appeared to be sitting with their lawyers. He had no idea the treat he was in for. Mark looked defeated; that was the first treat.

"Your Honor, I wanted to apologize. I humbly learned that I let my position as an officer of the law go to my head. I'm not guilty of all of the charges against me—"

"Mr. Stephens, let me remind you that you pleaded no contest. You already gave your plea, and it wasn't not guilty, so you're contradicting yourself. You cannot apologize and deny at the same time. Please proceed in honor and truth if you're intending to address how you got in such a disgraceful ordeal. This is very serious. Three people were murdered with ammunition and guns that you had in your possession.

You're being accused of robbing and bribing drug dealers, which is against the law. Are you here to beg the Court for mercy or to be in denial? Do you want to change your plea?"

"I'm sorry, Your Honor; I can't share everything I know because my life is in danger. There are people that I have to take the rap for because I don't want my family to get hurt."

"Mr. Stephens, again, do you have a basis for these claims?" The judge was becoming agitated and impatient with Mark's shenanigans.

Mark Stephens basically made a fool of himself and showed that he was no less arrogant or egotistical and still thought that he could outsmart other people, but actually outsmarted himself. He had his partner speak for him, and his mother spoke for him, but they were no more convincing than Mark was.

The list of people speaking against Mark was endless. Brandon was tenth. He spoke of the experience he had from the first day, when Mark pulled a gun on him.

"Your Honor, I worked hard my whole life. I lived by the book and followed rules. I had a mother and a father who were married. Christian people who instilled morals and respect in their sons. My father taught me not to be bitter, not to hate, not to be racist, to do the right thing. And because of the color of my skin, this man tried to destroy my life, my hopes, and my dreams."

Reigel asked the most provocative questions, and it was very apparent that Mark had a motive to plant the gun and the resources to do it. Brandon was shocked to see Jerry walk in and speak about the numerous times he committed unlawful acts for Mark, for Mark to only pressure and influence him to do more and more.

"His demands were never requests. Whatever he wanted

me to do, I had to do, or he would threaten to have me pay for my past crimes that he had helped me escape punishment for. Yes, it was wrong, but it started as one favor, then another, and then it became manipulation and harassment. I thought I would never be free from Mark's control. This man has no level of guilt. He would have never stopped."

Brandon turned around and noticed Grace had shown up, and Melinda was there as well. Melinda put praying hands up to show him that she was praying for him, and he nodded in thanks.

Escobar's lawyer told of Mark trying to set Escobar up and frame him for the murder of Cheesy, who was found in the ditch. The white girl who pretended to be an officer got on the stand and testified that Mark had shot Cheesy and that she had shot the twins for Mark because they were going to turn in evidence on him robbing them for $200,000. They had made a tape of Mark without his knowledge, and Désiré found it and turned it in to Mark's partner Paul, to whom she was now engaged.

"I had a life that was not a law-abiding life, but my man loved me, and he only worked for the mob so that we could live the American dream. He knew that Mark would never stop blackmailing him, and he began to worry about his safety. He never told exactly what was going on, but this tape was left in our safe. I want to thank my fiancé, Paul, for seeing beyond my past and loving me and reminding me that I'm worthy of a safe and great life and for giving that to me and my child." Désiré stepped down and then it was Grace's turn.

Grace got on the stand, as did Camilla Strong. "I don't know if I was intentionally being blind, but once I realized how much of a monster my husband had become, I knew that I had a duty to let the truth be revealed. He didn't care about me or our children and family. He cared about greed and money and obviously other women, as his mistress is here, probably feeling as betrayed as I am right now." Grace looked at Brandon as she stepped down, and her tears were not only for her pain of the realization of what her husband had become, but the opportunity she would never get to be with Brandon. He looked at Ciara and kissed her cheek when Grace was done to let both women know exactly where he stood.

Camilla spoke of Mark's emotional abuse, controlling behavior, and told of multiple instances that made her realize he was an officer who was involving himself in illegal activity and that she would eventually be brought down with him. "I'm so glad that Mark Stephens didn't end up ruining my life or my career." Camilla was given a pardon for helping Mark with stealing evidence and was put on four months' suspension from work but did not lose her job.

Mark must have blocked everything out because he sat there like a zombie staring into space. He must have been shocked into submission by the fact that he was about to go down and to prison for many years to come, if not the rest of his life.

When the hearing was over, Brandon, Escobar, and many others were vindicated by having their cases thrown out. There were sighs of relief and families hugging each other as each person learned that they were now free from further litigation.

"Mr. Mark Stephens, you will be remanded to Schuylkill Federal Prison for a term of twenty years." Almost everyone in the room cheered as Judge Young passed down the sentence.

They walked out of the courtroom, and to Ciara's surprise, there was a limousine waiting for her and Brandon. She looked confused as Brandon led her to the car and they got in. "What's going on?"

"We're going on vacation. Shit, I just got my life back. And my wife back." He kissed her long and hard, and she kissed him back.

"Yes, it's been a great couple of weeks, but let's not forget, I'm not a wife until I am, so let's not go there if you aren't ready for that conversation," Ciara said as gently and unaggressively as she could. "Where are we going? I'm excited about that! I need a vacation too!"

"Yes, change the subject. One day at a time. I just want to get on a beach and hopefully be able to get some. Shit, it's been over a year since I hit that," Brandon said.

"You know what? You better quit while you're ahead because you keep putting your foot all in your mouth right now. You aren't saying the right things, but because I'm about to be on a plane to somewhere, I'm gonna let it slide. So I don't even want to know where I'm going. I wish I had clothes, though."

"Your bag is already packed. Malika lay in your bed and told Aunt Gem what to pack while you were out the other day. I got everything covered."

If they weren't in the car, Ciara would've jumped up and down. Finally, this guy was acting like a man who knew how to love a queen. That's right, nigga. Get it right. Now you'll really be on your game if you have a muthafuckin ring in yo' pocket too. Ain't nothing like a gentleman who also has swag. You gonna get some really juicy pussy if you have that rock!

The following day, Ciara was on a beach with sky-blue water in Turks and Caicos, drinking a tall tropical drink, and Brandon was lying in his lounge chair next to her.

A band approached and stopped in front of them. Ciara thought, this is it. I'm about to get my ring!

The romantic melodies that came out of the native

musical instruments took her back to the day they met and how romantic their first few dates had been.

There were maracas and bongos and women dressed exotically dancing around them. Brandon got up and knelt down on his knee in the sand and gently took Ciara's left hand in his.

A box magically appeared from under his towel. Ciara's eyes popped wide open and followed his hand as it opened the box to reveal a canary-yellow emerald-cut gigantic center stone and the most beautiful ring that she had ever seen in her life. It was better than the first ring Brandon had given her, and it felt more meaningful. She didn't quite yet know why, but she knew it felt different.

For the first time, Brandon really poured out his heart to Ciara. "Lady, queen, my lover, my rider, my supporter, my helper, my comforter, my peace. My blessing, my gift, my soulmate, protector of my heart, the woman who prays for me, who has given me life outside of myself, the one who accepted me with all my flaws and fought for me to do better and be a better man, the one who wouldn't give up, who believed in me when I didn't even believe in myself. The one who won't take my excuses, who brings me joy and happiness, who makes me feel like a king. Our love is everything. It may have taken me a while to see, but I know you're the only one for me. I know that you were sent to me from Heaven above. You have taught me that Nothing Matters except God and love."

ACKNOWLEDGEMENTS

I give all Honor to Jesus Christ, the leader of my life. For his grace, mercy, protection, restoration and love.

I thank my parents, Cliff and Muriel and my sister, Laura for being the first family I knew. I thank my children Tori Sharan, SaniyaRain, Sierra Star, and Isaiah Sincere for giving me unconditional love and support and for giving me motivation and determination to do what I do for us. and being a major part of my purpose. I extend my love to my stepdaughter and her daughter, StarAsia and Aniyah and my stepson, Seven Sincere.

To my family and friends, I love you and thank you for being a part of my journey and a part of my experiences that have helped me have great stories to tell and memories of a lifetime.

To my partner in media, Lamartz Brown. We did it again! I would never have made it this far without you. We are gonna ride this thing out and never stop until God calls us home and when we meet up in Heaven, we will do it all over again! I truly appreciate you for being such a major part of my success in media and by being my brother in Christ! Thank you for putting up with me.

To all of the Editors, Manuscript Evaluators, Test Readers and Graphic Design Artist who made this project possible, I truly appreciate your hard work and effort in making my return to authorship, after ten years.

To my readers, followers, and supporters... "You give good love to Me!" In my Anita Baker voice. My "fans" have continued to show their loyalty to me even in my hiatus. And now I'm Back!

I hope everyone enjoys this story... we all have to know that sometimes the things that we think matter, really don't.

Peace, Blessings, Appreciation and Love!

To you All!

ABOUT THE *Author*

Public Speaker, Producer, Mentor, Writer, Social Giver, Filmmaker and Humanitarian

Since childhood, Ericka has always been a force of nature. Ericka has always been creative and a lover of the Arts. After graduating from Rutgers University in New Jersey with a degree in Communications, Ericka immediately began going after her dreams and passions in life and continues to reinvent herself today.

Ericka's first career after college was teaching, while beginning to write her first novel.

She taught language arts which includes reading, writing, public speaking, video critiquing, along with drama and script writing. She also used her knowledge of communications to help her students with conflict resolution, how to effectively interact with others, and to positively express themselves. To this day, Ericka continues to mentor and guide her former students, as well as others, through life.

During her years of being an educator, Ericka began to publish a series of novels, including her first title, "All That Glitters," in 2007, which addresses some of the most severe social issues like drug addiction, relationship abuse, family dysfunction, AIDS, lack of confidence and the results of having a lack of self-esteem.

Ericka's second novel came out just 2 years later in 2009 and was called "A Woman Scorned." She then released "A Woman Scorned 2 - Family Ties" in 2010, "The Robbin Hoods" and "A Woman Scorned 3-Déjà vu" by 2012. The release of this latest novel, "Nothing Matters" will be her first book release in ten years.

All of Ericka's books were written with one purpose only – to help people in need and to impact as many lives as possible, worldwide.

Ericka also plans to produce and turn her books into film and television series and has given herself the experience of producing independent films on YouTube to prepare for her break into the film and television industries; to reach even more people with the goal of proving her motto that, "there is nothing to it, but to do it". Ericka believes that there is no obstacle too big to conquer if you put your mind and body to work to accomplish your achievements. Ericka is a doer, a giver, and a great example of how determination can turn into success when you believe in yourself and decide to let nothing stop you from completing your endeavors.

Beyond writing and teaching others, Ericka's main priority is her family and closest friends, who support her along the way. They have been there through her novels, radio shows, internet talk shows, entertainment events, and film productions.

"There is nothing more important to me than my family," – says Ericka. And truly, all the things she is doing would be worthless if she didn't have her closest people around.

Beyond public speaking, teaching, and producing creative work for her fans and people around the world, Ericka plans to leave a legacy and a mark that will never be able to be deleted or erased. Long after Ericka Monique Williams is gone to be in the presence of God, and her Lord and Savior Jesus Christ her many productions will remain. She hopes you will enjoy her amazing work and use it as a guide to make your life better!

Made in the USA
Middletown, DE
12 July 2022

68872341R00146